T5-AWJ-280

FORK IN THE FALSE TRAIL

A TUCKER ASHLEY
WESTERN ADVENTURE

Fork in the False Trail

C. M. Wendelboe

THORNDIKE PRESS
A part of Gale, a Cengage Company

GALE
A Cengage Company

Copyright © 2021 by C. M. Wendelboe.
Thorndike Press, a part of Gale, a Cengage Company.

ALL RIGHTS RESERVED
This novel is a work of fiction. Names, characters, places, and incidents are either the product of the author's imagination, or, if real, used fictitiously.
The publisher bears no responsibility for the quality of information provided through author or third-party Web sites and does not have any control over, nor assume any responsibility for, information contained in these sites. Providing these sites should not be construed as an endorsement or approval by the publisher of these organizations or of the positions they may take on various issues.

Thorndike Press® Large Print Western.
The text of this Large Print edition is unabridged.
Other aspects of the book may vary from the original edition.
Set in 16 pt. Plantin.

LIBRARY OF CONGRESS CIP DATA ON FILE.
CATALOGUING IN PUBLICATION FOR THIS BOOK
IS AVAILABLE FROM THE LIBRARY OF CONGRESS.

ISBN-13: 978-1-4328-8264-8 (hardcover alk. paper)

Published in 2022 by arrangement with C. M. Wendelboe.

Printed in Mexico
Print Number: 01   Print Year: 2022

I would like to dedicate this book to Richard "Rick" Cunningham, friend, fellow Marine, and father-in-law.

ACKNOWLEDGEMENTS

I would like to thank rangers and the staff at the Nebraska Ft. Robinson State Park for their insights into Crazy Horse; the Edward Clown Family, descendants of Crazy Horse; the Nebraska Historical Society; and the South Dakota Historical Society. I wish also to thank Hazel Rumney, editor at Five Star, who dedicated so much to making this work of fiction historical and correct.

CHAPTER 1

Hack Reed pressed his face against the rusty, cold, iron bars of the Wyoming Territorial Prison. He looked up at the stars with his one good eye, the other blinded in a brutal prison fight and now covered by a black patch. He leaned against the weeping, damp, brick wall, thinking, *What I wouldn't give for a nice Waltham right now. Something so I knew* when *the festivities will start.* His partner before getting stuffed in this hole — Blade Tate — had visited him yesterday. "I know a feller —"

"How'd you get in here without getting thrown in *with* me?" Hack asked.

Blade looked around. "I'm not on any wanted posters like *my brother.*"

"You don't have a brother."

Blade lowered his voice. "That'd be you. At least that's what I told the turnkeys on this visiting day. Now you want to find out what I arranged or give me hell?"

9

Hack looked around, but the nearest prison guard stood leaning against a wall cradling a coffee cup outside the visiting area. "Tell me quick before they figure out who you are."

As he thought of Blade's flawless plan he'd fleshed out yesterday, Hack stood looking down at his cellmate, an aging old man who'd been locked up in various prisons across the territory since he was sixteen. The duffer cracked an eye and smiled at Hack through a toothless mouth. "You won't get to the front door — I know. I've tried more than a few times, and each time the screws and the stone walls beat me to a draw. Ended up in the hole. Every. Damn. Time." He shuddered as he scooted farther down into his blanket. "You'll just get yourself kilt, and then who would I get for a cellmate — someone not as . . . pleasant as you?" He laughed, triggering a coughing fit through his tuberculoid-ravaged lungs.

"Shut up, Pop," Hack said, straining his ears. But all he heard was the wind whistling through the bars and the cracks in the stone walls. "He's out there, Blade is. I'm to wait for a signal."

"What kind of signal?"

"The bakery blowing up."

Pop laughed, which triggered another

coughing fit. "So, they're going to smuggle some dynamite into the bakery in a loaf of bread. Maybe blow a cake to spring you."

"Damned old fool," Hack said. "Ever see flour dust when it gets close to open flames? It's like dynamite when it ignites. Every Thursday the bakery sells whatever the prison can't use to the public. Folks in town can buy from the bakery then. Blade bought a loaf of bread and slipped an old rustling partner on the bakery line some chaw to set up the explosion."

"You're screwed," Pop said. "Ain't nothing going to happen —"

"Got to be coming any moment," Hack said. "And it'll be *dramatic* is what Blade said. A distraction to end all distractions. Big enough that they could get a gun to me —"

"Don't hold your breath, my crazy friend," the old man said. "The only thing you'll get trying to bust out of here is lead in your gullet —"

An explosion shook the heavy prison walls, and the sky lit up, followed by another explosion. Sparks flew skyward from the direction of the prison bakery, and Hack pressed his face tight against the bars, looking down onto the courtyard below. Guards ran toward the fire that now engulfed the building. Some carried buckets. Others, shovels. All in a panic to reach that section of the prison before inmates were burned to death.

The guard on duty in Hack's cellblock jumped from his chair. He cradled a double shotgun in the crook of his arm as he ran to the window to look out.

A white flag fluttered. No, a white *rag* fluttered below Hack's cellblock, and he stood on his toes. His eyes adjusted from looking at the bright fire, and he spotted Blade Tate's upturned face looking frantically around, scanning the windows until Hack waved his own bandana through the bars. Blade uncoiled a rope and shook out a loop, twirling the riata over his head, looking up at Hack's window when he let loose with the rope. Hack snatched it before it fell and reeled it inside his cell.

Pop chuckled. "Is that your escape plan, genius? You going to lower yourself down to the ground? 'Cause if it is, I'm betting you won't fit through them bars."

Hack ignored Pop as he continued reeling in the rope while he kept an eye on the turnkey staring transfixed out the window beside the guard desk.

A *clanging* seemed loud in the small confines of the cell as metal hit the cell bars.

Hack pulled tight and grabbed onto the pistol tied to the end of the rope. He looked down, but already Blade had slipped back into the night while more guards ran to join the fire brigade.

Hack worked the gun between the bars and untied it from the rope, letting it fall back to the ground. With the sky lit up, Hack checked the Colt: six rounds of freedom. "Now you think I'm nuts?" Hack asked.

"You ain't got out the walls yet," Pop answered and sat up. "But this might be entertaining to watch you try."

Hack snatched his blanket from the bed and draped it over his hand as he turned to the cell door. "Guard!" he yelled. "Guard! Let me outta' here. I'm terrified of fire."

"Shut the hell up," the guard hollered back, but Hack yelled louder.

"Help me! I don't want to burn up. Help —"

The guard stepped from the window and walked to Hack's cell, the shotgun still cradled under his arm. "Now shut the hell up. The fire's at the other end of the compound. You're in no danger."

"But you are," Hack said. He thrust the barrel of the pistol through the bars.

The muzzle of the shotgun snapped up as

Hack cocked the Colt and leveled it at the guard's head. "You got kids?" Hack asked.

The guard's face turned ashen, and he nodded. "I got me two little girls."

"If you want them to see their pappy again, you best lay that scattergun down and unlock this here cell door."

There was but a moment's hesitation before the guard complied. He laid the shotgun down and took a ring of keys from his belt, fumbling for the right key. Metal scraped and clanked as he inserted it into the lock. Hack motioned for the guard to step away when he'd opened the cell door.

"Now get in the cell," he ordered, "and give me that flea-infested pillow of mine."

The guard bent to Hack's cot and handed him the pillow. Hack pressed the muzzle of the gun tight against it and shoved it into the guard's chest before touching off a muffled round. The guard staggered back a step before collapsing, smoke rising from the powder-burned feather ticking fluttering in the cell.

"What the hell you do that for?" Pop asked. "The man had kids."

"A casualty of battle, as we used to say in the War." Hack grabbed the keys from the lock and stuck them into his waistband.

"Ain't you even going to ask to come along?"

Pop covered himself with the blanket again as he averted his eyes from the dead guard. "And just where would I go? Ride the owlhoot trail? No, I'm here for the duration, brief though it may be." He nodded to the guard. "And don't expect me to wish you good luck."

Hack kept looking over his shoulder at the fire and smoke obscuring his run across the open field on the west side of Laramie. Sticky blood had crusted on his hand where he had shoved the sharpened bed spring into the outer guard's heart — the last obstacle to Hack's freedom — and he paused just long enough to catch his breath. He was — after all — no spring chicken. Looking at the top side of fifty, he had considered himself as aging well. But his bulky frame wasn't used to running. It was used to living in an eight- by twelve-foot cell listening to Pop's exploits, and Hack thought of the last time he'd had to run. From the Blackfeet? That had been mere months before the posse caught up with him and his men outside Rawlins after the robbery. He had nowhere to run then, unlike now as he searched the night for Blade Tate.

From across the field, Blade waved that same white rag to catch Hack's eye.

"Hacksaw," Blade hollered. "Over here. Down in the coulee."

Hack looked a final time at the burning prison bakery in the distance before sliding on his butt to the bottom of the ravine. He thrust out his hand, and Blade shook it. "Looks like your old rustling partner came through for us." Hack turned to Lowell Tornquist and held out his hand. "I thought they'd have hung you by now?"

Lowell had been with Hack and Blade and Big Nose George Parrot when they robbed the Union Pacific just outside Rawlins. It had been an easy mark — until expressmen concealed in the cars took umbrage to the gang's crime, and two of Hack's men had been killed by the expressmen and Hack wounded. The last he had seen of Blade and Lowell they were disappearing over a hill, riding fast away from the ambush.

Lowell stroked his long beard. He picked a flea out of it and tossed it away. "Seems like Blade here has a specialty for breaking convicts out of prison. They was fixin' to hang me in Billings for some bogus horse stealing charge when he busted me out."

"Even that weren't a cake walk," Blade said. "That posse chased us all across Idaho

Territory and even crossed the Canadian border after us until the Mounties shut them down. We laid low north of the border until we could make our way back here to Wyoming to bust you out, or we'd have come sooner." He slapped Lowell on the back. "But Lowell's gonna' be worth it — he's the only one I know who can handle dynamite."

Hack nodded. "The only way to get into express safes nowadays."

Out of the corner of his eye, Hack spotted a tall drink of water, skinny, looking like a snake on stilts, holding the horses. "Who's that?"

Blaide jerked his thumb at the kid. "That there's Jimmy Milk."

"What the hell's a Jimmy Milk?"

"About as fast a gun as you'd ever want riding with us," Lowell said.

"That's right," Blade said. "We picked him up right before we hit a train out of Omaha last month. He's as wild as a corn crib rat, but — what the hell — weren't we all when we were kids."

Hack motioned to Jimmy, and he ambled over, passing off the reins of the horses to Lowell. Jimmy stood a little shorter than Hack, but about a hundred pounds lighter. Wearing an oversized Montana Peak, and a

Schofield .45 slung low, he looked like every other dime store gunfighter depicted on Ned Buntline's novels. "Can you handle that thing?" Hack asked as he motioned to Jimmy's gun.

Jimmy smiled, and the next instant his Smith and Wesson was pointed at Hack. That fast. Hack couldn't follow the motion with his one good eye.

Jimmy smiled and holstered his gun. "That fast enough?"

"It is," Hack said. "But then I'm not armed." He grabbed Jimmy by the shirtfront and pulled him close. "Don't ever pull that on me again, kid. The next time I'll have my own gun." He faced Blade. "Just where *are* my guns?"

Blade walked to the far side of a sorrel fully sixteen hands tall. He fished into the saddlebags and came out with a holstered Colt that he handed to Hack. "This is your backup gun that was in your saddlebags when I caught up with that bay of yourn running hell bent for election after they shot you out of the saddle. And I . . . liberated a Winchester from a gun dealer in Deadwood." He patted the scabbard tied to the saddle before snatching a Stetson from the saddle horn and handing it to Hack. "And this is to cover that bald head of yourn."

Another explosion erupted in the cool night air, and Hack jumped, though the prison fire was a quarter mile away.

"Be glad to get away from here," Lowell said. "Blade's been looking over a railroad bank the other side of Salt Lake —"

"We're not going to Salt Lake," Hack said. "Or on any other job until I finish my business."

Blade took off his hat and ran his fingers through his long, stringy hair. "What you mean, we're not doing any jobs? I don't understand —"

"What you don't understand," Hack said, "is that I aim to find Tucker Ashley. First. Before I do anything else. Find and kill the bastard. Slowly."

"Hack," Blade said, "you're *free*. We have the whole country to ride to. The whole territory wide open to make some serious money, and you want to ride after Tucker Ashley?"

Hack took off his hat and stepped close enough to Blade that he smelled the tobacco smoke on the man's breath. "Look. Right here," Hack said, pointing to his face and pulling the patch away. "I got but this one good eye. What do you think about this other one, dead like it is? If Tucker hadn't goaded me into that fight and caught me unawares, I'd still have both of them! And my face wouldn't look like the south end of a cow going north."

"We all get in fights," Lowell said. "Sometimes we're the pigeon, sometimes we're the statue."

Hack thought back to that fight in the prison mess hall. The warden accused him of starting it when he snatched Tucker's piece of bread off his plate. But the way Hack figured it, Tucker — as thin as he'd become since arriving in prison — didn't need as much to fill his gullet as Hack did. "He caught me with a lucky shot to the chin," Hack said between clenched teeth. "And when I fell to the floor, the other prisoners goaded him into putting the boots to me. He kicked the hell out of me while the screws just watched. I spent a month in the infirmary mending up, hobbling around, getting used to seeing out of just one eye. No, Tucker Ashley will be in my gunsights real soon."

"Think about that," Blade said. "Even if you knew where Tucker was, this whole country" — he waved his arm — "can be ours. There's opportunity —"

"And there'll still be opportunity after I find and kill him."

"We don't even know where he landed."

20

"Sure, we do," Jimmy said. He took out a pouch of tobacco and sprinkled it onto a thin paper. "Ashley and that pard'ner of his, Jack Worman, got them a small ranch up Custer way."

Blade looked up at Jimmy. "How you know that?"

Jimmy rested his hand on the butt of his gun. "Heard it from an owlhoot who tried robbing the Deadwood gold coach. Said that Tucker and Worman have a small spread in the southern Black Hills now." He lit up the smoke, the flame illuminating his gaunt face before he blew out the lucifer. "I've been keeping track of Tucker Ashley. Folks say he's about the quickest man with a hogleg there is. Just killed Trait McGinty at the Hat Creek Station. But I'm faster than McGinty was, and I mean to hunt Ashley up on that ranch of his and prove he no longer is."

"Jimmy," Hack said, "make no mistake — Tucker's mine."

Jimmy shrugged, and Hack slapped Jimmy on the back. "I guess the kid's earned his pay for the day, knowing where to look for Tucker." He took the sorrel's reins from Lowell. "The sooner we find him, the sooner we tap into that opportunity you mentioned, Blade."

Hack swung a leg over the sorrel. It grunted under his weight and humped up until it settled down. "Seen Killdeer?"

Blade chin-pointed to the north. "My guess is he'll find us soon's we head out."

Hack grinned. "Good. Nice to have a man of the Crow's abilities in case Tucker manages to run off once we find him."

CHAPTER 2

Tucker stood overlooking what the Indians had left of their ranch. The army tent Jack and Tucker had called home until they could erect a proper house from the surrounding trees lay charred in the center of a hundred-foot black scar left on the mountain-prairie grass.

The shorthorn bull — their prized possession and the thing that would sire their heifers and earn them enough to expand their small ranch — lay bloated, the fly-buzzing carcass already being consumed by maggots that moved under the dead skin. As if warning Tucker away from the carcass. Away from the scene.

Tucker left the dressed elk on the back of his mule and led him to grass that the fire hadn't reached before turning back to the scene. He pulled his bandana up over his nose and walked a loose circle around the area. Lakota arrows stuck out of the bull —

a Sioux raiding party had come through. They had caught Jack by surprise, for how else could Tucker's friend have been bested?

Tucker sucked in a breath as he spotted a body partially hidden by the burned canvas tent. Jack? Tucker steeled himself as he peeled the canvas back — a Lakota warrior. Jack had at least killed one of his attackers before . . . what?

Tucker studied the tracks left by the Indians. They had made no attempt to hide their sign, telling Tucker they intended riding as fast and far away as they could, probably on their way to hunting grounds on the Powder River or the Shining Mountains to the west. But as he bent and ran his hand over the windblown tracks, trying to age them, the tracks clearly showed they dragged Jack behind their ponies. The Indians could only travel so fast dragging him behind them. He had a chance of catching them, then. But why not kill Jack here? Why burden themselves by taking him captive?

Tucker spotted a half-chewed plug of tobacco lying on the ground under an overturned water bucket. He squatted beside it and picked it up — Jack's tobacco plug he always kept close. Was Tucker's friend leaving sign for him? Jack rarely spit out a good chaw before it was plumb worn out. He pinched the dried tobacco between his thumb and finger: it had lain in the sun for a day. Perhaps two. The raiders had a good head start on Tucker. But with Jack barely keeping up by the drag marks in the ground, that would give Tucker a chance to catch them soon.

Light reflected off something lying under the dead Lakota, and Tucker was walking to the tent when riders approached. Two men — sitting horses more at home in a herd of unbroke mustangs — rode toward Tucker. The lead rider took off his floppy hat and ran his hand through his sweaty, greasy, gray hair while his partner — younger by twenty years, perhaps — rode to one side as he circled the remains of the ranch.

"Whoee!" the older man wheezed as he reined his horse beside Tucker. "It's hotter'n a whorehouse on a nickel night." He looked around. "This your spread, friend?"

Tucker nodded. "You know anything about what happened here?"

"I don't." He motioned to the younger man. "You know anything, Willam?"

Willam joined the old man. He stood in his stirrups, looking around. "No, Pa, but it looks like the Indians had their way with the whole damned place."

Tucker walked towards his mule grazing at the edge of the meadow where the fire had spared the grass. "I got no time to jaw. Sioux took my friend," he said over his shoulder when the old man said, "Whyn't you just stop right there and turn around slow like, friend. Oh, and drop that pistol of yourn."

Tucker looked over his shoulder at the man holding a Colt that he'd concealed under his hat. As Tucker thought about his chances of drawing before the man could get off a shot, Willam drew his own pistol and pointed it at Tucker's belly. "I'd do just like my pa says, 'cause this ain't our first encounter with rich ranchers like you."

Tucker carefully dropped his gun and said, "I'm not a wealthy rancher, and neither is my friend. This place was given to us —"

"Horseshit," the old man said. "All you ranchers have money. Now where is your money pouch?"

Tucker instinctively glanced at Soreback, and the father motioned to the mule. "Willam, grab his gun and fetch that mule over here."

Willam leaned over the saddle of his stunted pony and deftly snatched Tucker's Remington from the ground before riding to Soreback and grabbing the mule's reins.

Willam led him back to the old man while he stuck Tucker's pistol in his waistband.

"Watch him close like, boy," the father ordered and began rooting through Tucker's saddlebags. Within a moment, he came away with a pouch and untied the drawstring. "Whoee! We got this feller's poke." He stared at Tucker. "Thought you said you didn't have no money, friend?"

"I said we weren't rich," Tucker said. "That bag of dust represents months of panning Deadwood Gulch."

"Then you won't object to us helping ourselves," Pa said, " 'cause we're not rich ranchers like you."

"I got no objection," Tucker said, fighting down that rage, that hatred of people that had remained with him since that first day in prison and had never fully left him. "Just let me have my mule and gun so's I can go after my friend. Keep the gold dust and elk meat —"

"And have you come huntin' us?" Pa said. "By the way you wear that cut-down holster, I'd wager you're pretty proficient with it. No, Willam and I will just move along."

"I need my mule —"

The old man pointed his pistol at Tucker's head. "Don't make a fuss, hear? Just be grateful that we've left you with your life."

"My friend's been taken by the Sioux —"

"Then you best get after them on foot if you ever hope to catch them. Willam," his father said, and they turned and rode away at a slow trot, keeping Tucker in their gaze until they'd ridden fifty yards towards the far end of the meadow. As soon as they turned in their saddles, paying Tucker no more mind, he dropped to the burned tent and rolled the Indian off the object he'd spotted earlier. He bent over and grabbed his Rolling Block .45 the Indians had missed in their haste to get away.

He brushed dirt off the blackened rifle stock and off the four large rounds that he kept in a leather holder attached to the stock. He shook dirt out of the heavy, octagon barrel of the rifle and opened the breech, blowing dust away.

He looked up at the two highwaymen, now two hundred yards away, Soreback trailing behind Willam, elk carcass bouncing on his back. Tucker rummaged around the ground and found a small pouch containing the rifle's sight. He brought it to his mouth and blew hard. Dust shot from the sight, and Tucker duck-walked away from the dead Indian as he grabbed two shells. He stuck one between his fingers and chambered the other one while he sat back on

28

the ground.

The two men were more than three hundred yards off now, and Tucker drew his knees up. He rested an elbow on the inside of one, then rested the other elbow on the other knee. He adjusted the sight and took a deep breath before blowing it out.

Looking through the tiny hole in the back sight.

Focusing on the front blade at the end of the barrel.

Tripping the back set-trigger.

Pressing *ever* so slightly on the front trigger until . . .

The shot — when it came — surprised Tucker. As it should have if one was not to flinch with such a heavy-recoiling weapon. A moment later, Willam dropped off his horse. Soreback kicked the air, the elk falling to the ground as the mule ran off.

The old man turned in his saddle for the briefest time. He looked at his dead son only a moment before digging spurs into the flanks of his long-haired horse.

Tucker opened the breech. He placed a fresh cartridge in and once more set the back trigger, his second shot knocking the old man from his mustang.

Tucker chambered another round, expecting the worst, but it never came. Both men lay just where they had fallen.

Tucker stood and rested the rifle across his shoulders. He walked toward the dead men as Soreback looked on at the edge of the meadow briefly and began grazing. Would Tucker have time to bury the two highwaymen? "Not today," he murmured to himself. "And not tomorrow. I got to ride hard to catch up with Jack and the Indians."

CHAPTER 3

Mick Flynn fell on the slippery-wet forest leaves, and Jack Worman jerked him erect. "Damned fool. If we don't keep up, you'll be dragged to death. And with this" — Jack held up the heavy iron shackle encircling his wrist connecting him to Mick — "I'll be dragged to death along with you." If Jack could have distanced himself from the crude Irishman, he would have, if for nothing else than to get away from the smell. Mick was awfully water shy even before being dragged behind horses for miles in ninety-degree heat. These past days Mick had become as rank as a pissed-off civet cat.

The pony jerked them along behind, a long rope connecting them to the rider in back of the column of three Lakota raiders. Jack stumbled ahead, his throat dry, feeling as if he had been swallowing dirt, his lips cracked and bleeding. Since the Indians had raided his ranch and taken him captive, he had subsisted on whatever water he could scoop from puddles on the forest floor and ate whatever scraps of meat his captives tossed to him.

For as bad shape as Jack was in, Mick Flynn was worse. Two days after Jack was taken by Iron Hide and another Lakota, three other Indians had captured Mick twenty miles south of Deadwood. But why didn't they kill either of them right off?

"Where they taking us?" Mick said.

"I'm no soothsayer," Jack said. "How the hell should I know why Indians do what they do?"

The Indian in the rear — more a boy than a man — jerked the rope. Jack had started falling when Mick caught him, and they stumbled on. "Why don't they just kill us? And where *did* they get a set of iron shackles?" He stubbed his toe on a rock but maintained his footing. "Indians don't use shackles."

"Didn't you see that U.S. marshal's badge on that Iron Hide?"

"Who?"

"I told you yesterday, that big bastard leading these merry men." The Sioux headman stood a head taller than the others. With a thick back scarred from more than one Sun Dance ceremony and broad shoulders, the Sioux would say that he's *bloka,* and Jack knew he would be a handful in a fight with *any* man. Even Tucker Ashley, and his thoughts turned back to his friend. The last he'd seen Tucker, he had ridden out searching for game. "I saw a herd of elk grazing across the creek," he had told Jack five days ago. "I'll bed down after I make the kill and see you back here." Would Tucker pick up their trail, come after him? Jack wondered, then answered his own thought — *Of course Tucker would if he were still alive. Between Jack leaving whatever tidbits of sign for Tucker and the Indians making no effort to hide their tracks, Tucker would find them.* Jack only hoped he did so before he was dragged to death. Mick, he could care less either way.

"It just don't seem natural for an Indian to be wearing no badge," Mick said in his thick brogue.

"You can bet some poor marshal didn't just hand over that badge." Jack looked at Mick, but it didn't seem to register in the Irishman's dull mind. "He killed a marshal somewhere. Stole his badge. And his shackles."

"Well, he sure didn't steal it in Deadwood," Mick said. "Seth Bullock is the only law there —"

"Are you as dumb as you sound?" Jack asked. "There *are* other lawmen in this Dakota Territory beside Bullock."

Iron Hide held up his hand, and the column stopped. He yelled something in Lakota Jack couldn't hear, and the Indian tethering them — the boy Pale Moon — dropped off his pony and motioned to an aspen tree. "Sit," he said, his English broken, yet more extensive than Jack would have imagined. Since he was abducted, Jack had tried learning as much about his captors as he could, especially Pale Moon. Though he talked little, Jack had the impression that the young warrior had lived among whites at one time.

He motioned for Mick and Jack to sit beside a tree and tied the rope to it.

"So we're sitting like this again," Mick said. "Hurts my back."

"If you were actually used to hard work, it wouldn't."

"What you implying?"

"I'm not implying anything," Jack said. "I'm outright saying a thief like you isn't used to hard work."

Jack scooted so his back was against the tree, the pale trunk chewed off several feet high where elk had gnawed on the bark. He watched as Pale Moon took his water bladder from his saddle and looked to Iron Hide. The headman nodded, and Pale Moon tossed it to Jack. Mick grabbed for it, but Jack slapped his hand away. "Wait your turn!"

"Worman," Mick said, "when we get out of this pickle, I'm going to beat you like an errant child."

Jack took a long pull before he capped the water bladder and handed it to Mick. "Seems like you had more than enough chances to do that a few months ago." Mick and his brother, Red, had been in cahoots with the McGintys in and around Deadwood Gulch, robbing and killing miners for their claims. They had even cheated Jack and Tucker out of *their* claim in the Gulch. In the end, Red Flynn had been found beaten to death, while Mick would go on to face a miners' court and a sure drop at the end of a stout piece of hemp. If it hadn't been for Jack and Tucker snooping around about the crimes, Mick might be a wealthy and free man today. "Just how *did* you manage to cheat the hangman?" Jack asked. "Last I knew the miners had a California Collar with your name on it."

Mick smiled through his four remaining teeth. "They was stupid enough to post a dumb-ass kid to guard me while they argued among themselves. Some wanted to send for the territorial marshal and drag me back to Yankton for trial. Some wanted to string me up right then and there."

"Still don't answer how you got loose."

" 'Course it does," Mick said. "That kid watching me . . . well, he's taking a dirt nap right about now."

Jack shook his head. "You son of a bitch . . . you deserve what the Indians have planned for us."

Pale Moon returned and took his water bladder back. Mick waited until he was out of earshot before asking, "So you do know what they have in store for us?"

Jack motioned to Iron Hide. "Him and that stocky Indian were talking — they don't know I speak Lakota. They were to meet up with another raiding party in the Big Horns. That was before Custer stuck his nose into things on the Greasy Grass and got hisself killed."

"Meet up for what? Why the hell they keeping us alive?"

"We're to be sold as slaves. Seems like Iron Hide has a Nez Perce contact looking for men to sell to an Oregon sailing company —"

"So we're being shanghaied?"

Jack nodded. "The longest shanghai I ever

heard of. Iron Hide figures he'll have twenty poor souls in tow by the time he rendezvous with the other Indians. We need to figure out some way out of this . . ." Jack became silent as Iron Hide walked to where he and Mick were tied.

Iron Hide sat on a rock across from them and rested his elbows on his knees. "You two are holding up good. You're surprised I speak your language."

Mick stood abruptly, the chain jerking Jack with him. "You son of a —"

"Sit back down," Jack said. He set himself and pulled hard on the chain on his wrist. Mick fell on his face, and Jack hauled him back. "Just listen to what Iron Hide has to say."

"You know who I am?" the Indian said.

"What white man doesn't?" Jack answered. "Murderer of innocent civilians — farmers. Miners. People just making their way in this life —"

"Do not forget the white men who trespass on this sacred *Paha Sapa.* These hills black belong to the *Lakota Oyate.* Each and every *wasicu* deserved to be sent along the *Wanagi Tacanku* — "

"Spirit Road," Jack said and noticed Iron Hide look at him oddly. "I know a *little* of your language as well."

"Ah, yes," Iron Hide said. "Jack Worman — hunter of Lakota, scout for the horse soldiers — knows some of my language."

"And just where did you learn mine?" Jack asked. The longer he could engage the headman in conversation, the longer rest he and Mick would get. And they sorely needed rest. "From the white men you captured?"

Iron Hide shook his head. "No, from my half brother. He came to our lodge many years ago after some . . . trouble in Minnesota." He leaned closer to Jack, and the smile left his face. "You know Minnesota, where they hanged thirty-eight Santee Sioux." He paused for effect. "But of course you know." Iron Hide stood and arched his back. "My half brother's mother was *wasicu.* But that doesn't change the fact that you and your ugly friend" — he motioned to Mick — "are in for a long journey."

"Why not just kill us outright?" Jack asked, unwilling to let the Indian know he'd heard they were going to be sold.

Iron Hide paused as if it were the first time he'd been asked that. "You and all the other . . . people we capture will bring us much money. For ammunition. For guns."

Jack picked a clump of moss from the base of the tree and rubbed his bleeding wrists. "You think my government will stand aside while you kidnap white folks, especially after what your people did to Custer's Seventh Cavalry? The army will be even more determined to hunt you down and kill you."

"If it happens . . . is it not the desire of every warrior to die bravely in battle?" Iron Hide shrugged. "But I do not believe they will send many horse soldiers after us." He motioned to the others seated around on the ground, talking. One smoked a pipe, another had ripped out a clump of buffalo grass and rubbed his pony down with it. "Your army has more important things to do than to chase down a few *Sioux* passing through to hunting grounds to the west."

"The army *will* come after you," Mick said, jerking on the shackles hard. Jack had to brace himself, holding the dumb Irishman from reaching Iron Hide and doing something that would get them both killed. "Jack's right — the army don't cotton to white folks being taken. And cowboys and ranchers . . . miners don't either —"

Iron Hide tilted his head back and laughed. "It would seem that when *Bubuka* — Stumpy — found you a short ways from Deadwood, other white men were hunting you. He said he heard *hanging* when the hunters talked among themselves. I would think they would care less if you were my captive or if you were dead."

"Which is just what we're gonna' be," Jack said, "if we keep up this pace with little food and water."

Iron Hide shrugged again. "If it happens, it happens."

"And if we do not make it to the Nez Perce, you will get nothing for us," Jack said. "If we make it but can't even stand on our own anymore, you will get nothing."

"So," Iron Hide said, "the scout for the horse soldiers *has* been listening." He circled his arm. The others began taking their saddles off their horses, while Stumpy gathered firewood. "You *do* have some wisdom, Jack Worman. We will camp here for the night. And in the morning, you will be rested and able to run twice as fast. We will make better time tomorrow."

"Damn you," Mick said after the Indian had walked away. "Come tomorrow we're really gonna' be run to death. Who the hell is that big bastard who thinks he can evade the cavalry?"

"That big bastard" — Jack chin-pointed to Iron Hide — "has killed more white men in these Black Hills than any other Indian. The Lakota say he can weave dreams of success in battle, can impart to his warriors who follow him an uncanny glimpse of the future."

"Maybe he can dream up a glimpse of our future."

"Right now," Jack said as he watched Pale Moon approach, "our future runs just about the length of that rope they've been dragging us along by."

Pale Moon held his water bladder made from deerskin. He stopped beside Jack and dug into it, coming away with strips of dried meat for both. He turned and walked to a rock several yards away and sat looking up at the treetops, high, swaying with the stout breeze, and at chokecherry bushes clumped between trees, never paying his prisoners any mind. Too young and inexperienced to know Jack and Mick could still be dangerous. If they got loose of the rope and shackles.

"What a mess we're in," Mick said, gumming the strip of dried deer. He swatted at a swarm of no-see-ums, little gnats that had gathered around his face. "We gotta' get away from here pronto. Escape."

"Do you not see those Sioux?" Jack nodded to the Indians sitting beside their campfire. "Even if we haven't been run half to death and were in good shape, we would have a hard time besting them. They're about as fine a fighting man as ever was. And, in case you haven't noticed, they're armed, and we ain't."

Mick washed his meat down with a swig of water and motioned to Pale Moon, sitting with a faraway look. As if he, too, were wishing he were somewhere else. "That young buck there seems to like you more'n me. Tonight — when they're all sleeping — get his attention. Call him over close enough so's I can grab him. Snap his neck before he can holler out. We can use his knife to cut the damned rope and take our chances in the woods."

"As Jack Worman said before," Pale Moon said, walking closer to them, "you sound dumb. To escape is foolish."

"You *do* speak pretty good English," Mick said. "You've been holding back on us. Trying to fool us."

Pale Moon smiled. "Useful to know the . . . voice of your enemy. Especially one who wants me to get close to break my neck."

"Damn," Mick said, and Pale Moon went back to staring at the treetops.

CHAPTER 4

Jack sat upright with a jerk on the shackles, momentarily forgetting he was chained to Mick Flynn. "What the hell you doing —"

"Shush," Jack said, cocking an ear. "Listen."

As the morning sun just peeked over the Black Hills, the yelling of a man echoed off the jack pine forest, the sound seeming to come from everywhere. From nowhere, as sounds often did in these Black Hills. Coming closer.

The three Lakota sleeping next to the campfire leapt to their feet, instantly armed. The stocky, *Stumpy* man ran off into the brush with his bow, nocking an arrow even as he ran, while Iron Hide grabbed his stolen army Springfield. He motioned to Pale Moon, and the young man grabbed his own bow and melted into the trees.

Screams, yells. Nearing, people thrashing about when . . .

Horses broke through the clearing. Two Sioux, each with a captive roped to his pony and stumbling to keep up, halted their horses beside the campfire. The white man — twice Jack's age, wearing the overalls of a farmer, his hands bound together with a strip of rawhide — rushed at the Indians when the biggest of the pair kicked his horse in the flanks. The pony bolted ahead, knocking the man to the ground. The Indian dragged the man into the fire, hot coals burning his trousers. The Indian laughed as he tossed the rope aside, the man slapping his overalls.

The other captive — a girl holding her dress up as she ran — screamed at the Indian and rushed to the man. She dropped beside him and smothered the hot coals with her dress, her frizzled long hair dangerously close to the fire.

Iron Hide yelled, and Stumpy and Pale Moon emerged from their hiding places.

"What's happening?" Mick asked, straining against the rope securing him and Jack to the tree. "Who the hell are —"

"Will you shut that pneumonia hole for a minute and let me listen to what they're saying."

Mick became quiet, and Jack put his hand to his ear as he tried hearing what Iron Hide

44

was telling his warriors. "That man and girl were taken four days ago in a raid west of *Mato Tipila* . . . Bear Butte," Jack said. "Pretty ballsy with an army outpost garrisoned close by." Earlier this month, the army — at the repeated demands of ranchers and miners in the Black Hills region — had stationed a company of cavalry a few miles from Bear Butte with the promise of establishing a permanent fort there. Jack watched the Indians gesturing and telling Iron Hide about their raid on the man's farm. "Those two Hunkpapa must be good to drag those two away right under the nose of army patrols."

"I thought you said these Indians are *Sichangu Brule*?"

"Pale Moon is," Jack said as he cocked an ear towards the Indians. "Iron Hide and Stumpy are *Miniconjou*."

"Kind of a mismatch if you ask me."

"A mismatch good enough to kidnap both of us," Jack said, "along with those two."

The man rolled away from the fire, and Jack had to admire his spunk, even though he was flaunting death with every foolish outburst. He grabbed onto a pony's mane and hauled himself erect. "You sons of bitches are due for a killing —"

Stumpy drew a knife from his belt and hit

the man on the side of the head with the thick bone handle in one smooth motion. He fell to the ground, and the girl instantly dropped beside him. "Pa!" the girl screamed.

Iron Hide bent to the girl and stood her up. He ran his hand over the side of her head, feeling her hair. She slapped his hand away, saying things Jack couldn't quite make out.

Iron Hide nodded to Pale Moon, and the warrior dragged the girl towards Jack and Mick, her legs flailing the air as she tried to get away.

The older Hunkpapa, nearly as tall and nearly as heavy as Iron Hide, suddenly stopped talking and looked about. He spoke to Iron Hide, who motioned in Jack's direction. The man drew his knife and had started toward Jack when Iron Hide grabbed him by the arm and spun him around just as Pale Moon reached a tree next to Jack and Mick. The Indian jerked on the end of the rope threaded through the girl's bound hands, and she fell to the ground beside Jack and Mick. As Pale Moon tied the rope to the tree, she pounded on his back with her roped fists. "If I ever get out of these, I'll take that bow of yours and send an arrow through your chest."

Pale Moon remained silent, absorbing the feeble blows as he tied the girl to the tree next to Jack and Mick. She looked over at them as if seeing them for the first time. "Where'd you two peckerwoods come from?" she asked.

"In due time," Jack said and motioned to Pale Moon. "What's with that big Hunkpapa? He looks like he wants to scalp me alive the way he started over here with his knife."

Pale Moon deftly sidestepped the girl's kick to his shin, not that her bare and bleeding feet would do any damage. Pale Moon looked to where the big Indian stood glaring at Jack. "That is Grass, brother of Rabbit — the other warrior standing over that *wasicu*. Grass looked for his friend, Little Squirrel. But Little Squirrel travels the *Wanagi Takanku*."

"The Spirit Road," Jack said. "This Little Squirrel is dead, then?"

Pale Moon nodded.

"What's that got to do with me?"

"You are the one who sent Little Squirrel to the Spirit Road," Pale Moon said, keeping just out of the girl's kicking range. "Little Squirrel is the warrior you killed at your ranch. Now Grass wants to kill you."

"What choice *did* I have? You bastards attacked me. Killed my livestock. Burned what ranch I did have."

"True," Pale Moon said. He looked over his shoulder and, when Grass wasn't looking, said softly, "I would stay away from him. Iron Hide tells him do not kill you. But Iron Hide not always around."

Pale Moon stood and moved aside for Rabbit. He twisted the rope around his hand, dragging the man along as he held his bloody head where Stumpy had smacked him with his knife. Rabbit whipped him hard with the end of the rope until he stopped at the tree the girl was tied to. He tossed the end of the rope around the trunk, deftly catching it and tying it off.

The farmer shook his head and had gathered his legs under him to lunge at Rabbit when Jack said, "Were I you, I'd be as polite as possible right now. These Indians seem in a sour mood."

"Polite!" the girl said. "These animals killed my mother and little brother." She eased her father back onto the ground beside her. She ripped a piece of her dress and tied it around her father's bleeding head. "Take it easy, Papa. Be a bit before your head clears."

She looked up at Mick, then at Jack, where her gaze lingered for a mite longer. Though not much older than late teens, the crow's-feet around her eyes suggested she had lived a hard life those short years. Yet — with her flaming red hair and eyes as green as any meadow — she would be striking at any age.

"Where'd they capture you?" Jack asked. "I heard them say a ranch by Bear Butte."

The father scooted back against the tree and managed to sit up. He rubbed dried blood that had run down from his forehead out of the corner of one eye. The girl started dabbing at it with a piece of torn skirt, but the man waved her hand away. "Those two Sioux come at us at dawn just as I was walking to the barn to milk the cow." Tears filled his eyes, and Jack suspected it wasn't from pain of a busted head. "Little Joshua weren't but a month off the teat and was handling cow's milk real easy." He chin-pointed to Rabbit and Grass still glaring at Jack. "Them two attacked the missus and filled Joshua full of arrows. Before their screams even died down, I come running up to the house when one of them rode up behind me and knocked me arse over tea kettle."

"By that time," the girl said, untangling pine needles and grass from her hair, "they'd found me. Hog-tied me. Tied me and Pa to a rope around a pony's neck. Flanked their horses and dragged us for better part of a quarter mile. I thought they was going to drag us to death, but they stopped. They didn't speak any English, but they couldn't have told us to be quiet any better if they had. And from then on, they rode just slow enough that we tramped along behind them."

"How'd they manage to sneak past the army patrols?"

The father rubbed his head, but the girl slapped his hand away. "At one point," he said, "we passed within forty yards of a cavalry unit."

"Pa's right — them two didn't have to tell us anything. If either of us would have made a sound, they'd have slit our throats right then and there and hightailed it outta' there."

"Bear Butte is four hard days' trek from here."

"Feels more like four weeks." The man offered his hand, and Jack leaned across and carefully gripped the farmer's hand, bloody and scraped. Like Jack's and Mick's from days being dragged over rough rock and fallen timber. "Rory Tenpenny. And this here is my daughter, Erin."

Erin offered her hand, her grip firm, thick calluses showing she was used to heavy work. She reluctantly shook Mick's hand

and asked, "Who might you two be?"

Jack introduced himself, telling them how the Indians had raided his ranch, destroying everything he and Tucker worked for. "I managed to kill one of them before they roped me and half dragged me to death." He jerked his thumb at Grass. "It seems it was his best pard I killed back there. I'll be lucky if that Indian don't sneak up on me and slit my throat."

"And who are you?" Rory asked Mick.

Mick smoothed his hair back and smiled at Erin. "Mick Flynn. Late of the old country. Come here from County Limerick. And you, sir, you got the sound?"

"County Galway," Rory said. "What's a fine lad like you doing here in America?"

"I was just making me way in life when the Indians put the grab on me —"

"More like he was making for the hills to escape a necktie party," Jack said. "I wouldn't get too friendly with ol' Mick here . . . he'd slit your throat for a dollar and steal the pennies from a dead man's eyes."

"Worman, I'm warning you —"

"Shut that thing under your lip!" Jack said and turned back to Rory. "Fellow country-man Mick was no more off the boat from Ireland when got his nasty feet wet taking money from rich men who had gotten drafted during the war in exchange for taking their place. Not that Mick or his brother, Red, ever served a day in defense of their state."

"That's a lie!"

Jack ignored him. "And when they killed and robbed a few too many fellers in New York, things got hot for them. They come out West killing and robbing miners along Deadwood Gulch."

"Worman —"

Jack jerked on the shackles, and Mick fell over. "I'd trust Mick about as far as I could toss him."

Rory looked to Mick, then his daughter. "Don't matter. We're not going to be around any longer than we have to."

"It looks like we'll all be around one another until they sell us off," Mick said.

Rory motioned to Iron Hide. He squatted with the others around the campfire and now and again looked this way. "I'm not going to have *my* daughter violated."

"Violated?" Jack said. "What's that supposed to mean?"

"It means," Rory said as he took the bandage off his head amid Erin's protests, "that I'm not going to have my daughter in their presence where they can . . . have their way with her."

"Sexually?"

Rory jerked on the rope, but he was short of reaching Jack. "You keep a clean mouth around my Erin."

"All's I'm saying is it sounds like you figure these Indians are going to . . . rape her?"

Rory's face flushed. "I said —"

"I know what you said," Jack said, "but those Sioux won't touch her . . . *that* way. They might kill her and parade around with that long, red hair of hers dangling off their war lance, but she's safe from being molested. Folks just assume Indians will . . . have their womenfolk. Fact is, though, that they have their own sense of honor. At least these Lakota do."

"Pa's right," Erin said, looking at Iron Hide. She caught him looking back, and she blushed. "A girl can tell when a feller's got the eye for her. That big 'un's been nicer to me than he was to my pa since we got here."

"Nice how?" Jack asked.

"He asked if I was hungry. Asked if I wanted an extra swallow of water."

"Are you hungry?" Mick asked, looking her over. " 'Cause you seem to fill out that dress mighty nice." He looked at Rory sitting red faced against the tree. "Take it easy, Pops. There's nothing I can do when I'm tied to this fool." He held up his shackled hand.

"Of course I'm hungry," Erin said. "Thirsty as all get out, too, but Iron Hide wouldn't let me take any dried meat to Pa or water neither, so I told him where to put it." She felt her neck where the headman had caressed her. "But I'm afraid he won't stop hurting Pa."

"He won't be hurting either of us for very long," Rory said. "Like I says, we're getting out of here."

"Mr. Tenpenny," Jack said, "you two wouldn't have a chance of escaping those Indians."

"Hell, don't pay Worman no mind," Mick said to Rory. "If you got you a plan to escape, let us in on it."

"Pa's always got a plan," Erin said.

Rory leaned over and looked around Mick at the Indians. Iron Hide sat with his back to them while the others roasted meat over a fire and talked. Rory hiked up his pant leg and showed Jack a small knife stuffed down his boot. "I keep this little dirk sharp enough to shave with. Tonight, I'm aiming to cut these ropes, and me and Erin's going to be gone before they know it."

"Take me with you," Mick said.

Rory looked at the shackles connecting

Mick to Jack. "Even this here knife of mine's not sharp enough to cut through that iron."

"But you could cut the ropes," Mick pleaded. "Me and Worman can make our own tracks away from those Sioux once we're freed."

"Don't be a damned fool, both of you." Jack looked over his shoulder as Pale Moon stood and walked towards them. The young warrior laid four pieces of cooked deer meat on a leaf and set a water bladder between them. "Eat, sleep," he told them. "Tomorrow we make more ground."

Jack grabbed a piece of meat and began chewing on the deer, a young, dry doe by the flavor. "If you escape, both of you will wind up dead. Those Lakota are powerful trackers. They'll pick up your sign soon's they see you're gone."

"I know how to hide my tracks," Rory said, handing Erin a piece of the meat. "We'll make it."

"Look at this." Jack scooped up a handful of dirt and let it slip between his fingers. "Fine dirt like this easily shows a person's tracks —"

"Don't listen to him," Mick said, and Jack jerked the chain. Mick jerked it back, and Jack nearly fell over.

"I know tracking," Jack said. "I've scouted

for the army enough years to know what's poor tracking ground and what ain't. This" — he let dirt filter through his fingers again — "is *prime* tracking terrain. At least wait until we get to places with the ground more packed . . . by the rain. By the wind and animals. More rocks —"

"My daughter might not have until we find perfect escape ground," Rory said as he nodded to Iron Hide looking at Erin. "We're going tonight."

CHAPTER 5

Hack didn't spot his Mountain Crow
tracker until the wiry little man spurred his
pony out of the ravine toward their hasty
camp. Jimmy Milk had drawn his Colt, aiming at the Indian, when Blade stopped him
before he could fire. "Ease up, Son. Killdeer's ours."

Jimmy holstered cautiously, watching the
Indian ride easily toward the camp. He
reined his horse beside Hack and hopped
off. The man — old by Crow measure of a
warrior's age, with his leathered face host-
ing scars from battles past — held out his
hand.

"What's he want?" Jimmy asked.

Blade lowered his voice. "Tobacco. The
old scoundrel claims only tobacco can
loosen his tongue."

Jimmy guffawed. "And the prospect of
more money than he knows how to spend
doesn't get him to talking?"

"Killdeer's not about money," Blade said, digging into his pocket for his bible. He began rolling a smoke and said, "The Indian never took a dime from *any* of our jobs."

"Then why the hell does he ride with us?"

"For the excitement," Blade said. "For the love of the chase. And for the Sioux. The only thing the old man loves more than running white men to ground is killing Sioux."

Killdeer bit off a corner of the plug and handed it back to Hack before he started talking. He gestured wildly with his hand, motioning to the southeast.

"What's he saying?" Jimmy asked.

"Damned if I know. I can't talk Indian. You know what's he rambling on about?"

Lowell Tornquist shook his head and deftly skinned the feathers off the three grouse he'd shot. "That old Indian speaks as good as you and me when he wants to. He just knows it pisses us off when he talks Crow to Hack in front of us."

Killdeer stopped talking as abruptly as he'd begun and walked to his pony. He led it to the edge of the clearing and hobbled it there before grabbing a clump of grama grass and rubbing it down.

Hack stood for a moment and pulled his patch back from his eye as if he could see out of both. He looked to the southeast where Killdeer had gestured before walking to the fire. He grabbed the pot hanging over the coals and poured a cup of coffee.

Lowell skewered a grouse and hung it over the fire to roast. "Trouble, Boss, 'cause you look mighty worried since talking with the Indian."

"Posse's on our tail."

Blade snickered. "Wouldn't be the first time we had a posse after us. We'll lose them like we've always done."

Hack stared at Blade and shook his head. "We won't lose them this time."

"If we don't lose them, we can kill them," Jimmy said.

Hack ignored him and swirled his coffee around in his rusty cup. "Killdeer's right about this bunch — they won't be fooled. They won't be discouraged. There is nothing we can do that they won't find us." He sipped and scrunched up his nose at the burnt coffee before tossing it onto the ground. "Simon Cady is tracking for them."

"What's a Simon Cady?" Jimmy asked. He brought out his own kit. He trickled tobacco onto the paper as a gust of wind blew tobacco on his face, and he spit it out of his mouth. "Can't be faster than me."

"Simon Cady's a bounty hunter," Blade said.

Jimmy shrugged. "So, he's a bounty hunter. I gunned down two what came after me this spring in Tucson."

Hack glared at Jimmy. "You damned fool, they weren't Simon Cady." He stood and walked to the edge of their camp and stood beside Killdeer looking to the southeast. "Few men that Simon hunts down return alive," he said over his shoulder. "He's a better tracker than any Indian you ever seen. Except Killdeer maybe."

Jimmy started to speak, but Blade shut him up.

Hack turned back to the fire and drew his knife. He sliced off a piece of grouse as he told the piss-ant Jimmy Milk about Simon. "He tracked for Chivington's Colorado Volunteers. Led the good colonel and his soldiers to villages along Sand Creek where Arapaho and Cheyenne camped." He tossed a wing bone aside. "He earned a fearsome reputation to have on your trail even before Sand Creek. After the . . . massacre, it's said Simon was so soured on hunting Indians that he started going after white men. *Wanted* white man. None outsmarted him, and few came back alive."

Jimmy batted cigarette embers off his shirtfront. "I'm sure he bleeds like every other man. Let me get him in my sights —"

"You won't," Lowell said. "Hear tell nobody gets close with that big Sharps Fifty of Simon's. For as old as he is, folks say he can still hit a gnat's ass at a thousand yards."

"Age ain't got nothin' to do with it," Hack said. "He seems to get better with age."

Lowell laid another log onto the fire and sat back as it flared up. "Don't make any sense a bounty hunter tracking for the law. They can't be paying him much."

Hack chin-pointed to the Indian. "Just like him, Simon's not tracking for the money. This time it's about vengeance."

Blade stood and arched his back. "There something you ain't telling us about Simon?"

Hack considered keeping it to himself, but he could not lie to an old friend who had saved his hide more than once. "I killed Simon's woman."

"We're listening."

"It happened up along the Platte thirteen years ago. Oglala Sioux she were, her and her youngen. A boy. Simon had him a nice cache of wolf pelts that I had my eye on, all haired-up nice, as it was a particularly nasty winter. One morning when Simon was out checking traps, I waltzed into their camp to help myself to the pelts. Only problem was his woman had more gumption than I

61

bargained for. She cut me with a fleshing knife, and I had to shoot her when she came after me again." He spit tobacco that hit a rock with a *splat.*

"You said she had a youngster," Lowell said. "What happened to him?"

Hack looked away.

"Hack," Blade said, "what happened to the boy? Did you kill him, too?"

"What do you take me for?" Hack said. "Of course, I didn't kill him, even though a boy of six or seven would have been able to tell his daddy who killed his momma."

"What *did* you do with the child?" Blade pressed. "Did you find him a home? Somebody to take him in?"

Hack stood, rising to his full height, towering over Blade. Intimidating. "I left him to fend for himself," he sputtered. "Now don't look at me like that — I gave him a couple strips of dried bear."

"And just left him?"

"Hell, I weren't much older than him when I had to fend for my lonesome."

"What became of the boy?" Lowell asked.

Hack shrugged. "He weren't none of my concern. If he made it, he grew up a stronger man for it."

"Hack . . . what happened —"

"The cold got to him from what I heard."

"So, because you killed Simon Cady's woman and boy, he's after you with that posse?"

Hack nodded. "We'd better talk about this."

Hack peeked between two black jack pine growing in a *V* overlooking the shallow canyon made up of scrub juniper, stunted aspen trees, and currants, their red berries the color of fresh blood. The canyon started widening gradually enough a half mile to the east but became deeper, though Hack and his men had little trouble negotiating the sharp granite boulders the size of a horse. When they had ridden through the canyon yesterday, Hack hadn't been worried about anyone following, and he'd done nothing to hide their trail. Only occasionally had prison authorities sent a posse after escaped convicts. Hack felt a moment of pride that he was important enough to send a posse after him. But only for a moment as he thought of Simon Cady tracking in the lead. Could he kill Simon? Hack had no doubt in a fair fight with fists or pistols he could beat the old man. And when the time came, he would make certain it *wasn't* a fair fight. He'd make certain Simon's rifle was nowhere within his reach.

Hack propped his elbows on both trees and shielded the front of the binoculars with his hand preventing sun reflecting off the lens. He brought the glasses to his eyes, cursing Tucker. *If that bastard hadn't knocked my eye blind, I could actually have some use of a binocular.* He trained the glass onto the canyon below. The three-man posse worked their way up the shallow end toward where Hack's tracks led. Simon walked beside his horse ten yards in front of the lawmen, stopping now and again to examine the ground. Perhaps a crushed leaf or an overturned rock. Anything that might tell him how long it had been since Hack and his men had passed through the canyon.

Hack brought the binoculars down and rubbed his eyes as he looked around for his men. He couldn't spot them, and he would have been angry if he could, for Simon Cady could sniff out an ambush a half mile away it was said.

But then, no one set an ambush like Hacksaw Reed.

He whistled softly, and Blade poked his head out from under the juniper bush he laid under. He whistled back, and Hack knew his friend had his rifle and extra cartridges at the ready.

Hack looked around for Lowell and finally

spotted him. He blended in with the clump of squirrel tail he lay behind, careful not to anger their sharp spines, his gun cradled in the crook of his arm. He whistled back.

Where was Jimmy? Hack looked among the bushes and boulders lining the rim of the canyon and caught sight of fluttering high in a tree. Jimmy had crawled to the end of a large cottonwood bough, his bandana fluttering every time a gust of wind travelled up the canyon. *Damn him, I told that kid to check and make sure nothing was loose to attract attention.* There wasn't anything Hack could do about it now, except hope Simon or the law dogs didn't spot it.

Hack turned his attention back to the posse, now within three hundred yards. Jimmy and Lowell and Blade had discounted the posse earlier. They wanted to continue after Tucker Ashley, to find and kill him as quick as they could so they could resume their life of robbing other people's money. Blade, Lowell, and Jimmy — three votes to go after Tucker. But Hack had four votes. As much as he *needed* to catch and kill Tucker, he also knew that, if Simon wasn't dealt with now, the posse *would* catch up with them.

Hack put the glasses to his eye once more,

the lawmen now within two hundred yards of death. The posse worked their way among the loose rocks and cactus towards the natural choke point in the canyon. When the festivities began, it would be chaos with every man down there scrambling for cover where there was none. More importantly for Hack, Simon Cady would no longer haunt him as he rode the owlhoot trail.

Where was Killdeer? Hack scoured the canyon and the rim where the others waited. After long moments, he gave up finding the Crow and put the binoculars down. If the old warrior didn't want to be seen, he wouldn't be. But Hack was assured the Crow was somewhere in the canyon, arrows stuck in the ground beside him waiting to be nocked when the action started.

Hack would give the signal, as he did in other ambushes the gang had conducted. He had picked this spot, almost a foolproof position looking down, waiting for the column of men to enter the choke point where only a horse at a time could pass. How many times had he and Blade set ambushes for pursuing Union troops chasing his cross-border raiders, leading the blue-bellies into such a trap much as the lawmen were headed to a few moments longer?

He laid his rifle in the crook formed by both trees and set three more cartridges beside him. A hundred yards.

Hack had picked out a boulder fifty yards away. When the posse reached that, Hack would begin firing.

Simon stood from looking at a track and arched his back, looking around nonchalantly.

But nothing Simon Cady did when he was on a track was done nonchalantly. Nothing done by chance. Everything the killer did had a purpose. Even stretching.

He glanced up the canyon and seemed to stiffen for a moment. He turned to the lawman nearest him and spoke when . . .

A shot! And another as Jimmy emptied his Scofield pistol at the posse, the slugs impacting the ground fifty yards from them.

"Son of a bitch, Jimmy!" Hack yelled and fired at the lawmen, levering fresh cartridges into his Winchester, drowned out by Lowell and Blade firing their Henrys as fast as they could.

A lawman toppled from his horse, an arrow sticking out of his neck, even as another struck the croup of his horse and he stumbled. Killdeer. But even now, Hack didn't see where the Crow shot from.

Another lawman slumped over in the

saddle before Blade hit him again, and he slid down the side of his bloody saddle.

Simon. *Where the hell's Simon?* Hack spotted him running beside his horse, his hand clutching the saddle horn, swinging a leg over the saddle when . . .

His horse jerked away. Simon fighting to control it.

Hack concentrated on the front sight of his Winchester. Letting his breath out. Calm, even as Simon swung a leg once again over the saddle, pulling hard on the reins, grabbing for the saddle as . . .

Hack fired.

Simon jerked from the impact of the bullet hitting his back, and he slumped against the horse's flank. The terrified animal bolted down the canyon, running over dead lawmen, dragging Simon with it. "Son of a bitch is getting away!" Hack yelled and shot the horse. The bay hunched over from the bullet, but fright and pain kept the animal running headlong away from the choke point toward the shallow end of the canyon.

"Shoot Simon!" he yelled. Blade and Lowell opened up, their bullets kicking up dirt and hard rock just behind Simon's horse, as it disappeared down the canyon with Simon barely holding onto the saddle.

By the time Hack turned his attention

back to the last remaining lawman, he lay like the other two — their blood soaking up canyon dust.

Out of the corner of his eye, Hack caught movement. Killdeer sprang from his concealed position among the rocks, scalping knife in hand. A curdling scream erupted from his throat that sent chills down Hack's back even though he had heard the Indian's gleeful cries more times than he could recall. Killdeer straddled the first lawman and deftly lifted the man's scalp before turning to the other two bodies.

"Get to the horses!" Hack yelled at the others. "We gotta' get Simon."

Blade stood and ran to Hack as he reloaded his rifle. "Simon? Looked like you hit him pretty good the way he slumped over his saddle. He won't last long, if he ain't died already."

"Just get to the horses," Hack said. "I'm not going to feel safe until *his* scalp is hanging off my belt."

CHAPTER 6

Killdeer still smiled as he fingered the three scalps dangling from his belt, dried blood staining the front of his trousers as he bent and studied the tracks Simon left when his horse dragged him away. Even Jimmy could have followed the tracks if his one eye wasn't swollen shut where Hack had hit him for his screwup. The Crow stood and looked down the canyon and motioned to turkey vultures circling overhead. "They may come for Simon Cady, I think."

"I'm with Killdeer," Lowell said. "You hit him good, and now those vultures are waiting for us to leave so's they can swoop down and feast on Simon's corpse."

"If he's that bad," Hack said, "we'd have found his body by now. Let's keep on down there. I won't be satisfied until I see his body."

With Killdeer walking ahead of the others — stopping now and again to look at sign

70

— they slowly made their way down towards the canyon floor, Hack's head on a swivel. Sure, he'd hit Simon good — a man didn't fall over in his saddle like he did if he was all right. Still, he had heard rumors and murmurs over campfires for years how the man was bullet proof. That there was nothing that could stop him short of being run over by a herd of buffalo. *Just rumors. The man's no different than any other.* They came around two enormous boulders and saw what the vultures were feasting on: Simon's horse. "What the hell happened to Simon —"

A shot echoed loudly off the granite canyon walls a heartbeat before a chunk of rock *exploded* beside Hack's head, driving splinters of stone into his cheek, his forehead. He dove for the ground just as another bullet kicked up rock where he'd ridden a moment before.

Sharps!

Hack yelled at the others to get to cover, but they'd already leapt off their horses and hunkered down behind rocks, some barely big enough to conceal them from the big .50 caliber bullets. "Sound off!" Hack yelled.

In military precision, Lowell and Blade and Killdeer called out they were okay.

"Jimmy!" Hack yelled when he didn't answer.

"Jimmy's over yonder," Blade motioned to a cluster of rocks. "Kid's shaking worse than a dog passing a peach pit. I think he pissed himself."

"Some killer he is," Hack said, absorbing the silence, wondering when the next shot would come. "So much for Simon being down and out," Hack yelled to Blade.

"Don't see how he could still be alive the way you shot him."

"Apparently not good enough," Lowell said. "Where'd that shot come from?"

"I think he's in that stand of timber a hundred yards down thataway," Jimmy said, his voice breaking as he rubbed his split lip, courtesy of Hack's earlier beating. He low-crawled among the rocks and dropped behind the boulder where Blade squatted. "I think I see the top of his head —"

"You don't see nothin', you damned fool." Hack squatted behind his own little piece of granite rock, the only thing between him and Simon's bullets. He had counted the puffs of smoke after Simon's second round and how long it took to reach them. "He's at least six hundred yards down that canyon," Hack called to the others. "Only reason he didn't hit any of us right off,"

Hack said, picking shards of rock out of his cheek.

"I don't figure we can get to him," Blade said.

Hack agreed. This canyon was a good place to ambush the posse. It was just as good a place for Simon to pick them off if they showed themselves. They lay behind their own cover, things quieter than a horse thief after a hanging. No one moved. No one dared. Simon was down there somewhere with that Sharps buffalo gun of his ready and able to kill the next man foolish enough to leave cover.

"We can take him," Jimmy called out. He looked around his rock while he wiped sweat from his eyes. "He's got to have lost so much blood by now he can't shoot anymore."

"Hey, Jimmy," Lowell yelled. "Whyn't you test that theory of yours — stand up nice and tall and see if ol' Simon don't shoot you. If he don't, we'll know for sure he's down."

Jimmy remained prone behind his rock while Hack said, "Lowell's got a good idea, kid. Stand up there. If he kills you, it'll save me the trouble if you pull another stunt like that damn bandana thing again."

"I s'pose he ain't quite dead yet," Jimmy

said at last.

"I suppose not," Hack said.

Blade shielded his eyes from the sun as he looked down into the canyon. "What's the plan, Boss?"

Hack had no plan for approaching Simon without being drilled, and it angered him. Tucker Ashley had been so close before they had to set the ambush for the posse. He'd been within killing distance of only a few hours, but a simple ambush had gone awry. They'd made good time since picking up Tucker's trail at the ranch, but now this. Hack hated the thought of Tucker putting more distance between him and Hack. But he hated the thought of being ventilated by Simon's .50 even more.

Hack searched the canyon below. There had been no more shooting these last two hours. The turkey vultures had stopped circling overhead when they swooped down on Simon's horse, and Hack saw no more in the skies above the rocks. Was the bounty hunter still alive? Hack had to assume he was, alive and still lethal. If they tried backing out of the canyon now, leaving their rocks for cover, Simon could pick each one off. As much as he'd love Simon Cady's scalp, he wanted to keep his even more. If

Simon was dead down there — and he might be with the solid hit from Hack's Winchester — he resisted the urge to investigate.

Damn. The longer we're here, the more distance Tucker puts between us. But they had no choice. "Plan is," he yelled to the others, "is we wait for dark and back on out of here without any holes in ourselves to show for it."

CHAPTER 7

Two Oglala Sioux rode into camp, a young warrior holding a bleeding shoulder, while his older companion led his pony. Stumpy called to Grass, and he ran to the wounded man while Rabbit took charge of their horses. Grass helped the injured man to the ground and eased him to a log beside the fire and sat him down, the flickering flames playing eerily on their war-weary faces.

"What're they saying?" Mick asked.

"Don't you ever shut up?" Jack said.

"What *are* they saying?" Rory asked.

"If you both be quiet, I might be able to hear," Jack said.

Pale Moon stood from the rock he'd been sitting on some yards from where he'd been watching the captives and approached the fire. He stood well away from the others as the older Lakota gestured wildly with his hands. He motioned to the wounded man slumped against Grass, blood soaking his

U.S. Army woolen shirt he'd probably lifted from some dead soldier.

"The cavalry attacked them at Slim Buttes," Jack said.

"Where's that?" Mick asked.

"About thirty miles north of here as the crow flies," Rory said. "But what's the army doing this far into the hills? Thought that garrison by Bear Butte was there to protect us ranchers."

The Oglala motioned to the north, and Jack picked it up. "Seems like General Crook's been chasing after the Sioux ever since the Custer Massacre —"

"But that was two months ago," Erin said. "And the general just *now* caught up with them?"

"Ever try to catch a Lakota when he doesn't want to be caught?" Jack asked.

Erin shook her head. Even with jaggers sticking out of her tangled locks, she was beautiful. Even if she was tethered to a tree like he was, he thought her . . . attractive.

"Indians travel light compared to the army," Jack said. "I know — I scouted enough years for them. After I'd locate an Indian village and report back to the commanding officer, the whole bunch of soldiers — supply train and pack train and even wagons carrying fool reporters — would plod on, alerting the Indians miles away. By the time the dust settled and the noises the cavalry made died down, the Indians were miles away."

"Then how the hell did Crook catch the Indians at Slim Buttes?"

Jack held up his hand as he strained to hear what the old man told Iron Hide and the others. "Small detachment of soldiers attacked first, it seems. Kept the Indians busy until cavalry reinforcements arrived." A sadness was drawn over Jack's face. "American Horse was kilt in the fight."

"You act like you're sorry he's dead," Rory said, "even though American Horse was one of their leaders."

Jack nodded. "He was a headman."

"Then why the dour look? Just be glad another Indian's dead."

"I met American Horse once, negotiating for the army. He turned down the government's offer to move to a reservation, choosing to fight instead. But at least he was honorable. He had five hundred warriors close in the hills during the negotiations waiting to attack on his command, but he held them back. Allowed the army brass and us folks interpreting to leave unmolested."

"American Horse could have been one of the men who ordered my ranch raided, and you're sorry he's gone?"

"He didn't," Jack said. "Iron Hide ordered his warriors to kill your family and capture you." He turned to Mick and said, "Scoot here a little closer so's I can relieve the pressure some."

Mick moved nearer to Jack, who rubbed his bloody wrists tenderly. "All's I'm saying is that I respected the man as a fighter." He met Rory's fiery stare. "Same respect all fighting men have for one another."

"My Pa's fought enough times, so don't look down on him —"

"Shush," Jack said. "Iron Hide's arguing with them."

"About who's going to lift our scalps?" Mick asked.

"No. About keeping their camp here. Knifes on Top — that's the old man — wants to leave as soon as that young feller gets the bullet dug out of his shoulder. But Iron Hide wants them to stay the night until he finds out just where the soldiers are camped now."

The Indians ceased their argument as suddenly as it began. Grass draped a blanket around the wounded warrior and disappeared into the forest with Rabbit. "Well," Rory asked, "what's happening?"

"Iron Hide sent Grass and Rabbit away to

find out where the soldiers are. He doesn't want Knifes on Top and that one who's been shot to leave and accidentally show the army where this camp is."

"But it's dark," Mick said. "How are they going to be able to see anything at night?"

Jack looked up through the half moon peeking through the canopy of pine trees. "You'll be surprised what Lakota can see at night."

"Don't mean squat to me," Rory said, fingering the handle of his small dirk before slipping it back into his boot. "First chance we get, me and Erin's cutting loose."

"Good luck with that," Jack said. "I'd bet the Indians would have something to say about that."

Iron Hide bent and spoke briefly with Pale Moon. He turned from the campfire and walked back towards where the captives were tied. He walked around back of the tree securing Erin and her father and untied her. "Come," he said. He had begun dragging her toward the fire when she stopped and reared back on the rope, nearly jerking it out of the Indian's hand.

"What the hell's going on?" Rory asked, tugging on the rope held fast to the tree. "Where you taking my daughter?"

"Swan," Pale Moon said, "has a soldier's

80

bullet still in his shoulder."

"What's that got to do with me?" the girl said.

Pale Moon faced her. "Iron Hide saw you take care of your *ate*'s head after *Bubuka* hit him. You take out the bullet —"

"I'm not doing anything for you people. You killed my ma and brother —"

Pale Moon jerked her along. "You no choice."

"Help him!" Jack called out to Erin. "Or *you* might be killed."

"The only thing she ever took a bullet out of," Rory said as he looked on helplessly as Pale Moon dragged Erin towards the wounded man, "was my old hound dog once when he got between my gun and a coon. She don't know how to doctor a man hurt thataway."

"She better learn fast," Jack said.

Pale Moon let the rope fall at the feet of Iron Hide. He pulled the blanket back from Swan — a woolen one with *U.S.* in white letters across it — and gently eased her down beside him. He pulled a small skinning knife out of the coals and handed it to her before stepping back. She started to protest, but Iron Hide rose to his full height and laid his hand on his pistol. He said nothing to her but looked to her father, the implication obvious. *Use the knife on me or my warriors and your father will be shot.* She kept the hot blade away from Iron Hide and motioned to Pale Moon and Stumpy seated across the fire from Swan. "Hold him still."

The Indians held Swan down while Iron Hide slipped the shaft of an arrow between the young man's teeth and nodded to Erin. She hesitated until Rory called out, "You can do it, sweetheart."

She wiped her forehead with the back of her hand and began to probe the warrior's wound.

CHAPTER 8

Jack jerked on the shackles, and Mick moved a little closer, relieving some of the tension on the chains. "Wouldn't hurt you none to be a little gentle."

"And it wouldn't hurt you none to stop your snoring," Jack said.

"What about her?" Mick nodded to where Erin slept with her head against her father's shoulder. "She snores a passel her ownself." He wiped his mouth with the back of his hand. "But what I wouldn't give to let her snore next to me every night."

Jack jerked hard on the chain, and Mick jerked it back. "You quit having licentious thoughts about that girl."

"What kind of thoughts?"

"Immoral, you boob. Besides, she deserves some sleep the way she went to work on Swan even though she'd never dug a bullet out before. Now let's see if Pale Moon will let us go into the woods away from her. I gotta' take a leak."

Jack whistled to Pale Moon seated in front of the campfire. The young Brule had been assigned last watch, and he'd been doing the pecking bird the last hour. He fought to stay awake, his braids bouncing every time his head jerked up, waking him. He looked over his shoulder at Jack motioning to him and stood. He rubbed his eyes while his blanket fell off his shoulders. He walked over to Jack and asked, "What is it you need?"

"We got to pee."

Pale Moon shrugged. "Then pee."

Jack nodded to Erin. "Not in front of *her*. She might wake up and see us. Just let us go a few feet into the woods by that big tree."

Pale Moon smiled. "Do you think your manhood would frighten her, or are you afraid she wouldn't see it at all in the dark?" He walked around back of Jack and Mick and untied the rope while he drew his knife. He led them a few feet away, and they did their thing before the Indian led them back. He secured the rope to the tree again just as Rabbit and Grass rode back into camp. They said nothing as they tethered their ponies and started warming themselves over the fire. Iron Hide threw his blanket aside and crawled closer to the fire.

"What's happening?" Rory asked. He eased his daughter off his shoulder and back against the tree. He glared at the Indians and said, "I was hoping the army would have found them and shot the bastards."

"The army can't find buffalo tracks in the snow at night," Jack said.

"What's going on?" Erin rolled over and propped herself on one elbow. "Those Sioux came back? I was hoping they'd fall in a canyon somewhere."

"As you can see, sweet cheeks," Mick said as he flashed his four-tooth grin, "that didn't happen."

"You'll be kind not to talk to my daughter in that manner —"

"Or you'll do what?" Mick winked, taunting. "You'll cut loose your ropes and come over here and beat my ass?"

"Enough," Jack said. "They're talking about Erin."

Iron Hide and Stumpy spoke among themselves before whispering something to Pale Moon. He walked to where the captives feigned sleep and untied Erin's rope.

Rory lunged at Pale Moon, but the rope kept him away from the Indian. "What are you doing with Erin —"

"Easy, Rory," Jack said, "until we find out

what *is* going on."

Jack caught Pale Moon's attention. "Where are you taking her?"

"Swan," Pale Moon said. "His wound is green. She needs help him."

"Infected," Jack said.

Erin jerked on the rope again and lashed out with a kick that Pale Moon easily sidestepped. "Iron Hide says if Swan dies, one of you die." He nodded to Rory. "Maybe your *ate.*"

Erin settled down, and Pale Moon led her hobbling on her bare feet to where Knifes on Top knelt beside his young friend shaking violently under the blanket.

She moved the old man aside and motioned for the water bladder, tearing a strip off her dress. She soaked the cloth and began dabbing at Swan's forehead.

Grass stood with Rabbit off to one side as they told Iron Hide what they'd found in the forest, gesturing with their arms, speaking soft enough that Jack couldn't hear what they said.

When they had finished talking, Iron Hide turned and walked towards his captives. Mick scooted back as far as he could with the short shackle attached to Jack's wrist, while Rory looked defiantly up at the headman. "They saw many soldiers, Rabbit and

Grass," Iron Hide began. "So many horse soldiers in our *He Sapa* that they fear moving might draw their attention. It is wise to stay in the protection of this valley."

"How long?" Jack asked. If he had an idea how long they were to hole up here, he might be able to form a plan of escape. "How long will we be here?"

"A day," Iron Hide said. "Perhaps two. When the soldiers have tired of the chase and returned to their warm blankets and full bellies we will leave."

Jack knew Iron Hide spoke truth, for Jack had seen it many times with the soldiers — many young men out West living their first great adventure, only to be slapped with a dose of reality. Few soldiers had the spunk to continue on half rations or pursue Indians in a blinding snowstorm or intense heat wave. They would — Jack knew — rather hole up in some fort somewhere.

"We . . . your prisoners might not make it for you to sell," Jack said. "A day's rest will help us continue, but we need food. We can't live much longer on a few strips of dried buffalo or elk."

Iron Hide shook his head. "Always wanting more, Jack Worman. I will send *Bubuka* out and hunt deer tomorrow." He looked at Rory. "Your daughter . . . she is a fine

87

woman. She took that bullet out of Swan even though she had never done so before. And she helps him even now as the fever overcomes him."

"Not by choice she didn't help," Rory said.

Iron Hide said, "Still, she will make a fine woman to share my lodge with, once I have bargained with you men."

"Are you saying Erin and you . . ." Rory's face flushed red even in the dim light. "By, Gawd, she will share no teepee with you!"

Iron Hide shrugged. "We will see. I think that she will get used to being in my lodge."

Rory was struggling against the rope when Jack laid his hand on his shoulder to calm him, before turning to Iron Hide. "Those two Hunkpapa over there spoke of someone else in the woods."

Iron Hide nodded. "There is a *wasicu* in these hills. Who is it?"

"There are many white men in these woods," Jack said. "Hunters bagging game to sell in Deadwood to hungry miners. Miners themselves who went bust in the Gulch."

"But," Iron Hide said, "this *wasicu* follows us. Hunts us, Grass thinks." Iron Hide pointed to where Jack knew they'd passed a game trail this morning. "He is but a day's ride down that path. Hunting us."

"A lone white man?" Jack said. "Why tell me?"

"To let you know that I will send Rabbit down that trail to kill this man."

"Again, why tell *me* this?"

"Because it is said that Jack Worman — who scouts for the horse soldiers — knows everyone."

"Without seeing him, how *can* I know who this man is?"

"He is a man who sits tall on his big mule."

Jack stiffened and inwardly cursed himself for letting Iron Hide know he suspected who it was.

"So you *do* know him. Why is he so foolish to follow us? Alone?"

Jack looked away and remained silent.

"No matter. Rabbit will kill this man."

"Kill Tucker Ashley?"

Now it was Iron Hide's turn to stiffen at the sound of Tucker's name. He stood to his full height and his hand rested on his pistol jammed into his waist belt. "Tucker Ashley?"

Jack smiled. "The last man you want on your back trail."

"I do not worry," Iron Hide said, his voice breaking up as he turned and walked quickly to Rabbit. He spoke to him, and soon he and Knifes on Top rode into the night towards the game trail.

To where Tucker surely followed the tracks. Hope entered Jack's waking thoughts for the briefest amount of time. *Perhaps Tucker will find us.*

CHAPTER 9

Tucker turned Soreback into the wind, stroking the mule's neck, quieting him. *Rifle shots.* .44 Henry, maybe a Winchester. The sounds filtered through the thick forest below, hard to tell as the sound whipped through the canyon Tucker had passed through not half a day ago.

Firing coming from somewhere behind him.

Had someone been following him and was now engaged in a gunfight? Or was it some hapless miner or hunter who got ambushed by Indians, for there surely were Lakota — Cheyenne, too — roaming their sacred Black Hills?

Tucker had been so engrossed in picking up the Indians' trail as they dragged Jack along. He had paid scant attention to his back trail. He would have to be more careful in the future.

When the sun beat down overhead, Tucker

stripped off his sourdough coat lined with red and blue flannel and wiped his forehead before draping his hat over the horn. He turned in the saddle as he looked back, down ancient granite formations, this the highest place in the Black Hills. This place the Lakota called *Okawita Paha,* the Gathering Place, and from where he could see for miles in any direction. The Indians had separated for a brief time at the base of *Okawita Paha,* two warriors riding high, sitting their ponies just where Tucker sat his now. Their tracks showed where they had stopped now and again, turning their mounts, looking around.

Worried. About soldiers combing these hills, no doubt. After Custer and his regiment got their butts kicked on the Greasy Grass, the army threw another two regiments into finding and punishing the Indians. And Tucker had heard the company of cavalry garrisoned outside Bear Butte had joined the search.

He turned the mule towards the trail down off the mountain. He would pick up the tracks of the Indians once more when he reached the base.

Except this time, he would watch behind him.

■ ■ ■ ■

The mountain stood barely visible in the distant thick forest when Tucker stopped Soreback and dismounted. He bent over, looking into the sun, deciphering the tracks left by the Indians and Jack and . . . another captive? Jack's drag marks remained distinct where he continued struggling to remain on his feet while being dragged behind a pony. But this new set of tracks was also distinct, with the right foot pigeon-toed when he was able to jog behind the horse.

Two captives — Jack and this new one — walking close together, perhaps bound together by rawhide or a rope. But why were the Indians keeping them alive? By their inability to remain on their feet for long, it was apparent to Tucker that both men were at the point of exhaustion these many miles. How long would they last? Tucker wasn't a religious man, but he prayed now that he would find Jack before death rescued him from his ordeal.

Tucker led Soreback to a trickling stream. He rolled a rock on top of the reins before taking a bag of dried venison he'd bartered for a box of .45 ammunition from a wolfer half a day's ride ago. But dried deer got old, and — when a grouse took flight in the woods ahead — Tucker took his rifle from the scabbard, then replaced it. If he hit the bird with a buffalo gun, he *still* would have no supper. He had decided to use his pistol to bag a bird when Soreback's ears pricked up and turned toward where the bird had been bedded down.

Tucker stroked the mule's withers. "See something through the trees, pard'ner?" Tucker said softly. "Or do you just *feel* it," and immediately answered his own question: *he* felt someone lay in wait among the trees thirty yards across the creek.

He slowly slid his Remington from the scabbard as he looked around the small clearing surrounded by thick forest. Ten yards ahead and to the side off the game trail the Indians had taken sat a boulder large enough to hide a man. Tucker looked away, knowing one's peripheral vision often detects things looking straight on misses, and he spotted . . . a strand of black hair blowing on a gust of wind before it disappeared behind the boulder once again.

A man hunkered down behind that boulder. An Indian, more'n likely. He gripped the rifle tightly. *But Indians rarely ambushed alone.*

Somewhere close another Indian hid, waiting to spring their trap.

If Tucker cooperated, which he had no intention of doing.

He looked over the ground, his experience during the war telling him terrain could often be the difference between living and dying. He spotted a slight depression in the ground that could offer him temporary protection when attacked just as the *twang* of a bowstring cut the silence. He threw himself into the depression as an arrow *whizzed* past where he had stood a moment before.

A scream erupted from in back of him, and Tucker turned with the rifle.

A Lakota — seeming to fly through the air carried by a guttural, animalistic cry spewing from his throat — leapt from a tree branch, slashing the air with a long knife, black blood dried on the blade.

Tucker swung the rifle butt at the Indian's head.

He deflected it. The rifle sailed from Tucker's grasp and careened off a rock into a deep ravine, while the Lakota landed atop Tucker. Air *wooshed* out of his lungs.

He caught sight of another Indian — an elder — emerging from behind the boulder, his own knife in hand. The old warrior hobbled towards where Tucker and his opponent rolled on the ground.

The Indian laid all his weight atop Tucker, squeezing his throat with one powerful hand. His knife cocked overhead. Stabbing downward.

Tucker jerked his head to one side, and the Indian's blade sliced through the brim of Tucker's hat and buried itself in the ground beside his ear.

Tucker kneed the Lakota in the groin, putrid air *wooshing* out of him a second before Tucker grabbed the man's chin and back of his head and twisted violently. The Indian's head *snapped,* his body instantly limp, the old man nearly upon them.

Tucker rolled from under the dead Indian as the old man thrust low with his knife. Tucker drew his pistol and shot the man center chest. Tucker cocked his Remington to shoot him again, but it was unnecessary.

The old man stared at Tucker's feet, his eyes looking upward in that stare reserved only for the dead.

Tucker willed his shaky legs to be still as he walked to a log to one side of the game trail and sat. He took deep, calming breaths, feeling the throbbing in his forehead veins subside. He replaced the spent cartridge with a fresh one and holstered when he realized Soreback wasn't where he'd left him. Tucker whistled, but the mule didn't come for the wild turnip like he usually did.

"You can whistle until the air runs out of you, but that old mule of yours is gone," a voice behind him said.

Tucker turned to see a tall, skinny kid ambling from behind two pine trees, a Smith Schofield balanced in his hand as he pointed it at Tucker. "Oh, you can stand on up, if that's what you want to do. Just keep that gun of yours holstered."

Tucker faced the man. Even though he was little more than a youngster, he wore the haggard look of someone who'd grown up too fast. Of someone who wanted to *see the elephant* but didn't know where to look. Of someone who had killed a time or two and felt the *rush* of excitement as his opponent bled out at his feet. "Who the hell are you, and what did you do with my mule?"

The kid pushed his Montana Peak on the back of his head. Wispy, blond bangs fell across his eyes, and he brushed them away. "I cut your mule loose like I did those Indians' ponies." He grinned. "I hate to see critters not be able to run free like they ought to."

"I asked you who the hell you were."

The kid's grin faded. "I'm Jimmy Milk."

Tucker didn't know what Jimmy's game

was, but he was certain he had no good intentions toward Tucker. He breathed deep, relaxing breaths, knowing relaxed muscles reacted faster than tense ones, and said, "So you're Jimmy something-or-other. That supposed to mean something?"

Jimmy's face flushed red, a contrast to his pale complexion. "I've killed six men in stand-up gunfights. You'll be number seven."

A sinister sadness overcame Tucker. How many mothers' sons had come after him, only to be planted in the nearest bone orchard, their main sin wanting a reputation that they could take home and brag about. "You mean you *murdered* those six men?" he said, riling Jimmy, watching the kid's gun hand. "It doesn't have to be this way. All you got to do is walk away, and I won't kill you —"

"Kill *me*? I'm the one holding the gun. And yours is still holstered. Even you ain't that fast."

"But your hand's shaking, Son. It's probably sweaty enough by now you fear you might drop that Schofield. You know the slightest mistake, and I'll drill you where you stand." Tucker watched carefully Jimmy's hand white knuckled around the grip of the gun butt. Watched his thumb. Whenever Jimmy's thumb came over the top to cock the gun . . . "Bet you shot the others down without so much as a chance, too, just like you're planning on doing right now."

"You son of a —"

"Do yourself a favor, kid, and holster that hogleg. Back out of here and live to see the sun set. On my worst day I could beat you."

Jimmy stepped closer, and his voice broke when he said, "Folks will recognize me when I tell them I outdrew Tucker Ashley in a fair fight."

"But this isn't a fair fight, you snot nosed little bastard."

Jimmy's thumb uncurled from the gun butt.

Tucker breathed deep; his muscles relaxed.

Jimmy's thumb — as if in slow motion — dropped on the hammer.

Drawing it back. Cocking the gun when . . .

. . . Tucker threw himself into the depression in the ground. Drew his pistol when . . .

Jimmy's first bullet went wild over Tucker's head.

The second bullet hit Tucker's upper arm even as he felt his own gun buck from the recoil of the shot.

Jimmy stiffened, looking disbelievingly at the gun dangling from his hand, trying to cock the gun once more when Tucker fired again. The bullet struck Jimmy under his eye socket and his face *poofed* up dirt as he fell facedown on the ground. Unmoving.

For the second time in as many hours, Tucker had to sit on the stump to calm his shaking legs that threatened to give out. And, once again, he reloaded his pistol and holstered.

Warm blood pooled at the end of his wrist from the bullet wound to his shoulder. Tucker carefully unbuttoned his shirt and peeled the fabric away. The bullet had taken a chunk of flesh from his shoulder muscle but had not hit bone. He walked to Jimmy's body and snatched the kid's bright-yellow bandana from around his neck and slipped it around his shoulder and under his armpit. He clutched one end of the cloth in his teeth while he managed to tie a knot that would stay before covering it with his shirt.

He looked down at the dead Indians and at Jimmy Milk, momentarily feeling the need to say *something* over their corpses. Until he remembered Jack was but a day away now, and Tucker sorely needed to make up for lost time. If Tucker could catch one of the Indians' ponies and ride after

Soreback . . . until he remembered Jimmy saying he had cut loose the ponies when he did Tucker's mule.

But Jimmy had to have tied his own horse down the trail. Somewhere.

Tucker worked a loose circle around where he and the Indians had fought and picked up Jimmy's tracks leading down the game trail. Tucker broke into an easy lope, wanting — *needing* — to get to Jimmy's horse. *Needing* to get back on the trail before Jack died from exhaustion . . .

The *tracks* of Jimmy's horse, when Tucker spotted them only thirty yards away, showed a frightened animal that had been tied to a low hanging pine bough. The branch lay broken, the bark scraped off where the reins had abraded it, and Tucker could envision the terrified animal jerking its thousand pounds on the thin rein around the branch and running off.

Tucker was afoot.

He walked back to where the fight happened and searched the bodies for anything that might help him. He took the flint and cotton fire starter kit from the old Lakota and plucked Jimmy's ammunition from his belt. Tucker snapped open the Schofield and ejected the remaining four cartridges that were unfired, pocketing them. Though they were different from the Remington's ammunition and underpowered, they'd come in handy in a pinch. And Tucker felt there may be many *pinches* in the days ahead. He lobbed the Smith into the woods and bent to Jimmy once again. Tucker grabbed the kid's bible from his shirt pocket. He peeled off a paper and began rolling a smoke.

When his shaking hand holding the cigarette calmed enough, he walked to the rim of the deep ravine and looked down. His rifle lay shattered among rocks, the barrel bent at an ugly angle, the stock broken at the wrist.

He turned back to the game trail and picked up the tracks of Jack and the Indians. Being on foot, having only a handgun, no water, Tucker was less than hopeful that he would eventually catch them and save his friend.

But he had to try.

CHAPTER 10

Jack jerked lightly on the shackles, and Mick woke up. "What the —"

"Shush up, damned fool," Jack whispered, "and listen to me."

He looked over at Rory sawing on the rope encircling his and Erin's wrists to the tree. "They're fixin' to make a run for it, and I didn't want you waking up Pale Moon."

The young warrior sat by the fire, his body turned so he could watch the captives. *If he managed to stay awake.* His head had bobbed on his chest for the better part of an hour before settling on his chest, immobile. Soft snores reached Jack ten yards away that were only slightly louder than the other Indians sleeping close to the warmth of the campfire.

"Take me with you —"

Jack clamped his hand over Mick's mouth. "One more peep outta' you and I'm going to ask Rory for that knife of his and make sure you don't say another word. Now *shut up!*"

Swan moaned under his blanket, and Jack paused until the wounded man settled down into his fitful sleep before he scooted as close to Rory as the shackles would allow. "I can't talk you out of it?" he whispered.

"Here," Rory said and handed Erin the dirk. "Now cut your rope." He looked around Jack at Pale Moon. "This is going to be our best chance to get away."

"But you won't," Jack pleaded. "They can track a water bug across a lake and — no offense — but you're not exactly a woodsman."

"What's that supposed to mean?"

"You're a rancher. You couldn't hide your tracks good enough that they wouldn't find you. Hell, *I* probably couldn't confound my tracks so they wouldn't find *me.* And I'm pretty track savvy."

"Here, Pa," Erin said, freed from her rope that had rubbed her wrists raw and bloody.

"Maybe she's got a say in it," Jack said.

"Pa's an almighty smart man," Erin whispered. "If he has a plan, it'll work. Besides, I got no desire to be Iron Hide's woman. I'll go with Pa."

Jack looked back over his shoulder at Pale Moon still sleeping by the fire, an army blanket wrapped around his thin shoulders. "The only plan you have is to hide long enough to get away once you're free, but I'm telling you, they'll find you —"

"Thanks for your concern," Rory said as he helped Erin stand. "Just do your best to keep the camp quiet long enough to give us a head start." He held out his hand, and Jack shook it. "Once we're gone, I'll find an army unit and tell them about you two and what the Indians have planned for you."

Jack caught Erin's frightened look. In the darkness he could not see, but he knew right now her pupils were as wide as saucers at the prospect of what Iron Hide would do once he learned she and her father had escaped. But Erin had trusted her father's actions all her life. Even if it was a foolish decision, she would trust him again this night.

Unlike Jack, who didn't trust Rory to fool the Indians and *knew* their escape would be disastrous for them both.

Erin faced Jack a final time, her eyes meeting his for a long moment before she turned and followed her father into the forest.

"Hope it's not long before they find the cavalry," Mick said under his breath. "Thank God we'll be freed from these bastards."

"You *are* a damned fool," Jack said.

"What'cha mean by that?"

Jack chin-pointed to the Indians sleeping around the campfire. "Once they wake up and realize Rory and Erin have escaped, they'll be madder 'n hell. It won't take them long to find the Tenpennys. Then we'll all suffer for it."

When Pale Moon screamed, Mick and Jack sat up as one. Iron Hide and Stumpy threw off their blankets and stood, rubbing sleepers out of their eyes a moment before Grass leapt from beneath his blanket. They ran after Pale Moon leading Iron Hide towards Jack and Mick and where the rope securing the Tenpennys lay frayed on the ground. "How far you figure they got?" Mick asked, wild eyed watching the Indians approach.

"Not far enough," Jack answered.

Iron Hide rushed to the tree where the Tenpennys had been tied and examined the ends of the rope before looking around. He spotted the tracks where the captives had fled and told the others to mount up.

He turned to Jack and asked, "When did they leave?"

Jack shrugged and squinted as he looked into the rising sun peeking through the forest. "Four, maybe five hours ago, when it was *Bubuka*'s watch. They slipped away so quietly —"

Iron Hide *slapped* Jack hard across the face. He fell backwards against Mick, who scooted as far away from Iron Hide as he could. "You lie, Jack Worman. The one-who-scouts-for-the-soldier chiefs can tell when the morning dew was disturbed. How long it takes for the smell of broken branches and crushed leaves to filter through the wind." He grabbed Jack's face and squeezed hard. "The smell is strong. They have been gone for an hour. Maybe two." He let Jack go and looked angrily up at Pale Moon. "Besides, *Bubuka* would never fall asleep when it is his turn to watch. Now when exactly —"

"Were I you," Jack said, rubbing his face stinging from the blow, "I'd worry about Tucker Ashley."

Iron Hide stood and looked around the camp nervously. "Knifes on Top and Rabbit have found Ashley by now and killed him —"

"Then why are they not back at camp by now?"

Iron Hide said nothing, and Jack exaggerated a grin. "Because Tucker killed *them*. And you know it."

107

For a brief while, Jack thought Pale Moon and Grass had lost the Tenpennys' tracks. Iron Hide had sent them to track Erin and Rory and bring them back. Grass had volunteered to remain in camp and watch Jack and Mick, but Iron Hide didn't trust Grass alone with Jack. The memory of him killing Little Squirrel still soured in the warrior's mind, and he had been sent with Pale Moon.

Iron Hide looked into the sky, judging the time just as Jack had: three hours they'd been gone. The headman glared at his captives now and again, stopping several times to reassure Swan he would recover from his bullet wound. Between waiting for the soldiers to leave the Black Hills and the Tenpennys' escape, Iron Hide was in a sour mood. "I should have driven my knife into you long ago," the Indian had told Jack as Grass and Pale Moon disappeared into the woods.

"Why, just because I didn't tell you when Rory and the girl escaped?" Jack asked. "I doubt you would have done so if you were in my place."

"If I could not get much money for you, I

would cut your throat . . ." He fingered the handle of his skinning knife hanging off his waist. Iron Hide stalked off and resumed his pacing around the camp. Jack knew the Indians needed to be gone from the Black Hills if they were to deliver their white men in exchange for his precious guns. And the Tenpennys' escape put a burr under Iron Hide's saddle.

"Think they made it?" Mick asked as he chewed the last of the deer meat Iron Hide had tossed their way.

Jack stared at the Irishman, thick bags hanging under his red-rimmed eyes like bags of wormy flour hanging in a storekeeper's back room. Jack wondered if *he* looked as bad, concluding he probably did after being half dragged, half starved this past week. "I was hoping they might have made it, but I doubt Rory or his daughter made it far at all."

"But they had a couple hours head start."

"That only means that — when the Indians capture them again — they'll be that much more exhausted when they come back. They don't *belong* in the woods. The Indians will find them soon enough. They'll —"

Grass broke through the camp clearing, Erin kicking the side of the pony as she lay across the saddle. Her hands were trussed up with strips of rawhide, her bare feet were cut and bleeding, the toe of one foot showed where a cactus needle had penetrated all the way and stuck out. The Indian shoved her off the horse, and she hit the ground, rolling over, sitting up. Glaring.

Still defiant.

Iron Hide walked to her and had bent down to help her stand when she swung with both tied hands. He deftly drew back. She lost her balance and fell back into the dirt beside the fire. "Stand her up," Iron Hide ordered.

Pale Moon grabbed Erin by the shoulders and jerked her erect. She crow-hopped on her bleeding foot as Iron Hide and Grass looked down on her. "It was a foolish thing you did, you and your *ate.*"

She glared at Grass and lunged at him, but Pale Moon held her firm. "If I ever get a gun or a knife or a bow in my hand, I'm going to kill you."

"But you will not get that chance," the headman said and took hold of Erin's rawhide binders. He scowled at Pale Moon. "Because of your failure to stay awake, we have a long delay. See to it that Swan is fed. We break camp in the morning."

Iron Hide dragged a hobbling, screaming

Erin Tenpenny away from the campfire and into the woods, her cries of protest growing fainter as the forest swallowed her cries. "What's he going to do," Mick said, "have his way with her? Or kill her?"

Jack rubbed his face, still stinging from Iron Hide's slap three hours ago. *Damn, that man's strong.* "He will not molest her."

"I don't know," Mick said. "That big bastard had *the look* about him when he took her away."

"He fancies Erin as his next woman," Jack said. "I do not think that he will harm her."

"Then why drag her away?"

"Perhaps to *make her think* that he intends having his way with her. After all, that's what everyone in the frontier here believes — that all Indians rape women captives at will. They do have their own code of honor."

"Then why —"

"Perhaps he intends frightening her as a warning of future escapes."

"That might be, but where's Rory? Pale Moon and Grass came back with just the girl."

Jack motioned to Grass bending over a pot of meat boiling over the fire. Heavy, tooled leather suspenders were hooked to his trousers. Just like the fancy ones that had held up Rory's trousers. When he was alive.

Agonizing shrieks interrupted the quiet evening. The Indians around the campfire stood and looked to where Iron Hide emerged from the forest dragging Erin Tenpenny behind him. An Erin with patches of her hair cut away, looking to Jack as if she had the mange, her scalp bleeding from a dozen shallow cuts.

She wailed as she limped beside Iron Hide, the cactus thorn still sticking from her foot. Her red hair that had been cut off now dangled from Iron Hide's belt as he noticed Jack glaring at him. "Tie her up," he ordered Pale Moon and threw her on the ground beside the young warrior.

She buried her face in her hands, crying, her shoulders shaking, and Jack sorely wanted to go to her. Tell her everything was going to be all right. *If* Tucker caught up with them.

Iron Hide walked to where Jack struggled with his restraints and scowled down at him. "Why does Pale Moon have to do all the camp chores?" Jack asked. "Things a woman ought to be doing?"

Iron Hide looked over at the young warrior as he brought in more firewood to stack in the depleting pile away from the blaze. "He is my *tahnhan*."

"And that is how you treat your first woman's brother?"

"If it were any other warrior, I would have killed him outright for falling asleep. Pale Moon lives *because* he is *tahnhan*. Besides, his shame is his biggest punishment."

"I overheard you arguing with Grass . . . what happened out there?" Jack motioned to the forest. "What happened when he and Pale Moon ran down the girl and her father?"

Iron Hide took out a red clay pipe and filled it with tobacco. "The father . . . fought bravely when Grass caught up with him." He tamped the tobacco down with a piece of deer horn. "The *wasicu* had a small knife, and he attacked Grass with it. Grass killed him." He looked once again at Erin as she sat on a log, bending over, gripping the cactus thorn with her teeth and pulling it from her foot. "She fought them as a *Lakota* woman would do."

"Why didn't Grass kill her, too?" Mick asked.

"Because he knows she is to be my woman," Iron Hide said immediately. "And because Swan still needs her."

"And this band of yours," Jack said, waving around the campsite with his hand, the shackles *tinkling* against one another, "will you still be alive once Tucker Ashley finds you?"

A tic.

Just a slight nervous tic at the corner of Iron Hide's eye that Jack nearly missed. One of those involuntary muscle spasms that told Jack the headman was, indeed, worried about Tucker.

CHAPTER 11

One moment Hack was holding out his cup for Lowell to refill it, the next moment Killdeer stood inside their camp circle walking towards the fire. As if he'd blown in with the rain and the wind the thunderstorm brought a couple hours ago. The Crow said nothing as he squatted beside Hack and held out his hand. "Damned vulture," Hack said and handed Killdeer his plug of tobacco.

Hack waited until the Indian had bit off a corner and was thoroughly chewing it — indicated by a soft *humm* emitting from Killdeer's throat, the only emotion Hack ever saw the man make. Except when he was killing an enemy. "Well," Hack said at last, knowing he could not rush the Indian's explanation, "did Jimmy kill Tucker or not?"

"Jimmy Milk was a fool. Tucker Ashley shot him twice." A slight smile passed across Killdeer's face as he grabbed a cup and the pot of coffee resting over the coals. "And he killed two Sioux." He grabbed Jimmy's Schofield stuck down his trousers and handed it to Hack. "Tucker Ashley threw this into the woods."

Hack picked it up and snapped the top of the pistol open. Empty. "Jimmy have ammunition on him for it?"

"He did not."

Hack tossed the gun aside. "Don't do us any good — our Colt cases won't fit into this." He pointed to fresh scalps hanging from Killdeer's trousers. "The Sioux?"

He nodded.

"Sioux, you say," Blade Tate said as he emerged from the trees buttoning his trousers. "I thought the army was driving them back to the reservations."

"It would seem," Killdeer said, choosing his words carefully, "that the soldiers attacked the *Snakes* by Slim Buttes. Many were killed."

"Damn." Hack spat tobacco juice into the fire and stood. He kicked a rock, and it caromed off a dread stump. "We got Sioux hereabouts besides Tucker Ashley to worry about."

Killdeer sipped. "Not to worry. Kills the Deer will deal with the *Snakes* when the time comes. We *should* worry about the

116

horse soldiers. They search for Sioux who escaped into the Black Hills. If they find you" — he pointed with his coffee cup — "they will take you prisoner."

"I'll be damned if I'm ever going back to prison."

"Might be your wish," Blade said, "but you might not have a choice. By now, your escape from the Wyoming Territorial Prison has made all the newspapers. And the army surely knows it, too."

Lowell stood and threw the dregs of the coffee pot onto the dirt before setting the pot down and picking pine needles from his long beard. "We wouldn't stand much of a chance with the cavalry. I vote we light outta' here. Go south. I hear those Mormons down Utah way are ripe for the pickin's."

Hack stepped around the pile of firewood and stood facing Lowell close enough that Hack could reach out and squeeze his throat closed if he wished. Even though Lowell sat tall in the saddle, he looked almost small looking up at Hack. "This is not a democracy," Hack said between teeth clenched hard enough to break them. His face and neck flashed red, his jaw muscles clenching and unclenching. Blade had brought Lowell along because he worked dynamite. But right now — with no use for a powder monkey — the man didn't seem to fit in. "I'll have Tucker Ashley's head in my saddlebags before we break off and head south. Understood?"

Lowell backed away out of Hack's reach. "I was just throwing out an alternative —"

"That you might as well forget," Hack said, feeling his anger subside. He'd need enough of that rage when he met Tucker. "Unless you want to ride out on your lonesome?"

Lowell held his hands in front of him as if to ward off the suggestion. "I got no truck with you. Blade says it'll be well worth riding with you once we bag Ashley."

"Good." Hack turned back to the fire and the rabbit roasting over the coals. "Now all we have to do is catch up to him."

"That will not be hard," Killdeer said.

"How the hell you know that?"

"Because he does nothing to hide his tracks," Killdeer said. "I do not think that he knows anyone follows him."

"Can you pick up his trail again?"

Killdeer held out his hand. "I could if I had fresh tobacco."

Flickering flames cast eerie shadows over the three men sitting around the campfire.

118

"Killdeer's been gone longer than I expected," Lowell said. He had formed dough from flour he'd stolen somewhere and wrapped it around a stick. He held it over the fire to cook slowly. "You figure Tucker spotted him and got the best of the Indian?"

Blade guffawed. "You've never worked with the Crow before. Tucker wouldn't even *know* the Indian was close. He could put the sneak on the man and cut his throat before he even knew Killdeer was on him."

"Then if he kills Tucker . . ." Lowell stopped abruptly.

"Finish it," Hack said. "You think if Killdeer kills Tucker that it will free us to look at some bank or railroad jobs."

"It crossed my mind," Lowell said.

"Let it just *cross* that pea brain of yours that Killdeer won't touch Tucker. He knows the man is mine alone."

"You hate him that much?" Lowell said.

"This," Hack said and pulled back his patch covering his blind eye as if to remind Lowell, "is the reason. Tucker puts the boots to me in prison. Sent me to the infirmary, but the sawbones couldn't save it. Not that they tried all that hard. And that's why Tucker will be all mine." He spit a string of juice that *sizzled* on the hot coals. "If I'd known Jimmy was going after Tucker, I would have killed the kid myself. God help the poor SOB who takes Tucker out before I get the chance."

They sat in silence, and Hack pulled the heavy duster tighter around him against the cold, grateful for the stage company. The Sidney to Black Hills stage had been gracious enough to part with the duster — usually loaned to passengers to protect them from the dirt along their trip. Except Hack relieved them of the coat, along with the strong box and a fine pocket watch he'd lifted from one of the passengers at the scene of the robbery two days after the prison break. As he stared into the fire, he felt anger build inside him. The prison had kept his own watch when he entered, and he would have liked to get it back. But he'd settle for the stolen watch to tell him just how long Killdeer had been gone.

Hack bent to the meat cooking over the fire and had drawn his knife to slice a piece off when Killdeer *appeared* at the peripheral edge of the fire. "Ashley is no more than a quarter mile," he chin-pointed, "through the woods."

"Quarter mile!" Blade said. "He ought to be a lot farther away."

Killdeer broke off a leg of rabbit and began chewing. "He is on foot. His mule is not with him. He sits by his campfire. Like you do now."

"Like we *were* doing," Hack said. He brushed grease off his shirt and handed the Indian a branch from the pile of wood. "Show us where Tucker is exactly."

Killdeer drew a rough map on the ground showing where Tucker was camped along a stream still running fast from the spring rains. "This creek," the Indian said, "flows strong. And loud. It will surely . . . how you say it, mask our approach. He will not hear us if we are careful." He drew another line in the dirt. "And this short ridge will hide us. Let us get close."

"You got close enough that he didn't hear?" Lowell asked.

Killdeer looked over at Lowell and nodded. "I was close enough that I could have killed him and had his scalp hanging from my belt" — he glanced at Hack — "if you hadn't ordered me not to."

Hack studied the map carefully before standing and brushing wet dirt off his trousers and gesturing to the others. "Me and Killdeer will approach the camp using that ridge line as cover. You two" — he motioned to Blade and Lowell — "will follow the creek. You guys will get there before we do, and I want you to wait. Make sure he doesn't escape. And make damn sure you do not kill him."

"There is something else," Killdeer said, studying the map he had just drawn. "Something is not right."

"What's not right?" Blade said. "We put the sneak on Tucker and hold him long enough for Hack to get there."

Killdeer continued studying the map. "Tucker Ashley's fire is too big."

Hack chuckled. "That's it? You think he wants to warm himself by a hot fire is not right?"

Killdeer met Hack's gaze and chose his words carefully. "Tucker Ashley is a hunted man. And hunted men keep their fire low."

"You said before that Tucker don't know we're on his trail," Hack said.

The Indian stood and looked into the forest, toward where Tucker was camped a quarter mile away. "This one . . . he is different. He . . . leaves tracks even *you* could follow," he told Hack. "I feel that he knows we hunt him now."

Hack waved the air. "Don't worry about it. In an hour, Tucker will be planting sunflowers, and we can get on our way to a nice, fat bank."

"We're off, Boss," Blade said as he checked his pistol before walking to his horse. "How will we know when to put the grab on him?"

"When my first shot kicks up dirt beside him." Hack had started towards his sorrel when Killdeer stopped him. "We go on foot."

Hack paused. "You're right. We don't need a horse to nicker or the clomp of a hoof to give us away."

"That is good," the Indian said, "for this Tucker Ashley is said to be *ahpal'aake*. A *ghost*. One that kills."

What little moonlight filtered through the trees offered scant illumination of the path that Killdeer and Hack picked their way on. "Hold up a moment," he said softly to Killdeer. Hack had stumbled through the forest and thick underbrush, tripping now and again, jaggers raking across his arms, his face, cutting tiny rivulets that oozed blood. "I'm not quite as nimble as you," he said and sat on a fallen tree to catch his breath.

Killdeer sat beside him, and Hack noticed the old man didn't wheeze. The Crow looked out into the night, his head on a swivel, looking for what?

"What you see?" Hack asked.

Killdeer shook his head. "Nothing. Everything. One does not lower his caution when he knows there are Sioux nearby."

"You ain't gonna' go off hunting Sioux just when I'm about to take Tucker?"

"It is what I do," Killdeer answered simply.

"It is said that your people have been bitter enemies for many years."

Killdeer looked into the forest as he spoke. "My people and the Sioux have been *iskoochiia* — enemy — for so long —"

"Why?" Hack asked. "What caused your tribes to hate one another?"

The Crow paused, mulling over the question. "I do not know. It is what my people do — hunt and kill the Sioux. It is told over smoke holes in our teepees on cold winter nights that there have been great battles between my people and the *Snakes*. It is . . . just how things *are*. It is my duty." He faced Hack. "As much as it is your duty to kill this Tucker Ashley."

Hack understood that. Even if he and Tucker hadn't fought — and even if Tucker hadn't beaten him, humiliated him — the two men represented different paths of life. One that would have been on a collision course anywhere. Under any circumstance.

Hack stood and arched his back. "How much farther?"

"Close," Killdeer said, and Hack recognized the worried look on his face. "What is it?"

"It is that fire," Killdeer said. "I still believe it is too high and too hot for a hunted man."

Hack slapped the Indian on the back. "That means after we put the grab on Tucker, we'll be able to warm ourselves all the better."

"And when we do . . . put the grab on him, what then?" Killdeer asked.

"Then I beat the snot out of him until he can't even move. Before I kill him."

Killdeer's hand brushed his skinning knife, and he looked out past the campfire again. "This Tucker Ashley . . . I think that sneaking up on him will not be easy. I think that he escapes."

Hacksaw shrugged. "As much as I'd like to beat the hell outta' him, perhaps you're right — perhaps we'll just ventilate him where he sleeps."

CHAPTER 12

Mick sat up, the chain between them clattering. "Riders coming in."

Jack scooted back to sit against the tree as he looked over at Erin. She had wailed through the night about Grass killing her father and about Iron Hide cutting her hair that she had been so proud of. Jack had given her his Stetson to wear to cover her head, even though it was a size too big, and it drooped down as it rested on her ears. That had helped for a while, but she now sat with her face buried in her arms that hugged her bent knees. She rocked back and forth, murmuring something. "Erin, are you all right?"

She pushed the hat back from her eyes and looked at Jack. "What?"

"Are you ok?"

She forced a laugh while she swept her hand over her damp eyes. "Sure I am. I'm tied to a tree and haven't eaten much for

126

three — or has it been four days? My father was murdered in front of me, and that head-man cut off all my hair. Besides that, I'm just fine." She sat up and glared at Grass standing beside Iron Hide awaiting the riders return to the camp. "But I am going to kill that bastard."

Iron Hide stepped aside as the riders broke through the trees, and Jack sucked in a breath: "Blue Boy" he breathed, the Lakota's horse barely stout enough to carry the huge Santee Sioux.

"What's a white man doing running with Indians?"

"He's not white — he's Indian. Gets his complexion from his white mother . . . his size from his Oglala father."

"Know him then?" Mick asked.

Jack nodded, his eyes transfixed on the Indian. "Technically, I guess you could say he was Oglala, though he calls himself a Santee. His mother left his Indian father and took Blue Boy to her relatives in Minnesota. He was caught up in that massacre in '62 there when the Indians killed all those whites, and Blue Boy fled ahead of a hangman's noose."

"You act like you're afeard of him," Mick said.

"You would be, too, if you knew what he's

capable of. He kidnapped Tucker's woman from her mercantile store, and Tucker hunted him down. He damned near kilt Tucker until he got the best of Blue Boy. But I thought he left the territory after that."

"How'd Tucker best somebody that big?"

"A miracle, I'm thinking," Jack answered, watching Blue Boy step off his horse, a large army mount with the *U.S.* branded on its flank.

He stepped toward Iron Hide and stood at arm's length before saying something Jack couldn't hear.

Jack got Pale Moon's attention, and the young Indian walked over to them, watching Blue Boy over his shoulder as he neared. He stopped in front of Jack and Mick and stood looking in awe at Blue Boy.

"They pard'ners or something?" Jack asked.

"Half brothers," Pale Moon answered. "Iron Hide is *sunkaku* to Blue Boy."

"Iron Hide is Blue Boy's younger brother then," Jack said cursing himself that he hadn't realized it sooner. Iron Hide had said enough that Jack ought to have known he and the renegade Blue Boy were related. "What's he doing here?" Jack asked. "Heard there was bad blood 'tween them." Tucker had told Jack the story that Blue Boy and his younger brother had gotten into a terrible fight as youngsters, with Blue Boy cutting his brother with a knife. Shortly thereafter, Blue Boy's mother took him and lit out for Minnesota to be with her family. But that fight had earned Iron Hide his name when the medicine man had a difficult time sewing the knife wound closed in the boy's *iron hide.*

Pale Moon glanced at Erin murmuring to herself and held up his hand. "We learn why he is here in this camp if we listen."

Iron Hide and Blue Boy spoke again before he whistled, and seven more haggard warriors rode into camp. One rode slumped over the neck of his pony, crusted blood covering a leg while another walked beside him leading both his ponies. Bloody bandanas were wrapped around two other Sioux breaking from the trees. A broken shaft of an arrow stuck out of the flank of one scrub pony stumbling along, and Jack was certain it would have to be put down. *What I wouldn't give for even that arrow-stuck pony and my freedom from Mick Flynn.*

"What're they saying?" Mick pressed Pale Moon.

Pale Moon ignored him and walked towards where the newcomers painfully dismounted their horses. "They said," Jack explained, "they're fixin' to roast the Irishman slow over a roaring fire."

The color left Mick's face. "Really?"

Jack laughed. "No, fool. They didn't. Just figured I'd give you some grief."

"Then what *are* they saying?"

Jack cupped his hand to his ear. "Blue Boy and his raiders were camped at Slim Buttes when the soldiers attacked. They were caught flat footed. Got the hell shot out of them before they managed to skirt the buttes and fled down thisaway."

Iron Hide motioned to Pale Moon, and the young Lakota joined them for a moment before returning to where the captives were tied. He walked around Erin and began untying her rope.

"What are you doing?" she demanded. She jerked free from Pale Moon's grip before he wrapped his hand around the rope and dragged her toward the other Indians.

"You help Swan," Pale Moon said. "Now you help Little Water. His leg bleeds much."

"The hell I will!" Erin kicked Pale Moon's shin with her bare foot. His leg buckled, but he managed to stay upright as he dragged her along. "You bastards killed my pa, and you expect me to help you?" She kicked again, missed, and fell to the ground, but

130

Pale Moon continued dragging her along.

"They might kill us all if you don't help him," Jack called out as Pale Moon threw Erin onto the ground beside the wounded Little Water.

At the sound of Jack's voice, Blue Boy straightened. He walked to where Mick and Jack were tethered, and Mick backed up as far as he could get, Blue Boy towering over them both. All color drained from Mick's face as he stared up at the Santee.

He looked curiously at Mick for a moment before squatting in front of Jack. "I thought that was the voice of Jack Worman — army scout. Hunter of innocent Sioux —"

"And I thought that was Blue Boy, killer of the innocent when you burn farms, kill women and innocent children," Jack blurted, throwing common sense to the wind. This man in front of him could snap him in two if he detected weakness. But the only thing Blue Boy respected was courage. "And now," he held up his shackle and jerked Mick closer, "you will profit from *selling* us?"

"Selling you?" Blue Boy scooted closer. "Sell you for what?"

Jack forced a laugh. "What for? *Mazaska igni.* To raise money, of course, and the great Santee Blue Boy will profit from the sale of captives he and his brother has."

Blue Boy stood and backed away as if he were backing away from the Devil himself. "I know nothing of selling you. How could I — we have been fighting the horse soldiers since they entered these Black Hills." He walked to where Iron Hide talked with Stumpy and one of the newcomers. "We need to talk, *misun*," Blue Boy said.

Iron Hide backed away from Blue Boy and waved his arm around the camp. "I trust all my warriors. Say what you wish."

"So be it." Blue Boy pointed to Jack and Mick, and he looked down at Erin tearing her dress into strips for a bandage. "These *wasicu* . . . you have captured them to *sell*?"

"For money. Yes," Iron Hide said. "To buy guns. And ammunition, to drive the white men from our sacred *He Sapa*. Has not that always been our wish, you and me?"

Blue Boy paced in front of the others standing around listening to the brothers argue. "It has. But this," he motioned to Erin, "brings us no honor. To kill the white man, yes. But not *this*."

Iron Hide looked to his warriors as if for support. "We will get many guns after the sale of our captives. And for those whites we pick up along the way —"

"Killing a white man is something the

soldier chiefs can forgive over time. But taking just one *wasicu* as a slave — especially a woman — is something they will *never* forgive. They will send many soldiers after you. And they will find you."

Iron Hide laughed, and Stumpy and Grass took his cue and laughed as well, glaring at Pale Moon, who stood silent off to one side. "The soldiers cannot find buffalo tracks in the snow let alone find us. We have waited here two days, time enough for the horse soldiers to tire of looking for Lakota in these hills. They have surely left by now."

"What'd they say?" Mick asked. "Looks like they're ready to kill one another."

"Don't bet on it." Jack interpreted what the brothers were arguing about.

"You think that's right, that the army has given up looking for Indians in these mountains?"

"If I were a betting man — which I am if we ever get back to Deadwood — Iron Hide is right about the army. It is almost a certainty that the cavalry has given up the hunt. Don't hope on them saving us."

"It sounds like Blue Boy doesn't want us to be sold. He wants us freed, by the sounds of it."

"As usual, you can't think right. Blue Boy doesn't want us freed. He wants us *dead.*"

133

"I speak truth, *misun!*" Blue Boy's voice rose once more. "The soldiers will follow you and find you. And worse, they will find me and my warriors."

Iron Hide laughed again, though he stepped back from Blue Boy. "The only one who follows us is a lone white man riding his clumsy mule."

Blue Boy stiffened. He looked over at Jack and seemed to finally connect who Tucker was tracking. "A mule you say?"

"Tucker Ashley," Iron Hide said, nodding. "I sent two men back to kill him. He will follow us no more."

Blue Boy's legs wobbled, and he sat on a log beside his injured warrior. He glanced down at Erin bending over the wounded man. She had torn away his trousers and dribbled water over the bullet wound. "If this *is* Tucker Ashley who hunts you, this is *worse* than the soldiers looking for us."

Iron Hide waved the air as if dismissing Blue Boy. "I sent Rabbit and an Oglala who rode in with Swan." He nodded to the Indian returning with firewood cradled in his one good arm. "Rabbit and Knifes on Top —"

"The old man?" Blue Boy asked. "He was in camp when the soldiers attacked us." He shook his head. "*That* is who you sent with

Rabbit to kill Ashley?"

Iron Hide's face flushed. "They are both good men."

"It will take more than just good men to best that white man. *When* did you send these men back to kill Ashley?"

Iron Hide looked away. "Yesterday."

Blue Boy kicked a rock with his foot. "Then they are surely dead, and Ashley continues hunting you." He motioned to Jack. "Because you have taken his friend over there, he will not stop."

"You are afraid of this white man, then," Iron Hide said before he stopped, realizing what he had accused his brother of.

Blue Boy rose slowly, his chest heaving, the muscles in his thick neck tensing, and Jack recognized the controlled rage he had seen on the big Santee once before. He stepped closer to Iron Hide, who could step no farther before he fell into the fire. "I do not kill you because you are my brother." Blue Boy lowered his voice so that Jack barely heard the threat. "But if you accuse me of cowardice in front of my men again, I will forget we share the same *ate,* and I will send you along the *Wanagi Tacanku* before you wish."

Iron Hide's hand shook as he took his red clay pipe from his pocket and dipped into his tobacco pouch. He tamped it down with an antler bone before lighting it and handing it to Blue Boy, stem-wise. The Santee looked at for a long moment before accepting the pipe. He drew in a puff and handed it back, the argument between brothers over.

The others saw all was right once again and sat in front of the fire building it up, while two more took their bows and disappeared into the forest to hunt meat.

"What are they saying?" Mick asked, "and don't give me that cock-and-bull about wanting to roast an Irishman over hot coals."

"I think Blue Boy's worried that Tucker's on our trail."

Mick's stomach growled. They hadn't eaten since this morning, and it wore on him and Jack. "I doubt that big Indian ever worries about anyone."

"Tucker could have killed Blue Boy a couple years ago but didn't. And Blue Boy could have killed Tucker. Seems like they reached some sort of mutual agreement to fight another day." Jack listened to his own stomach growl and hoped the hunters would bring back a fat doe. "That day might be coming up if Blue Boy has a notion to find him now that he knows Tucker is somewhere close in the hills."

"What will you do now that you have fought the soldiers and escaped?" Iron Hide asked Blue Boy.

He accepted the pipe again and drew deeply. "We will go to Deadwood town where miners have squatted on our land. We are not many, but we will kill them one by one when they leave town. We will make the *wasicu* sorry that they trespassed on our land."

"I will be there as well, brother," Iron Hide said, "as soon as I take these white men — and many more along the way — to sell for weapons. We will come back here with guns." He motioned to Blue Boy's .44 Colt. Blue Boy had wrapped a strip of rawhide around the barrel and loading lever to prevent it from falling apart as the heavy gun recoiled. "We will have new guns. Ones that don't break when you fire them."

Blue Boy looked at Jack and Mick and nodded to Erin, squatting beside the wounded Lakota as she wrapped his leg with a strip of her torn dress. "No good can come of this. Me and my men will leave as soon as Little Water recovers."

Blue Boy stepped over the fire pit and bent beside Little Water, who gritted his teeth as Erin doctored him. "Will he live?"

"If we take his leg off," she said. "His infection had spread, and there's nothing I can do for him. If we had an army doctor . . ."

"Leave us," Blue Boy said and told the others, "we will talk between us, me and Little Water. Leave us."

"What's going on with them?" Mick asked.

"You heard Blue Boy — he wants to talk alone with his injured man. My guess is he's asking if Little Water wants to be taken to an army surgeon to have the bullet taken out, or stay with Blue Boy and have the leg lopped off."

Blue Boy propped Little Water's head up, and they spoke in hushed voices. The wounded Indian fingered his *wophiye* hanging around his neck with a leather thong, the medicine bundle giving him strength even as he lay dying.

After long moments, Blue Boy simply said to Pale Moon, *"Peji hota."*

The young warrior walked to his beaded saddlebag and came away with a stalk of sage. He handed it to Blue Boy, who spoke to Pale Moon. He nodded and stood Erin up, walking her back to where Mick and Jack were tied, and secured her to the tree.

Blue Boy held the sage and lit it with a

138

burning twig before gently cradling Little Water in his arms and walking into the woods. No one stopped them. No one questioned them. But the others looked after them with a profound sadness as they knew what was about to happen.

"What's going on?" Jack asked Erin after Pale Moon rejoined the others around the fire.

"I couldn't do a thing for him," she said, and Jack saw genuine sadness in her face. As much as she despised these people, she had done all she could for Little Water. "He did not want to be taken to an army surgeon."

The other Indians sat around the fire. They spoke among themselves in quiet, almost reverent, tones for nearly an hour until . . .

. . . a shot rang out from the direction Blue Boy and Little Water had gone.

"What the hell —"

"That was a .44," Jack said. "Blue Boy's big ol' Colt be my guess."

"He just killed his own man?" Mick asked.

"Little Water knew he was dying," Erin said as she pulled Jack's hat farther over her patchy head. "Blue Boy could have taken him to a white doctor, but Little Water refused. That would mean surrender, and there is no surrender in these people."

CHAPTER 13

A noise behind Tucker alerted him — the snapping of a twig. Perhaps the rushing of pine needles under foot. No more than ten yards in the trees. Good.

Someone approached him from his backside, and he slipped off the thong securing his gun to his holster. Whoever was putting the sneak on him confirmed Tucker's suspicions: that Jimmy Milk had *not* been working alone. That someone besides the dead gunslinger hunted Tucker. But who? He'd collected dozens of enemies in his life as a scout and bounty hunter. All he knew was that the one in the forest behind him was good.

Tucker turned his ear to catch any sound. He closed his eyes, willing his breathing to slow, his heart to slow when . . . another snap of a twig, farther down the trail. Leaving. But the one who hunted him would return with more cutthroats he was certain.

He piled more branches onto the fire, then, for good measure, laid on two more large logs. The flames licked higher, sparks crackling, the odor of burst pine and ash filling the air. A fire one could see for a mile. A fire bright enough to temporarily blind any man at night.

He kept the thong off his pistol and mentally made his plan.

It wouldn't be long now. By the time the killers made their move, Tucker's night vision will have returned.

Tucker knelt behind an enormous black jack pine as big around as a wagon wheel and turned his collar up to ward off the stiff needles rubbing his neck from the low hanging branches. He had put another log onto the fire before leaving for the safety of the trees, avoiding looking into the light as he watched the dark woods. Moonlight peeked through the trees. Just enough that he will be able to spot movement when it came.

He was certain it would come. And soon.

He swiveled his head, closing his eyes, picking up a crackling of leaves underfoot fifty yards into the trees. A deer or an elk? Perhaps until a sharp *snap* of a branch told him it was the hunters: no deer or elk would put its foot down on a fallen twig.

He breathed deeply but saw no movement, no one sneaking into his camp, no one approaching the rolled-up blanket stuffed with grass until . . .

Another branch broken. Rustling of clothing against a boulder. Clumsy men not used to the woods. Not used to hunting a man like Tucker as they pushed branches aside before breaking from the clearing on the other side of the fire. They led with their rifles, muzzles jutting from brush before darting back to the safety of the trees.

Tucker drew his gun. He saw their outlines and could kill both in as many seconds when *something* caused him to pause. A heartbeat later he saw what his instincts warned him about: shadows of two more men, faint in the glint of light. They made their way through the trees from the ridgeline he himself had used for cover when he approached this camping site.

He inched back farther into the protection of the low hanging branches. How many more men hunted him, for they surely were not alone? A moment ago, he could have killed the first two. He might even be able to kill one or both of the second set of killers. But how many *more* stalked the woods after him?

He waited, breathing deeply, willing his

heart to slow, waiting for them to make the first move and reveal just how many were out there stalking him.

The first two men stumbled through the trees a few feet before separating. They went in opposite directions, flanking the campfire and the stuffed bedroll beside it — *Blade Tate*. Tucker recognized the killer, but not his partner. Blade had ridden and robbed with Hacksaw Reed for years, and it would be no surprise if he still rode with him. They stopped, thirty yards apart, waiting for the other two Tucker had spotted. Or making certain Tucker didn't escape?

A sudden wave of an arm; a brief shadow across the camp as the second pair inched their way from the woods to stand at the edge of the trees, and Tucker sucked in a breath: *Hacksaw Reed.* The last time he saw the cross-border raider he was in the prison mess hall. He had jumped Tucker and tried stealing his food. Big mistake for Hacksaw, and he shouted that he would find and kill Tucker even as the turnkeys were carting the big man to the infirmary on a stretcher.

Hacksaw sat on a stump partially hidden by pine branches, his partner standing back several feet, yet close enough to the fire that the flames illuminated his craggy face. Tucker recognized the small man's over-long and thick nose that had once been splayed across his weathered cheeks. His long braids hung freely over his chest, his medicine bundle — a small beaded leather lizard — was woven into his one braid. That man among the hunters who did not look into the fire.

Kills the Deer.

Tucker cursed to himself. As good a man tracker as he was, Kills the Deer was a legend among his people. And among the Lakota whom the old man had hunted and killed for decades. Tucker had no illusions about evading these men as long as the Crow tracked for them.

But he could slow them down.

Tucker moved cautiously to the other side of the pine tree where he could better look at both sets of men separated by thirty yards. Hacksaw and Kills the Deer worked their way around the far side of the camp. Soon they would have all directions covered, preventing any escape by Tucker, springing their ambush. Still, he didn't know if more men ran with Hacksaw or not.

Tucker backed deeper into the trees and began working his way around to the opposite side where the man that had approached with Blade knelt with his rifle propped against a bush. Tucker carefully picked up his feet, testing the ground for branches or pinecones before putting his weight down. Watching the man stare into the fire, stare at the bedroll lying there, inching through the trees when . . .

A twig *snapped* underfoot.

The man's head turned around, staring in Tucker's direction.

Tucker looked away. *The eyes draw the eyes,* he repeated to himself, knowing the man had been looking in the direction of the fire for so long his night vision was shot. For the time being.

After tense moments, the man turned back and continued staring at the grass-stuffed blanket.

Tucker stood within ten yards of this man, yet he knew he could not approach without being heard. And he *needed* to be hands on with him. Knew he *needed* to carry out his plan if he hoped to slow Hacksaw and the others down long enough to find Jack.

Hacksaw finally stood from the stump and followed Killdeer through the trees until they stopped ten feet from the clearing. If Tucker were to make his move, it had better be before they were all in position to launch their attack.

Tucker bent, and his hand found a fist-sized rock. If he could lob it to this side of the campfire, draw his man's attention that way, Tucker might slip the last few yards undetected. He checked Hacksaw and the Crow: they remained where they were, waiting for Blade to work his way closer.

Tucker cocked his arm and lobbed the rock into the trees across from the clearing.

The man's eyes instantly turned to the sound, snapping his Henry to his shoulder as Tucker . . .

. . . crept closer, three yards separating them. The man's focus toward the sound . . .

. . . now within grabbing distance.

One more step.

The man's head snapped around to the sound behind him. He swung his rifle to meet Tucker.

Too late.

Tucker set himself and hit the man hard on the neck. As he collapsed, Tucker wrapped his arm around him and eased him soundlessly to the ground, catching his rifle a heartbeat before he hit the dirt.

Tucker looked about. Hacksaw and the others had heard nothing of the man Tucker had choked unconscious.

It was time for Tucker to begin slowing the hunters.

■ ■ ■

The man — big and broad shouldered — had been a handful. He tried lifting the man and the rifle, too, and had to lay the man's Henry on the ground to lift him over his shoulder. Tucker carried him farther back into the trees, stopping now and again to catch his breath until he was twenty yards away from his campfire. He laid him carefully on the ground just as he regained consciousness.

The man looked up at Tucker with a wild-eyed, frightened look about his face as he tried mumbling through the bandana tied around his mouth. He struggled against his hands bound with his own galluses, his boots lay beside his filthy bare feet, and his holster was empty after Tucker shucked the man's Colt into the brush. He squatted beside him and asked, "How many more are there riding with Hacksaw besides the Crow and your partner?"

The captive remained silent. Tucker drew his Bowie and caressed the man's cheek with the back of the blade. "I'm not going to take that gag off just yet. Now you nod or shake your head: are there more men riding with Hacksaw?"

The man shook his head.

"I don't see any horses . . . you all come on foot?"

The man nodded.

"Crap," Tucker whispered to himself. He had hoped Hacksaw and his ambushers had ridden close to the camp before sneaking the rest of the way on foot. What Tucker wouldn't give for a horse right now, and he cursed Kills the Deer, for surely it was the Indian who had sneaked within twenty yards of Tucker's fire an hour ago. And it was surely the cagey old Crow who told the others to approach the camp quietly on foot.

"Don't go anywhere," he told the man and walked a few yards closer to the trees. He parted branches until he spotted Blade leaning against a tree at the far side of the fire. He stared at the bedroll with his rifle shouldered, the barrel peeking out from the bush.

Tucker strained to spot Kills the Deer and Hacksaw, seeing the big man bring his rifle to his shoulder and aim at the bedroll.

And open fire.

The hills reverberated with the sound of three rifles firing as fast as the ambushers could operate the levers and jerk their triggers. Wool blanket material *sputtered* into the air; dirt chipped into the fire from the impact of the bullets on the grass-stuffed bedroll. Shell casings hit the ground beside the shooters, and Tucker saw Hacksaw getting a piece of hot brass down his neck. He crow-hopped as he clawed at the hot metal inside his neck and tossed the spent cartridge aside.

The firing ceased, and Hacksaw thumbed fresh cartridges into his rifle. He shouldered his rifle again while he walked into the clearing just ahead of the Crow and Blade Tate. "Go check his bedroll," Hacksaw ordered, and Blade warily approached. He stuck the barrel of his rifle under the blanket and tossed the bedroll aside.

Hacksaw ran to the shot-to-hell bedroll and cursed. "That son of a bitch set us up." He dropped to one knee and looked about nervously. "He might be in the trees getting a bead on us right this moment." He motioned to the Indian. "Cut his sign. If he was here not an hour ago, he couldn't get far. Unless what you saw was just that stuffed blanket."

"It was no blanket," Killdeer said and began working a wide circle around the campsite.

Hacksaw moved closer to the protection of the trees and said to Blade, "You and

Lowell comb that stand of trees to the west . . ." He looked about. "Where the hell *is* Lowell."

"I don't know," Blade said. "He was with me a few moments ago —"

Hacksaw moved from the trees and grabbed Blade by the collar of his coat. "What do you mean, you don't know?"

Blade looked frantically around as if realizing for the first time his partner wasn't there. "We split up once we got close enough to the campfire." He jerked away from Hacksaw and nearly stumbled over a pile of firewood. "We was waiting for you to start the party, just like you said." He looked around again. "I don't know *what* happened to Lowell."

Tucker moved back from the trees to where Lowell struggled needlessly. It was only a matter of time before Kills the Deer picked up his sign. Tucker needed to complete his plan quick and light out. It was time to make more chaos to slow Hacksaw and his men down enough to allow Tucker to catch up with Jack.

Tucker squatted beside Lowell and drew his knife. "If there were any other way, pard, I'd do it. But I'm on foot, and I need to slow Hacksaw down enough for me to hightail it outta' here." He pushed the man over and grabbed onto his legs. "This is gonna' cripple you for now. But your muscles'll heal back up after Hacksaw tends to you. Long after I'm gone."

Lowell's eyes widened looking at the long blade. He thrashed around to get away from the Bowie, but Tucker held him down. Tucker hadn't lied — he really did not want to cut the man. But in so doing, he wouldn't be able to stand on his own. And sitting a horse would be hard, slowing the band of killers down. The others would *have* to help Lowell, and that would give Tucker time to . . .

. . . in one smooth motion he sliced first one of Lowell's Achilles tendons, then the other. Not deep enough to cripple him permanently, but deep enough that — when Tucker snatched the bandana from Lowell's mouth — his screams would attract the others. But by then, Tucker would be well away from the camp and back onto Jack's trail.

Lowell's face contorted in agony, thrashing about, looking at Tucker with pure hate. Lowell was rolling on the ground when Tucker bent to him. "Now you can scream," he said and snatched the bandana from Lowell's mouth.

Lowell's painful anguish cut the night air, sending shivers up Tucker's spine a moment before he slipped into the forest just as Hacksaw and the others ran headlong through the trees toward the screams.

As the cries grew fainter with distance between them, Tucker hoped the ambushers would be too busy tending to Lowell to make time for Tucker right then.

Still, there was Kills the Deer. Now that Tucker knew he tracked for Hacksaw, he'd have to be more careful with his trail sign. That meant it would slow *him* down laying tracks to confound the Indian.

And that would mean he might not reach Jack in time.

CHAPTER 14

Blade reached Lowell Tornquist a moment before Hacksaw broke through the trees. Blade stood staring down at Lowell flailing the air with his legs.

"For God's sake, untie him!" Hack ordered.

Blade laid his rifle on the ground and dropped beside Lowell. He cut Lowell's suspenders securing his wrists, and they dropped to the ground, stained with blood. Tears cut rivulets down Lowell's cheeks as Blade held his feet from thrashing around. "He cut me!"

Blade gently pulled Lowell's legs up to ease the tension on the gaping wounds.

"Easy now," Hack said. He squatted beside Lowell. "Stop your squirming around, and let me see how bad it is."

Lowell gritted his teeth when Hack pulled Lowell's trouser leg up over the wound before easing his legs back down onto the ground. "It's bad," Hack said. "You're not going to be able to walk as bad as you're cut." He turned to Blade. "Go back to camp and fetch the horses."

"We going to get that bastard?" Lowell managed to blurt out, trying to keep his feet off the dirt.

Hack took Lowell's hat and set it on the ground before gently resting his feet on it. "Getting Tucker . . . that's the *only* thing I've been thinking of since he beat me and put out my eye, you know that. Oh, I'm going to get him all right."

"This hurts bad," Lowell said, unable to position his feet any way that they wouldn't hurt more.

Hack patted Lowell's shoulder. "I know. Soon's Blade returns with the horses and water, we'll get your wounds cleaned up."

Killdeer walked from the trees and stood beside the fire. He motioned to Hack while he grabbed a stick and squatted in the dirt. "Found Ashley's sign," he said and began drawing a crude map in the dirt. "He left in the direction Blade and Lowell entered the woods to sneak up on his campfire. Used their tracks tramping through the trees to mask his own. Here is where he broke out." The Crow drew a line that meandered through the hills. "He walked a shallow ravine to hide his escape. For a man on foot, he travels fast."

"But we can catch him?"

Killdeer shrugged. "I do not know. It will take time helping Lowell. He cannot walk, and we will have to ride slowly if at all — he cannot sit the stirrups." He grinned. "He is no Indian."

Blade rode into the clearing leading the other horses and dismounted before tying them to a tree. He took a canteen looped over his saddle horn and dropped down beside Lowell. "God, this hurts so bad, Blade."

"Understood," Blade said. "Let's clean up those cuts. You'll have to turn on your side. Can you do that?"

Lowell's jaw muscles clenched tight as he gingerly turned onto his side.

"This is going to sting a mite," Blade said. He pulled up Lowell's trouser leg and trickled water over the blood already crusting in the wound.

Lowell screamed as Blade used the last of the water to flush out the blood. "Got an extra bandana in my saddlebags," Blade said and ran to his horse.

Hack walked away from Killdeer and back to Lowell. "Blade'll have you cleaned up in no time." He looked down at the injured man as Blade returned with his bandana. He ripped it into two long pieces and tied them around each leg even as Lowell's wailing echoed off the granite rocks surrounding the campsite.

Blade set the canteen aside and scooted closer to the injured man. "I'm gonna' put you on your horse careful like —"

"No," Hack said, "you're not." He motioned Blade to step away from Lowell. "He wouldn't be able to ride worth a damn. He'd just slow us down —"

"What are you saying?" Blade asked.

"I'm afraid Lowell's on his own."

"You're going to leave him out here alone? Hurt and with Sioux hereabouts?"

"Got no choice. We'll pick him up on the way back."

"We'll be lucky if he's not buzzard bait by morning."

Hack stepped around Blade and said to Lowell, "Killdeer found your rifle in the dirt and laid it there by the fire. We'll put some more logs on to keep you warm —"

"Dammit," Lowell said, "just put me on my horse."

"Grab hold of him," Hack said to Blade. "And be careful."

"Thanks," Lowell said but stopped short when they set him beside the fire. "What the hell you doing? My horse is over that-away."

"Sorry," Hack said. "You'll just slow us down. We've lost too much time already. Tucker's got a start on us."

"I can ride," Lowell pleaded. He tried standing but only made it a foot before he fell back to the ground. "Don't leave me here. There's Sioux close by."

Hack walked towards Lowell's horse and said over his shoulder, "Sorry, but I'll be damned if Tucker's going to get away from me. And your chestnut might make the difference in us catching him or not."

"Leave me my horse —"

"We'll bring it back when we pick you up."

"You son of a bitch!" Lowell yelled. "I'm going to kill you —"

"Which is why I put your rifle well out of your reach. By the time you drag yourself over by the fire and grab it, we'll be long gone. But I'll leave you some dried deer and a half canteen of water. I'm not totally heartless."

Lowell tried dragging himself across the clearing to his rifle as he screamed at Hacksaw walking to his horse.

Lowell's screams pierced the night air, still wrenching his body along the ground as he struggled to reach the gun before Hack was out of sight. *I was smart not to lay Lowell's rifle too close to him,* Hack thought as he rode behind Blade and Killdeer into the forest. Into the night.

CHAPTER 15

Simon Cady put a few more small branches onto the fire — not enough to flare it up and give his position away, but enough to cut the chill that ran through his bones from the mountain air. It amazed him how days in the Black Hills could be so brutally hot only to drop fifty degrees by nightfall.

He sat under pine branches that would dissipate the smoke as he held the stick with the ground squirrel over the flames. With his shoulder giving him fits, he hadn't been able to shoot worth a damn, and he'd been lucky to bag this squirrel with a snare he'd set.

But that would change, he knew, as the recent itching told him the wound was healing. When Hacksaw's men had shot him, the bullet had passed through his upper back and shoulder, tearing flesh and muscle before exiting.

He cursed Hacksaw Reed as he turned

the squirrel over the fire. He tested the meat with his knife: *not quite done,* but then he wasn't used to eating a rodent barely large enough to silence the growling in his empty stomach. But it would give him strength to continue.

And continue he would, for he would not let Hacksaw live. "I'll bet you think I'm foolish enough to go after someone as dangerous as Hacksaw Reed with this bum shoulder," he asked Soreback. The mule said nothing as he continued hanging its head, and Simon didn't know if the critter was dead on its feet or just sleeping.

He had found the mule wandering the Black Hills two days after Hacksaw had ambushed the posse and shot Simon's sorrel out from under him. No, he recalled, the mule had found *him* as Simon struggled to walk with his shot shoulder. Soreback had come up to him and stopped a few feet from Simon, hanging his jughead as if wanting to be consoled for losing his master.

But where *was* Tucker? From the tracks, Simon saw that Hacksaw and his gang had been following Tucker, who was hot after a band of Lakota. Made no sense to Simon that Tucker would hunt Sioux, for he'd not known the former army scout to harbor a grudge against the Indians.

Soreback seemed to wake up as he snorted, like he had snorted when he walked into Simon's dry camp. The saddle had been empty, but the saddlebags contained things Simon had lost when he had to leave his dead horse at the ambush canyon and run for his life: flint and steel to start a fire. Thread for sewing torn sourdough coats and that Simon had used to sew shut the bullet holes.

He'd been lucky that day, riding his horse for another five hundred yards after it had been shot before it succumbed to the bullet in its lung. Simon had thrown himself clear of the gelding and crawled to a rock-protected part of the canyon where he could fire on the approaching killers. That he hadn't hit any that he could confirm wasn't his saving grace, but rather that Hacksaw must have *thought* Simon was in far better shape than he was. Even Hacksaw wouldn't think about coming up against Simon's Sharps .50. He had lost consciousness then, and when he came to, it was dark with Hacksaw and his gang probably thinking Simon was dead. But wise enough not to go into the rocks to find out.

He tested the squirrel meat and found it done. "You're lucky you can eat grass," he told the mule. "I might prefer it over this stringy rat with a tail." He split the meat with his knife and ate slowly.

Soreback had remained at Simon's side, never hobbled, never tied to any rock or tree, as if he wanted to stay close to the bounty hunter. As if he knew Simon would eventually find Tucker. The mule walked to Simon and sniffed the meat before dropping his head to a clump of buffalo grass and grazing. Simon had misjudged Soreback's friendliness that first day and tried mounting him. The mule had balked and backed away, and Simon had given up — he couldn't chance sitting the animal if he didn't want to be sat. The last thing Simon needed now was to be bucked off Soreback and open the wound.

He sipped carefully of what water remained in Tucker's water bladder that had been looped over the saddle horn. He would have to ration it until he came across a creek, and he capped the bladder. While he finished eating the squirrel, he thought how truly lucky he'd been these days, with the only cloud on Simon's horizon being Kills the Deer. He thought back to what he knew about the Crow, for a man didn't go against his enemy without thinking him through. Simon would eventually catch up with

Hacksaw. And the Indian would be with him.

The Crow — hiding among the rocks in the canyon — had shot the lead deputy from the saddle with one shot from his bow at no less than forty yards, something even Simon could not do with a bow. Kills the Deer had run to the three dead posse members in turn and scalped them in as many minutes. Simon had heard around Lakota campfires about how the Crow sneaked among their camp and killed sleeping men, lifting a scalp before evaporating into the night. Eluding the Lakota while still killing his enemy was something that amazed Simon.

He finished the squirrel and scooped up a handful of dirt, rubbing it into his hands to absorb the grease from the meat. "Don't look at me like that," he told Soreback. "I *am* going to kill Hacksaw," he said, thinking back to the times he had stopped at the territorial prison to see if Hacksaw was still there. Each time Simon checked, Hacksaw was safely locked behind bars, but that was all right — Simon was a patient man. He could wait until the killer was paroled or served his sentence to kill him. So when he learned Hacksaw had killed two guards and escaped, Simon jumped at the chance to track the man down. The posse just didn't know Simon would never let Hacksaw live to see the inside of the prison again.

And once when he visited the prison to inquire about Hacksaw, he had spotted Tucker Ashley swinging a heavy hammer with others, turning a pile of rocks into dust. At first, Simon had chuckled that Tucker would wind up in prison for something as simple as knifing a cavalry officer and beating another in a barroom fight in Cowtown. But the more he thought of it, the more Simon realized Tucker had done much worse and not been imprisoned for it.

Simon stood painfully, grabbing onto the saddle to stand, feeling the pain in his shoulder throb. He took Tucker's shovel from the saddle to bury the squirrel carcass before he broke camp. There were Lakota in these hills, he knew, and, though he had no truck with them, he was certain they wouldn't look on him with likeminded civility. No reason to make it any easier to see where a white man had camped, and he turned the dirt over the bones.

He sat on a rock and uncapped the water bladder once again before peeling his shirt off his shoulder and easing the bandana down his arm. He trickled just enough water over it to flush out dried blood crusted on the stitches before slipping the bandana back over the wounds. *I've had worse than this.* But many other times, he had his woman to tend to him.

His woman.

Rain Water, and he smiled at her memory. The Oglala had found Simon with an arrow sticking out his side one winter, courtesy of a Blackfoot raiding party at the base of the Shining Mountains. She had hidden Simon, doctoring him, keeping him warm until his strength returned and the Blackfeet gave up hunting for him.

Simon had stayed on with Rain Water, hunting and trapping, and a year later, Touch the Trees was born. He grew up straight and tall for his age, loving the time spent with Simon, learning the ways of the man of the mountain, hunting and trapping and using what nature had given him to survive.

But he hadn't survived past his seventh year, when Simon found the boy slumped over his dead and scalped mother, both frozen. Simon had set them on a scaffold, then, and mourned their deaths in the way of the Lakota before working out the tracks that told the entire story, of a woman who'd been shot, her body violated. The boy, wishing to live no more, had just laid atop his mother as if thinking his heat would save her.

Simon had come close to catching up with Hacksaw, until he was caught after robbing the train outside Rawlins and sentenced to the territorial prison. But Simon would come close to Hack once again as soon as his strength allowed.

Soreback came to Simon once more and bent his huge head to sniff Simon's long, gray hair, the first true sign of trust and affection from the animal. He allowed Simon to stroke his muzzle before walking back to the grass to graze. Perhaps tomorrow he'd try saddling the mule and riding again.

The sooner he did, the sooner he'd send Hacksaw Reed to hell.

CHAPTER 16

That evening as the sun set, Blue Boy gathered up his men. They had mourned the death of Little Water, their wails filling the air throughout the day. When they had completed their death vigil, Blue Boy announced he wanted nothing to do with his half brother and his scheme to sell white captives.

"What're they yakking about?" Mick asked.

"You never miss an opportunity to shut up," Jack said. "But do it now so's I can hear."

"I welcome your men," Iron Hide said as he looked up at Blue Boy sitting his pony. "You do not have to go. Join us."

"Kill them, yes. But this" — Blue Boy waved to the captives roped to their tree — "will only bring you trouble. Besides, by the time you gather more white men and sell them, we will have driven the *wasicu* from

He Sapa. There will be none left for you to fight with your new guns."

With not a backward glance at Iron Hide, Blue Boy and his warriors rode silently out of camp.

Jack whistled to get Pale Moon's attention, and he walked over. "I take it Iron Hide won the argument — we're not to be killed?"

Pale Moon nodded while keeping an eye on Iron Hide and the others as they prepared for the night. "Blue Boy. Left in anger over you."

"The soldiers will find us —"

"The soldiers left the mountains. Grass and Swan found soldiers breaking camp. Moving out."

"Thought Swan was too sick hurt to move," Mick said.

"He healed enough to travel." Pale Moon nodded to Erin. "Because of her."

Erin lashed out with a vicious kick that fell short by a foot when she hit the end of her rope. She struggled against the rawhide thong securing her hands. "Let me loose for just a moment! I'll show you what I think of you murderers."

Pale Moon backed away and smiled. "Not for all the dried buffalo in Sitting Bull's camp."

When Pale Moon had walked back to sit beside the fire with the others, Erin said, "I'm getting out of here tonight. You two coming with me?"

"Girlie," Mick said holding his hand shackled to Jack so she could see it better, "maybe you don't see so good, but me and this fool Jack Worman are shackled together. And even if we got out of these, what do you expect us to do, gnaw through this rope around the tree?"

Erin leaned as close as she could and looked around Jack to the Indians. They paid them no mind, busy with preparations to leave at sunup. She was reaching under her dress when she paused. "You both look away."

"Now why should I do that, girlie?" Mick said, staring at her dress.

Jack jerked hard on the shackles, and the chain went taut, digging into Mick's wrist. "If Erin's got a plan, look away like she says."

Jack and Mick averted their eyes for a moment until Erin said, "Now you can look." She palmed a small skinning knife, the blade not much longer than her thumb, and tucked it back under her skirt. "Where'd you get that?" Jack asked.

"Little Water," Erin answered, keeping an

eye on the Indians. "He had it tucked into his moccasin. Stumpy took the big knife stuck into Little Water's trousers, but he missed this one. I palmed it when Blue Boy and Iron Hide were arguing about what to do with us."

Mick chuckled. "What do you think you're going to do with that little bitty blade? It ain't hardly big enough to slice through a deer hide."

"It's big enough to cut through these." She held up her hands. Since she was captured after her and Rory's failed escape, Iron Hide had ordered her wrists tied tighter. She had tried to relieve the pressure on them, but her wrists were raw. "It's big enough to slice through this rope. So you two in?"

"Count me out," Mick said. "I saw what happened to your pappy when he tried to get away. I'll take my chances that the army finds us."

"Well, you can count me in," Jack said. "I believe Pale Moon when he says the soldiers packed up and left the hills. I sure don't want to be sold to some slaver."

"Jack, me boy," Mick said, "did it occur to you that — if I stay — you have to stay. Compliments of these infernal shackles."

"Not if I saw your damn fool hand off

171

with that little skinning knife. Then I'd be free of you for good."

"Now wait a damn minute —"

"Wait a damn minute nothing," Erin cut in. "We have to decide if you two are going with me. If so, we have to make plans pronto."

Jack jerked hard on the chain, and Mick winced in pain. "What's it going to be, Mick, *me boy* — am I going alone with your bloody wrist dangling from these chains?"

"All right. All right," Mick blurted out. "But we ain't gonna' make very good time bound together like we are."

"We'll worry about that once we're free," Jack said under his breath as he leaned closer to Erin. "What's your plan?"

Jack watched closely as Swan — sitting his night watch beside the fire — swayed, fighting to stay awake. He had wrapped his blanket tightly around him against the cold, as snores came from the other Indians lying under their own blankets around the dying fire. Swan's head bobbed on his chest until it settled. Still.

When Erin and Jack and the reluctant Mick Flynn had concocted their plan, Jack was certain Pale Moon would be assigned the midnight watch — new warriors often

172

were. They were confident he would fall asleep during his turn to guard the captives as he had when Erin and Rory made their failed escape. But having Swan as midnight watch was even better, for the wounded man lacked strength, his injuries sapping his energy. His trek into the woods looking for the soldiers earlier in the day would have tired him even more.

Sawing noises coming from Erin's rope caused Jack to look at her for a moment before resuming watching the Indians.

"Just a minute more," she whispered and continued cutting away at the rope securing her to the tree. It dropped free, and she crawled to Jack. "Cut this rawhide offa' my wrists," she said and handed him the knife.

The knife easily sliced through the rawhide, and Erin rubbed her wrists. She took the knife back and whispered, "Keep watch" before low-crawling to the tree where Jack's and Mick's rope was tied around.

"I don't know about this," Mick said under his breath. In the faint moon, his eyes were wide and frightened as he stared at the Indians. He held up his hand, and Jack quickly wrapped his hand around the chain to silence the rattling. "Running through the woods shackled together is gonna' make a passel of noise."

"Rattling these chains will get us caught quicker. We just might make it if we go easy like I told you to do," Jack said. "All you have to do is go slow and step *right* where I step. You keep your fool mouth shut, and we just might slip away."

"To where?" Mick asked. "You said yourself those Indians can track a bug across a lake."

"Even Indians can't track in the rain," Jack said, motioning to thunder clouds boiling to the west. The temperature had dropped twenty degrees just in the past hour, and Jack hoped *someone* in the Black Hills was doing a rain dance. "If we're lucky, it'll storm like hell and erase any tracks."

"And how are we ever going to get these off."

"I don't know right now." Jack felt the rope drop away, and he looked over at Erin. She chin-pointed to Swan snoring as he sat beside the fire. Jack motioned her over and murmured, "When we head through those trees, go slow." He turned to Mick. "You keep your hand over this chain so it don't make noise."

"What the hell you going to be doin'?"

"Concentrating on finding the best and quickest way away from here. Confound them until we can find us a place to hole

174

up." Jack knew this part of the Black Hills from when he was scouting for the army three years ago. Few places in the Black Hills were flat, and this area was no exception. Mountains rose steeply a hundred feet high and dropped as steeply away on the other side only to be flanked by more hills dotted with trees and granite bounders. There was no easy way to evade the Indians on foot. Jack figured the Indians would think they had fled along one of the many beaten down game trails that intersected the hills, which made it easier for running away. They had better fool their Lakota pursuers, for there were only three hours left before the sun rose for them to find a hiding place where the Indians couldn't spot them. If Swan and the other Indians didn't awaken first.

Jack had thought out where to go and knew the only way to flee was where the Indians didn't expect them to. He prayed that confounding their trail long enough would give them a chance to find one of the shallow caves carved out of the face of a hundred granite cliffs in this part of the Black Hills. All they needed was to mislead the Indians long enough to plan their next move. If they made it that far.

"Ready?" Jack said into Erin's ear.

Her legs trembled, no doubt reliving the last time she had tried to escape with her father, and Mick gathered his legs under him. Jack looked a last time at Swan by the fire. What was left of it. In his exhaustion, Swan had failed to keep the fire going, and it had died to embers, as deep snoring arose from him, the faint flames barely showing where the others lay sleeping.

Jack nodded to Mick, and Erin walked hunched over, going slow, eying the Indians. When they reached their first goal, the thick trees at the edge of the clearing, Jack stopped and looked back at Swan. He hadn't heard them cut the rope. He hadn't heard them sneaking away. He just remained sleeping sitting in front of the dying coals, blanket still wrapped around his shoulders, rising and falling with his deep breaths.

Jack just hoped Swan didn't topple over and alert the others.

CHAPTER 17

Tucker squatted at the base of a tall pine and juniper covered hill, keeping an eye on his back trail while eating what was left of the rabbit that he had snared early this morning. Now that he knew that Kills the Deer tracked for Hacksaw Reed, it had taken Tucker longer than he wanted to catch up with Jack. Tucker had taken great pains to confound the Crow, but whatever he did to conceal his tracks was little more than a delaying tactic, for Kills the Deer would be able to work through anything that Tucker did to fool him. His only advantage was knowing Hacksaw had been slowed to take care of the wounded Lowell Tornquist.

Tucker took the skin and the bones of the rabbit and walked ten yards farther up the hillside. He left the rabbit carcass where the wind could take the scent to scavengers. Last night he'd heard a mountain lion scream somewhere in the hills, and coyotes talked with one another steadily through the night. By now, they may be hungry and catch the scent of what was left of the rabbit, destroying what little sign Tucker left of his meal.

He returned to the spot where he had skinned and cooked the rabbit and heaped dirt over the coals. Kills the Deer would undoubtedly find it, but Tucker made sure it would be harder for the man to age the campfire. Harder to determine just *how* long it was since Tucker was there.

He walked twenty yards down the hillside to the place where he'd last spotted the Indians' tracks last night, before the moon tucked behind the clouds and he could no longer track them. With a stick, he had circled one faint pair of boot tracks: Jack's boots, the track showing where his friend wore the outside of the heel down. But among the other captives being dragged along with Jack, it was hard to tell how many more there were. And hard to tell how many Indians remained in the band. He had killed two, but how many more were left alive?

Last night at the base of the hill among trees guarding the game trail, Tucker had spotted a broken spider web high among the trees. Too high for a walking man to disturb. Like Jack had swatted at the web with a coat to break it to let Tucker know he had passed here. So, Jack still had his wits about him. *How long would he, though, being dragged behind a pony along with the others?* But, for Tucker, tracking the Indians who made no attempt to hide their sign, along with Jack's tidbits he left — a piece of torn bandana in a chokecherry bush, a piece of off-white muslin like a woman's dress shoved into the ground, a corner sticking out to flutter for Tucker's attention — had made it easy.

But how long would Tucker be able to evade Hacksaw and his killers? Half a day perhaps? Long enough for Hacksaw to allow Lowell time to heal, long enough that he could sit a saddle.

Tucker started along the trail winding through the hills between rocks, through shallow valleys making it easier for the Indians to ride. The Lakota had hunted these hills for so long — ever since driving the Cheyenne out — they knew every trail. Every switchback that would conceal them as they rode undetected. No wonder the army never caught up with them in *their* Black Hills. They had passed down their knowledge of trails to others like a good rancher passes along to his son the ways of the cow and horse business.

The ranch. Tucker thought back to the great plans he and Jack had talked about over many a campfire. With the acquisition of the shorthorn bull, they had finally envisioned their ranch coming together, grazing the lush mountain grasses of the southern Black Hills, and Tucker felt his neck flush warm. The Indians had destroyed all that he and his friend had wanted and planned. But worse than killing their bull and heifers, the Indians had taken Jack. That made Tucker's anger rise even more.

And the apprehension that he'd felt over-coming him since he and Jack actually *had* their own ranch. It was what Tucker thought he always wanted — to settle down. Raise a few cows. Maybe some horses. But when it came to fulfilling that dream, he found himself second guessing himself. He had ridden the trail of excitement for so long, confronting danger and death nearly every day, that he concluded ranching might not be for him after all. Thinking he might have taken the fork in the road unsuitable to him.

That old excitement returned once he came upon the ranch destroyed and his friend abducted.

He walked beside the tracks, easy to fol-low with the captives stumbling behind the

Indian's barefoot ponies. He had stopped and bent to run his hand over a track when . . .

. . . a covey of quail flew up from the trees a hundred yards behind him.

Tucker dropped into a crouch. He walked bent over to the safety of the nearest trees ten yards off the trail just as two does darted from the direction of the quail and disappeared over the hill.

He willed his heart to beat calm as he closed his eyes, relaxing all his senses, when he caught . . .

Familiar voices — rising and falling with the wind whistling through the pines down the valley — reaching him. He could almost imagine Kills the Deer giving Hacksaw and Blade hell for talking so loudly. How had Lowell been able to ride with his hamstrings sliced? They should be miles behind as they rode slow enough that Lowell could keep up.

Tucker opened his eyes, looking around for things these woods would provide to help him evade the killers. The forest, always the forest had helped when he needed it, and he started up a steep slope to the nearest stand of pine. He walked quickly, making no attempt to hide his tracks. As if he wanted Hacksaw and his killers to follow *right* where he laid his tracks.

Which he did.

CHAPTER 18

Soreback nipped at Simon as if it was the mule's obligation if someone besides Tucker tried riding him. Simon first attempted sitting him again this morning, only to have the mule sidestep away. He had spent the better part of the morning talking softly to the mule, stroking his neck, and giving him a wild turnip Simon had dug up. When at last Soreback let him test the stirrup, Simon sucked in a breath, cradled the Sharps in the crook of his arm, and swung a leg over the saddle.

The mule hunched up, craning its neck back. He bared his teeth, *clicking* just out of the reach of Simon's leg, and Simon quickly gave Soreback another wild turnip as a peace offering. After tense moments, the mule settled down and stood still as if Simon had always ridden atop him on a crisp Black Hills morning. "That turnip was going to be my supper tonight, in case you feel guilty about it."

Soreback didn't answer but chomped on the turnip. "Hope you know where we're going; there's no more of those," he said and nudged the mule's flanks.

Soreback walked the granite rocks, picking his way around cactus and juniper, through bunchgrass and saw grass that would have sliced a horse's legs. As the mule plodded toward a towering hill, it remained sure-footed where Simon's sorrel would have balked, walking over this granite, cutting flakes of loose ground where the gelding would have slipped.

At the top of the hill, Simon paused, overlooking the trees and the valley of rocks and meadows below, hoping to catch a glimpse of Hacksaw. Since Simon had been able to ride Soreback, he had made up for time, leapfrogging sign Hacksaw's gang had left. They hadn't hidden their tracks, and Simon smiled: Hacksaw hadn't figured Simon survived that bullet to his back. And if he did somehow live, he would have been wounded and afoot, days behind the killers, never able to catch up to them. Simon patted the mule's neck. "Soon's we catch up with Hacksaw, maybe we'll look for . . ." He stopped and looked up.

Vultures circling overhead a couple hundred yards to the west caught Simon's attention. He slipped the rifle out of the scabbard as he coaxed Soreback slowly down the hill, the stench of a fresh corpse always distinctive. As he neared a rock formation covering half an acre of mountain meadow, he noticed dozens of vultures feeding on a body on the ground. He'd heard somewhere the vultures feeding like that were called a *wake,* and he saw why — sadly, there was little left of the body. As Simon urged the mule closer, the vultures took flight, revealing a naked white man devoid of his scalp lying close to a day-old campfire.

Soreback locked his legs, refusing to go farther, and Simon stepped carefully off the mule. He approached the scene, walking a wide circle around the corpse, reading the ground soaked with black blood. Four arrows stuck out of the body feasted on by the buzzards, bits of shirt and trousers ripped away by their powerful beaks. Simon held a bandana over his nose as he bent to the corpse and pulled one of the arrows out. *Lakota.* Three, by the looks of their moccasin tracks.

He tossed the shaft aside and stepped back to look at the victim. The tendons at the back of his feet had been cut, and Simon struggled to recall the last time an Indian had done that to a white man. Lakota mutilated *wasicu* often *after* killing them, but he'd never known a Sioux to cut a man like that.

Simon aged the death at a day, perhaps less: it was hard telling when vultures decided they wanted an easy meal. He bent and ran his hand over a moccasin print in the dirt, careful not to pull the stitches in his shoulder. The edges of the Indian's track crumbled, and he brushed dirt off his hand on his trousers. He stood and walked to where Soreback stood eying the dead man. *One of Hacksaw's men.*

He led the mule away from the body and left Soreback to graze on buffalo grass lining both sides of the trail. Simon walked a circle well away from the killing scene until he spotted a scuff mark on the face of a rock leading to the broken branch of a skunkbrush. He picked the branch up and brought it to his nose. It lacked the normal pungent smell of skunkbrush, and he confirmed his guess: a day since Hacksaw and his gang passed this way.

He tossed the branch aside, recalling Rain Water steeping the bark of such a plant to make a tea when he had a cold, and of her forcing Touch the Trees to chew on berries of the bush when the boy developed a toothache. Would he ever drive them from his memory? He doubted it, but he could make certain Hacksaw Reed never hurt another woman. And would never leave a boy to fend for himself in zero-degree weather.

Simon looked again at the direction the tracks led — to the northwest. If he could get atop a tall hill . . . he spotted a towering granite peak a half mile away rising above the tops of other high hills.

He had Hacksaw's direction of travel; now all Simon had to do was think a step ahead of him like he'd done with most of the men he pursued for the price on their heads. Except this one was not for any price, but for the sheer pleasure of sighting down the barrel of his rifle at the killer's chest.

Simon halted the mule at the base of the granite peak. Looking up, he realized just what kind of view he would have for miles around. *If* he made it to the top, with the steep hill even a task for a mule. And that was with a man with no bullet holes in him. With the loose shale, tumbling down was a real possibility. Still, he *had* to climb it. "We're going on up to the top, pard'ner," he said softly to the mule and nudged his flanks. Soreback inched his way up the loose shale covered with shards of sharp rocks without protest, without prodding, as if the mule enjoyed walking in rough country. Simon leaned over on the saddle and set himself in the stirrups as he clutched tightly to his rifle, expecting Soreback to topple over backwards as he ascended the hill.

When they reached the summit, the mule stood with his great chest heaving, spittle wetting his muzzle. Simon stepped out of the saddle and rested his rifle on a rock before grabbing the water bladder. He poured half the water into his hat and held it for the mule to drink. "Wish I had another turnip to give you," he said. "You deserve it after that climb you just made."

When Soreback had lapped all the water out of the hat, Simon took a short pull himself before looping the bladder over the saddle horn and walking to the edge of the butte, looking down over the Black Hills that he could see for miles in all directions. Nothing moved. No sign of Hacksaw Reed and his killers *or* Tucker, but they had to be down there somewhere. Simon had thought of the direction where the Indians Tucker followed might have gone. And where Tucker went, Hacksaw was not to be far behind. As he looked down into the deep draws at the base of high hills, Simon knew any one could hide a man. Or a gang of men.

He turned back to the mule, standing with his head hung as if mourning his owner. "Tucker will show up eventually," Simon said, patting Soreback's neck as if consoling him, before opening the saddlebags. When Simon was nursing his festering wound three days ago and having no luck hunting game, the mule had sauntered up to him and stood much as he did now. Simon had gone into the saddlebags and found some airtights: a can of peaches, two cans of oysters, a can of beans that he had eaten right off, giving him strength to continue after Hacksaw. Now all that was left of Tucker's food in his saddlebags was the last can of oysters.

He set the can on a flat rock and grabbed Tucker's telescope. Walking to the rim of the butte, he squatted low and extended the glass, scanning the ground below, paying particular attention to the draws and the forest dotting the woods. He brought the telescope from his eyes and was rubbing them when . . . movement caught his attention. A glint off *something* at the edge of the forest. Just for a brief moment and then gone.

He looked to the trees once again. Stillness.

Except for a doe and her fawn, leaping over a deadfall of aspen, running swiftly away from the trees before they disappeared down a deep coulee. Running from what?

He was looking through the glass once again, following where the deer had jumped from, when he spotted hiding among the pine and juniper . . . *Lakota.* Seven in a raiding party. Two of them climbed atop boulders scattered along the game trail. Sun reflected off brass tacks stuck into the stock of a trade rifle held by the Indian who towered over the rest, his back to Simon. Two others slipped the bows off their backs, and each had nocked arrows as yet another pointed down the trail, gesturing, talking among themselves too far away for Simon to hear them. Four hundred yards down? Five hundred perhaps?

He began searching trees in the direction the Indians pointed but failed to see anything until . . . emerging from a stand of black jack pine and carefully parting rabbitbrush nearly as tall as he walked Tucker Ashley. He was bent over studying the ground, probably working through sign that the Indians he trailed had left.

"I wish you luck with those Sioux," Simon

said to himself and closed the ship's glass. He stood and walked to Soreback. When he stowed the telescope in the saddlebag, the mule eyed him, the whites of his eyes showing fierce like some wild mustang ready to stomp the nearest man. "Don't look at me like that. I got no desire to see your human hurt, but I aim to kill Hacksaw Reed. I ain't got time for those Indians. And helping him out now will only show Hacksaw where I am if he's anywhere near. And, if I work it right, I can set up the sweetest ambush for Hacksaw coming out of those rocks below you can ever imagine."

He took the reins and had put a moccasin in the stirrup when Soreback sidestepped. Simon had to crow hop to extract his foot before he fell down and opened his wound. "What's wrong with you?" he asked the mule, though not expecting any answer from such a jughead. "Thought you and me were pards now. Thought we had us an agreement."

Simon gathered the reins once again and was holding onto the saddle horn, balancing his rifle in his free hand, when Soreback stepped back, jerking the reins out of Simon's hand, tugging on his shoulder, and threatening to pull the stitches out. The mule walked several yards away and stopped, looking back at Simon. "So now you're not going to let me throw a leg over you?"

The mule remained still but kept his eye on Simon as if the beast could tell — a quarter mile down on the forest floor — Tucker was about to be ambushed.

Simon walked to Soreback and ran his hand down the mule's neck. "Hate to be shamed by a damned mule — but I figure you're right. I need to help Tucker and worry about hunting Hacksaw afterwards."

He took the ship's glass from the saddlebag again and walked to the edge of the butte, snapping it out as he walked, his back and shoulder throbbing from the bullet wound. He set his rifle on the ground and lay at the edge of the butte. Looking down toward the trees, he spotted Tucker again — unaware that Indians lurked in ambush no more than a hundred yards along the game trail. Looking at a rock. Studying sign, Simon was certain.

Until Tucker rolled the rock away, and his hand shot out and grabbed . . . a snake? It writhed in Tucker's hand, fighting to get free as Tucker drew his knife. He cut the snake, but it still fought him as he walked back to the trees. "Just what the hell are you doing down there with that rattler?" Simon murmured to himself. "Catching supper?"

Simon brought the glass down and rubbed his eyes. When he put the telescope to his eyes again, he saw that the Indians had positioned themselves to take advantage of the rocks for cover.

Waiting.

Just a few more moments before Tucker was in range. Simon had witnessed the man's skill with a pistol before, but even Tucker wouldn't be able to best seven Lakota Sioux lying in ambush.

Tucker dropped back into the trees a few feet and tossed the snake over a branch. "What the *devil* are you up to?" Simon laid the ship's glass on the ground beside him before slipping the deerskin sheath off his Sharps. He rolled it up tight for padding as he moved a large rock to him and laid the rifle sheath on it.

He took his peep sight from the bag tied around his waist and blew dust from it before screwing it to the back of the breech. From his bag, he grabbed five large, heavy cartridges loaded with bullets he had painstakingly paper-patched the day before he rode with the posse chasing after Hacksaw and set four on the ground beside him.

He picked up the glass and looked a final time. Tucker had emerged from the trees once again and squatted, looking at sign, oblivious of the Indians among the rocks now but seventy yards away along the trail.

Simon set the hammer at half-cock and opened the breech of the rifle. He blew on a cartridge, inserted it in the chamber, and closed the long lever locking the action. He guessed the Indians were five hundred yards away, the angle steep, and he adjusted the sight as Tucker's red bandana caught Simon's eye: forty yards from the Lakotas.

Thirty yards. He could barely make out at this distance that two of the Indians had nocked their arrows, their bows at full draw.

Simon set the butt of his rifle tight against his uninjured shoulder. "I can't recall the last time I shot this here buffalo gun left handed," he said and switched shoulders, even knowing the heavy recoil of the rifle might open up his wound.

He picked out the Indian atop a bounder wearing a U.S. Army tunic.

Let out his breath.

Set the back trigger and rested his finger *lightly* on the front trigger. He breathed deeply once more before slowly letting out his breath and . . .

Barooom! The recoil of the rifle moved Simon back several inches. Blood weeped through the bandana and down his shirtfront from his shoulder as he opened the breech to load another cartridge. He grabbed the telescope. His bullet had caught the Lakota center chest, and he lay where he'd toppled off the rock. The others crouched behind their cover, arms waving in different directions, none knowing just where the shooter was.

But where was Tucker?

Simon looked to the trees once again. Tucker lay under a low juniper with just enough room to stick the barrel of his pistol out.

The Indians gestured to one another, no doubt wondering who would be soaking up the dirt next. Simon set the ship's glass aside and asked Soreback, "Think your human can take care of himself now?"

Simon got — and expected — no answer as he took up the spyglass. The Indians had withdrawn from the rocks towards where their ponies were tied, looking as if they intended leaving hastily when . . .

. . . Simon drew in a sharp breath. *Blue Boy*. Gathering his men, pointing in the direction where Tucker lay waiting for the Indians to attack. "I thought that renegade bastard was dead," Simon said when he realized the Indians hadn't turned to *leave* — that they had begun working their way in a large circle. If they continued, they would be successful in flanking Tucker. He would have no chance against all of them. "I got no choice now," he told Soreback. "They might figure out where I am if I shoot again, but I got to take one more shot, pard."

CHAPTER 19

Jack dropped onto his stomach and — because he was shackled to Jack — dragged Mick to the ground with him. Though Jack didn't hear Erin behind him, he knew she followed his lead. She had proved as stealthy and as quiet as any Indian this last mile since they'd broken from the Lakota's camp. The same could not be said of Mick. "What the hell you doing —"

Jack clamped his hand over Mick's mouth. When he quieted, Jack eased his hand from the Irishman's mouth and pointed to a rim two hundred feet high. "There's Indians up on that rim."

"And they'll find us, if you don't shut up," Erin said as she low-crawled to where Jack and Mick lay. Mud caked her dress as it did Mick's and Jack's clothes from the light rain that threatened to turn into a downpour, if Jack read the thunder clouds right. "You've been like a bull in a dress shop — bustin' through trees," he told Mick. "Stumbling along like you have been. No wonder they were able to pick up our trail so easily. Now we got little chance."

Jack parted branches of the chokecherry bush they hid behind and spotted Swan up on the hill. Lightning flashes illuminated his face, but he made no effort to hide himself, no effort to be silent as he looked for the captives. "The Indians know *just* where we are," he whispered.

Mick muffled his guffaw. "The hell they know. Just look at that Swan up there. He's lookin', but he don't see nothin'."

"Swan," Jack said, "is the *only* one up on that hillside."

"They gotta' be there?" Mick asked.

"See any of the others?" Jack answered.

"No."

"There should be four Indians beside Iron Hide. And all I see is Swan."

"Hell," Mick said, "the rest of those Sioux are more'n likely up there with him somewhere. Or under blankets with this rain like it has been the last hour. We just can't see them."

"I say Swan was left up there as a decoy. To make us *think* they're atop that ridgeline."

"If you're right," Erin said, looking slowly

around, without turning her head, "they're down here with us. Somewhere."

"We laid a false trail back up that draw," Jack whispered. "That ought to throw them off long enough for us to make for that canyon I was telling you about." When Jack had last scouted for the army three years ago, it had taken him to this part of the Black Hills with deep canyons and gorges, hundreds of dug out caves where animals often made their homes. Any one of those places could offer them sanctuary until night fell again and they could formulate a plan.

"Jack." Erin tugged on Jack's shirt and lowered her voice as she pointed behind them. "They're on to us."

Jack clamped his hand over the noisy chain and slowly turned to look behind him. Iron Hide looked at the ground as he walked a hundred yards behind, flashes of lightning illuminating his angry face, stopping now and again to pick up a rock. Sniff a leaf or a broken branch. Jack knew the Indians tracked in the absolute hardest conditions — rain. Grass walked to one side of Iron Hide, Stumpy the opposite side, both men watching, letting the headman track their escapees while Pale Moon hung twenty yards back leading the horses.

"They'll be on us in minutes," Erin said.

Jack turned back and looked around, studying the terrain. "We gotta' get outta' here pronto." He told Mick, "If you value your life, keep your hand over this chain and be as quiet as a hung man after his necktie party."

Mick's eyes widened, and his legs trembled as he started to stand. "We gotta' make a run for it —"

Once again, Jack clamped his hand over the Irishman's mouth. "Keep quiet and get up slow and easy."

Erin stood cautiously, looking back at the Indians now within fifty yards of them, working out their trail. She walked hunched over, using the thick chokecherry and juniper bushes leading to thick trees to mask her movement.

Jack led the way, carefully parting branches as they walked through the bushes, careful not to rub against them, careful not to make noise. Feeling the shackles joining him to Mick Flynn shudder.

Iron Hide paused and bent to the trail. He stood smiling and was looking in the direction the captives' tracks led when . . .

Mick looked behind him past Erin, his wide eyes frightened like a steer in a lightning storm. Ready to bolt. *Needing* to bolt, and Jack — too late — recognized the panic that washed over Mick's face. He burst past Jack, knocking him off his feet, crashing through the bushes, caroming off a tree. Mick dragged Jack along the wet ground, oblivious to the dead weight at the end of his wrist, never looking back at the pursuers.

Jack tried gaining his footing, but Mick ran headlong through the brush. With branches gouging his face and granite rocks scraping his knees, his legs, Jack was only vaguely aware that Erin ran beside him, trying to help him up as the Indian's yelps grew louder, closer.

"Stop!" Jack yelled, but Mick paid no attention. He dragged Jack along over rocks and cactus. Trousers hooked on a rock and ripped. "Stop so's I can get up —"

A shot. Another and . . . . a *thud*. Mick staggered two more steps and fell to the ground. Jack felt the chain slacken, and he dropped beside Mick. "Get up!"

Mick lay face up, his eyes already glassing over, a gaping hole in his chest where the bullet exited, leaking his life onto the ground as cries from the Indians grew louder.

"Drag him over here!" Erin shouted. "There's an overhang we can fit under down this hillside," she pointed.

Jack threw Mick's arms over his neck and *grunted* as he hoisted the dead man's body over his shoulders and stumbled under the Irishman's weight. He staggered to where Erin stood waving him closer to the edge of a hillside. Jack followed her, sliding down on rain-soaked leaves to where she knelt at the edge of a shallow cave. "I got to throw them off," he said, struggling to keep erect with Mick's dead weight.

Jack looked about. Twenty yards across a clearing, a stand of trees stood beside a game trail, trampled on by deer and elk over the years. Jack repositioned his grip on the dead man and wobbled toward the game trail. He stumbled down the trail for another twenty yards, scuffing the ground, leaving easy tracks before he ducked back into the trees. He kicked off his boots and snatched them up as he lightly walked — as lightly as a man could with an extra hundred-seventy pounds on his back — working his way back towards Erin, the sounds of the Indians running towards the rim of the hill loud, nearly upon them.

He followed Erin hunched over into a shallow cave three feet high, barely big enough for two people let alone two and a dead man. Jack stooped low entering the cave, praying there were no bears or mountain lions living there, and dropped Mick's body onto the moss-covered cave floor. He heaved heavily from the effort while he put his boots back on. He sat with his back against a damp rock wall, sucking in stale air smelling of rotting vegetation while he listened to the Indians running down the hillside. One warrior slipped and fell and sounded as if he hit a rock stopping him at the bottom.

"Where could they have gone?" Stumpy said to another man in Lakota. "Your bullet hit that white man."

Jack dropped onto his belly and wiggled toward the cave entrance, looking out at the Indians studying the ground. "There should be much blood," Stumpy said, "even in rain we should see blood." Jack agreed, feeling sticky blood soaking his back where he had draped Mick's body.

"Tracks lead to those trees," Grass said as he joined the others. "But I lost them."

Swan stumbled toward them holding his shoulder. He stood out of breath looking on as Iron Hide said to Stumpy, "You and Grass go back to where I shot the man and work out where we could have lost them." He turned to Swan. "I'll take Pale Moon and go to those trees. You," he laid his hand on Swan's good shoulder, "go back to camp. Stay warm by the fire. You look as white as the men we are hunting."

"How could they have gone this far," Pale Moon asked, "in the dark?"

"It is Jack Worman," Iron Hide said. "It is said he is clever. But in another hour the sun will be up. We will find them."

When the Indians split and disappeared into the woods, Jack dragged himself along with the dead Mick Flynn farther back under the rock overhang and sat beside Erin shivering, wet. He wanted to put his arm around her, warm her, comfort her. But with Mick shackled at the end of his arm, it made it nearly impossible. "Will they find us?" Erin asked.

Jack nodded, though he was certain she couldn't see him in the darkness. "When it gets light, they will be able to work out our sign. We fooled them only because God blessed us with rain."

"But our tracks were washed away the moment we made them," she said as if in protest. "They can't follow us —"

"We broke branches running from them. Flattened brush. Kicked rocks over. Things that will allow them to work our tracks once it gets light. But you" — he laid his hand on her shoulder — "can make a run for it."

"Me?" Erin asked. "What about you?"

"With this," Jack said, holding up his wrist chained to Mick's body, "I wouldn't get far. But you can."

"Are you saying I ought to just leave you?"

"That's *just* what I'm saying. Alone, you might have a chance —"

"We're in this together, Jack Worman. I ain't leaving you."

"Don't you understand what I just said — dragging Mick along will leave us with *no* chance of outrunning them."

"Then get rid of the Irishman," she said. "I never liked him anyway."

"Get rid of him . . ." Jack said and stopped when he realized what she was suggesting. But as gruesome as it might be, she was right. "Ok, then, give me that little skinning knife."

"What for?"

"I'm going to use it to get rid of Mick's body like you said."

Erin handed Jack something that pricked his hand. "Sorry," she said. "It's my hat pin."

"Where'd you get that?"

"Right before Iron Hide cut off my hair, I took it out and slipped it into the folds of my skirt. I was going to jab it into his eye but never got the chance."

"Why didn't you tell me before you had it?"

"Just now remembered it when it stuck me." She handed him the pin.

"You want me to jab ol' Mick here in his dead eye?" Jack asked.

"Jack Worman, are you that dumb? Have you never picked a lock before?"

"I have," Jack said. "Outside Fort Abe Lincoln." When Jack scouted for the army, he had fought with an army lieutenant. Jack told the officer a Cheyenne war party was waiting in ambush a half mile ahead and suggested the officer divert half his company to surprise the Indians at their flank. The lieutenant disagreed. Jack insisted. When the lieutenant laughed at Jack's suggestion, he punched the officer, which rewarded Jack with a new set of shackles. Just like the ones he wore now. As the company rode into the ambush with Jack pulling up the rear, he had grabbed a fishhook from his saddlebags and easily picked the crude lock in time to join the fight just as the Cheyenne sprang the ambush.

Jack dragged Mick close to relieve the pressure on his wrist and inserted the tip of the hat pin into the hole. He worked it around, feeling the teeth of the lock, but after ten minutes he pulled it back out. He waited for a moment before re-inserting the pin and . . . the tip of the hat pin depressed the teeth, and the lock released. He swung the arm of the iron manacles aside enough that he could slip his hand out and dropped his iron on the floor of the cave beside Mick. Jack rubbed his tender wrists and felt the circulation returning.

"Sounds like you got shuck of the Irishman," Erin said. "*Now* we can make a run for it."

"Not hardly," Jack said. "Those Indians will eventually track us right back to this little cave, raining or not."

"So getting rid of the body was a waste of time?"

"I didn't say that. Come on over here."

Erin crawled to where Jack lay at the mouth of the cave looking out. He pointed to two tall buttes eerily lit by flashes of lightning that seemed to come closer by the minute. "At the base of those hills is a cave big enough to hide a horse. Believe me, I have. Take that trail," he pointed to a break in the brush and trees, "and you'll end up there before sunup."

"You aren't going with me?"

"I'll meet you there. Right now, I got to take ol' Mick here and make him something he was never in life — useful."

"I don't understand," she said, her voice breaking as she laid her hand on Jack's shoulder.

"What I aim to do is cart Mick's body well away from that trail you'll be taking. When the Lakota find him without me, they'll figure I went that direction. It won't fool them for long, but it'll give us both enough time to make it to those caves. Right after I pay the Indian camp a visit."

"Go back there? You'll just be walking into a trap."

"I don't think so. The Indians are looking for us, and no one's at their camp right now except Swan, and he didn't appear like he will be any problem. With this rain picking up, I can slip in and be gone. They'll never know I was there until they come back and see their things gone."

"But why?" Erin asked.

Jack looked out of the cave a last time before he hoisted Mick's body onto his back. "Because that's where the weapons are."

CHAPTER 20

Blade Tate threw pine branches off his face as he struggled to keep up with the smaller Killdeer riding his scrub pony. The Crow deftly dodged overhanging branches and lay down on the neck of his pony when he couldn't dodge them. Unlike Blade, who had scrapes and cuts on his face and neck and irritating pine needles down his back. "Hold up there a minute," he called out. "My buckskin's a little too big to slip through these brambles like your pinto."

"We got no time to slow down," Hack said, taking his licks from the same branches and jaggers as he rode behind Blade and the Indian. "Tucker's out there and making better time than us, though I don't know how, him being afoot. You'll just have to keep up with Killdeer."

Two quail took flight from the brush, and Hack instinctively snapped his rifle up before lowering it. The last thing they needed was to alert Tucker that they were still on his trail.

Hack barely ducked a pine branch that Blade snapped back as he rode past, and his thoughts turned from Tucker for the moment to Lowell Tornquist. He *thought* he hoped Lowell had survived on his own. Hack nearly beat himself up thinking about taking Lowell's horse when he thought that — even if the man could stand with sliced tendons — he wouldn't have been able to crawl into the saddle and ride. *I had no choice. At least I left him with his rifle and some dried meat. But his horse . . . I almost feel bad about taking the chestnut along. But with a horse, Lowell just* might *somehow be able to come after us. And Lowell is a hell of a shot.*

The path Tucker took through thick brush had turned easier this last half mile when he had once again travelled a well-worn game trail. Killdeer didn't stop to examine Tucker's tracks once he took the trail, his boot prints visible even to Hack when . . . Killdeer stopped suddenly.

"Catching your breath, huh?" Blade said and reined in beside the Crow.

Killdeer looked sideways at him before turning his pony around to face Hack. "This man's trail *too* easy now. Leaves us *too* much sign. Does not hide himself anymore."

"Just makes it easier to track him," Hack said. "Means we ought to catch up with him sooner than we figured. Now let's get going."

Without another word, Killdeer nudged his pony's flanks and resumed along the game trail that meandered through a meadow. The path cut toward wild plum bushes before it headed into the tree line, and they had ridden into the trees thirty yards when Killdeer stopped abruptly once again. He tilted his head upward, testing the air like a wolf sniffing the wind. "Tucker was here."

Blade laughed. "Of course, he was here." He pointed to Tucker's tracks. "Even I can see that."

"Blade's right," Hack said. "Look at those boots prints, dug in like they are. Just like the man's out for a Sunday stroll in St. Louie." He paused. How many times had the Crow been right? How many times had his instincts saved his life and Hack's when the Indian *sensed* an ambush? Or danger. "You feel something?"

Killdeer looked across the small meadow to the trees on the other side. "It was nothing," he said and bent over and whispered something to his pony. He started cautiously across the clearing, his head on a swivel, watching. Looking for that danger his inner *Indian* told him lurked nearby, and the hairs on Hack's neck stood at attention. And stayed that way the thirty yards across the clearing as he watched Killdeer looking about for another Tucker ambush. Only when they had entered the trees did Hack relax when . . .

. . . Killdeer shouted a warning in Crow that Hack couldn't understand. The Indian threw himself from his horse, and Hack and Blade did so as well as a huge pine log swung in a lazy arc across the pathway Tucker had walked. Killdeer's mustang reared on its back legs, the whites of its eyes wild, frightened. The log hit the pony, bounced off, and hit Lowell's chestnut in the jaw. Both horses stumbled. Lowell's horse faltered, its broken jaw causing his breathing to become labored, pained. Painful snorts loud in the quiet forest. It went to its knees, sucking in great gasps of air.

Killdeer's pony toppled over onto its side, its neck lying at an obscene angle.

Hack drew his pistol and crouched behind a dogweed bush.

"He is not here." Killdeer picked himself up off the ground and brushed stickers from his head as the log — suspended from an overhanging branch by braided switchgrass — lost its momentum and slowed to a shallow arc.

Blade stood, his own pistol drawn, looking for the source of the mayhem: Tucker Ashley.

Hack lowered his Colt but did not holster it as he walked to the mortally wounded horses. He was aiming his pistol at Killdeer's pony when the Indian pushed the muzzle down. "I won't have a critter suffer," Hack said, stepping around the Crow.

"Hack's right," Blade said. "We can't leave them like that."

"It make too much noise," Killdeer said, "unless you want Tucker to hear you fire."

Hack decocked his Colt and holstered. "We can't just leave them —"

"I will take care of it my own way," Killdeer said. He drew his knife and knelt beside his pony, talking softly while he stroked the animal's neck.

Hack and Blade turned away. In a moment both horses were bleeding out, and Killdeer wiped his blade on his trousers before sticking the knife back into his sheath.

By the time the Indian had dispatched the horses, Hack and Blade had mounted theirs.

Killdeer took the bow off his back and held an arrow loosely between his fingers. "Will you leave me on foot, like you did Lowell Tornquist?"

Even if he wanted to leave the Indian, Hack knew he could nock an arrow and let it fly into Hack's heart before he could draw his pistol. "Not hardly. You're the only one who can find Tucker."

"Hell," Blade said, "even I can track Tucker, as easy as he's made it."

"Damn fool," Hack said. "Can't you tell he made it easy for a reason?" He nodded to the log hanging across the path. "He wanted us to ride right down this trail. Besides, you're going to be too busy making sure your horse don't falter under the extra weight."

"What extra weight?"

Hack nodded to Killdeer. "He's going to ride in back of you —"

"The hell he is."

Hack nudged his horse closer to Blade. "We got no choice."

"Why don't you have the Indian ride in back with *you*?" Blade asked.

"Because," Hack answered, "I'm only about fifty pounds heavier than you to begin with." He grinned. "And because I *said* you

214

two are a couple until we can find more horses."

CHAPTER 21

Hack rode with his rifle slung across his saddle. Expecting Tucker. Expecting another ambush. *Where the hell are you, old friend?* Hack looked around the trees. He hated to admit it, but the man had proven to be incredibly resilient since Killdeer got on his trail at the ranch. Hack should have caught Tucker by now, being on foot. Instead, he had forced Hack and his men to slow down, watching everything, knowing Tucker could kill them at any moment. He had set up the deadfall with the log injuring two horses. Eating away at time they should have been on the man's trail. So, as they entered a part of the forest with thick trees and under-brush, they were particularly cautious.

"You still think he's waiting for us?" Blade asked over his shoulder.

"He's here," Hack said to Blade riding ahead of him. "I would expect nothing less of Tucker."

"You sound as if you like him or something," Blade said as a pine branch swiped across his face, cutting tiny rivulets of blood across his cheek, and he cursed.

Hack thought of that. At the territorial prison, he had run roughshod over the other inmates, none wanting to cross the big man with the nasty reputation. At least that's what the warden accused Hack of when he visited him in the prison infirmary. Hack didn't see it that way. In his mind, all he was doing was what any top dog would do with his pack — pushing his weight around.

Until Tucker was admitted to the prison. He had stayed clear of Hack, but that didn't stop Hack from chiding the man. "Not much without your guns," Hack taunted him nearly every day at the mess hall. "You're mighty fast, from what I hear, but I don't see a gun strapped on you now."

Tucker had not answered him then nor any other time. Just one of those guys who wanted to serve out his sentence and go on with their lives.

But Hack had other plans for the man with the reputation as a quick gun. In prison, he was just another convict to be preyed upon. Tucker seemed almost meek, never confronting Hack's provocations. Until he had pushed Tucker too far that day in the mess hall. Hack kicked himself in the ass that day for misjudging Tucker. Hack thought the man deadly poison with his guns, but just another man without them. That Tucker beat him in a fair fight and continued stomping him, putting out his eye, continued working on Hack's mind. But it also brought a newfound respect for the man's capabilities. "Sure, there's some things I admire about Tucker," he told Blade. "Don't change anything, though — I'm still going to kill him when we catch him."

Hack avoided a branch and said to Killdeer, "Are we gaining on him?"

The Indian slid from the back of Blade's horse and bent to the ground. He ran his hand over a boot track and brought a handful of dirt to his nose as if he could smell his quarry. "We are close. An hour ago, I think, he passed this way." He stood and looked into the trees as if he could see through the forest. "Tracks more easy to follow."

"It just means he's getting tired, running from us on foot." Blade slipped his Henry from the rifle scabbard and held it loosely across his saddle. "I got my own score to settle with him, making me ride with the Indian."

"Just remember when the time comes that we run him to ground," Hack said. "The man is mine."

Killdeer swung his leg over the back of Blade's horse, and they started cautiously into the trees. The thick woods in this part of the hills cut the light, and Hack's night vision began to kick in. He looked about the woods and slowed, expecting an ambush. But none came.

As they neared the spot where the forest thinned, a doe jumped from her day bed among some buffalo grass.

A bluebird took flight in front of Blade's horse, the buckskin shaking its head as the bird flew by its nose.

He saw Killdeer stiffen.

Hack felt his heart race. His pulse throbbing strong in his neck. What had caused the deer and bird to fly off so suddenly? Hack took deep, calming breaths. *They* had spooked the forest critters, riding among the creatures, and he had settled his rifle back across the saddle when . . .

. . . Blade yelled.

Killdeer hurled himself off the back of the horse.

Blade thrashed around, flailing the air with his arms. Horse rearing. Throwing him to the ground.

Hack snapped his rifle to his shoulder with one hand, keeping the reins taut with the other. Stepping off his horse, expecting Tucker.

Until Hack saw the snake's fangs imbedded in Blade's neck. He seized the snake and jerked it away right before smashing it to the ground and stomping on its head.

Killdeer drew his knife and cut off the snake's head.

"What the hell?" Hack stepped towards the rattler. With no rattles. "How the hell does a rattler get into a tree?"

"It hung down from that tree," Killdeer said, pointing to a large pine. "Tied with a piece of braided grass. I did not see it in time."

Hack dropped beside Blade, while Killdeer looked impassively down at him, Blade's hands clutching his throat. He looked up at Hack with a pleading look, unable to speak, foamy spit drooling from the corner of his mouth. "You can do nothing for him now," Killdeer said.

Blade grabbed Hack's shirtfront, the other hand clawing at his throat as if he could diminish the poison coursing through his body. Hack held his friend's head, talking softly, assuring him when . . .

"He is gone," Killdeer said and walked to

the rattlesnake's body still writhing beside the trail. He picked it up and a slight smile crossed his face. "This man we seek . . . he is cunning. He cut the rattles off." He picked up the snake and drew his knife. "But he provided us with food."

"Not snake again?"

Killdeer shrugged. "Do you see any other game hereabouts?"

Hack looked at the rattlesnake. Killdeer had no problem eating it, but Hack had enough of snake meat these last days. "We have no time right now to eat," he said and walked to his horse. He took the short shovel tied to the saddle and returned to stand over Blade.

"We bury him *now*?" Killdeer asked.

"Not we," Hack said. "Me. He was my friend. You go on ahead. You have Blade's horse now. Find Tucker. Slow him down if you can. But" — he held up his finger as if scolding a child — "but do *not* kill him. That will be my pleasure."

"I will find this man," Killdeer said, "and slow him down as you ask. But" — he tapped the heel of his knife in the sheath shoved inside his trousers — "after you kill him, I take his hair."

CHAPTER 22

Tucker flinched when the heavy rifle shot echoed among the hills. He had hunted enough buffalo that he recognized that sound — a *Sharps*!

He threw himself behind a juniper bush and wriggled under it as he drew his gun, parting low-hanging branches and looking about. Ahead some thirty or forty yards along the game trail sat a cluster of rocks perfect for an ambush site, but he saw nothing. No one.

He looked about as far as he could see, but he knew the shot came from a great distance away by the sound bouncing off the granite rocks to the west. Unless the shooter fired again, he had no idea where the shot came from. Or what the shooter had fired at. Or who shot the buffalo gun.

He lay hidden by the juniper for many moments when . . .

. . . behind him a twig *snapped.* A rock

rolled down the hillside behind him in the trees and hit the trunk of a chokecherry bush.

He remained prone under the juniper, willing his breathing to slow, his heart threatening to burst from his chest as he caught sight of a Lakota not twenty yards behind him. Bent over. Studying the ground. Not looking in Tucker's direction.

The Indian stood and called to another, who emerged from the trees ducking to avoid the high branches across the trail — *Blue Boy.* The killer of white men bent to where the other Indian pointed and, after a moment, stood and looked in Tucker's direction.

They had worked out his direction of travel.

It was only a matter of time before they were upon him, and he scooted farther under the bush. He worked his way around to face them as he fished the four forty-five cartridges from his pocket that he had taken from Jimmy Milk's gun. Though they were less powerful than his own, they would be welcomed, for he did not know how many warriors Blue Boy had. This may be, he reasoned, his last chance to use *any* pistol rounds.

The Indians stood thirty yards down the

steep trail — out of most men's pistol range. But not Tucker's. He had often taken game at distances farther than this, and he was confident he could hit *one* man. But as soon as he did, the others would know where he was. *How many rode with Blue Boy?* He didn't know if Jimmy's four extra rounds would be enough, and he silently prayed that the man with the Sharps would help him once again. Didn't know if the shooter would wing more rounds on the Indians.

Blue Boy called out, and another Indian ran up the trail. He spoke to Blue Boy for a moment before fading into the trees. Tucker caught sight of him working his way behind him, though he was sure the Indians didn't know *exactly* where he was.

But they soon would if the Indian sneaking up on his backside succeeded in picking his way around and coming up behind him.

He holstered his pistol and low-crawled under the bush. He inched toward where the Lakota sneaking up on him would have to pass. When the warrior had walked ten yards into the trees again, Tucker squatted behind the trunk of an enormous pine and drew his Bowie. He cocked an ear, straining to hear the man when . . .

The Indian — muscles of his thick back straining his muslin shirt — walked a few yards through the trees. He held a stone war club beside his leg as he crouched, looking around. A moment later he rose, walking another few yards to kneel beside a snowberry bush, its white and pink flowers contrasting with the warrior's swarthy complexion. *Another few yards and he will be within knife range.*

The Indian suddenly turned toward the tree Tucker hid behind, and Tucker looked at the warrior out of his peripheral vision. Had he s*ensed* where Tucker was concealed?

The Lakota looked warily about before he resumed studying the ground.

Tucker stood from behind the juniper and inched through the underbrush, gripping his Bowie tightly. When he killed this Indian, the others might be alerted. Unless he killed this man quick. Noiselessly. And made a run for it before the other Indians heard the commotion.

Tucker stepped with the toe of his boot, feeling the ground beneath before putting his full weight down, approaching the man at his back.

Step with the toe. Test the ground.

Step with the toe. Test the ground. Put weight down when . . . the foliage underfoot gave way with a *snap* of a twig under his boot heel.

The Lakota turned, his eyes wide as he stared at Tucker's Bowie cocked over his shoulder, his arm coming down. The warrior screamed a warning and swung his heavy war club, grazing Tucker's arm as he sliced the Indian's forearm. He backed away, circling Tucker, balancing his war club in his hand, as blood dripped from his wound.

Tucker's arm ached from the heavy club's blow as he matched the man's movement, his knife held low as . . .

The Indian rushed in, swinging the club, air *swooshing* past Tucker's head. He jerked away just as the stone swung past him. The Indian smiled as he rushed in again, cocking the war club over his shoulder when Tucker kicked him in the gut. Air rushed out of the man, and he fought to stay on his feet. Tucker stepped into him, but the Indian leapt back just out of reach of Tucker's thrust.

Blue Boy's shouts grew loud, matched by the sound of more Indians running this way.

A shot. A Sharps and — from the direction of Blue Boy — a man screamed in pain. Blue Boy or one of the others? Tucker had little time to dwell on it as the Indian rushed in, swinging his club in front of him, when he . . . paused and turned his head toward the cries of the warrior somewhere behind him. And, in that fatal pause, Tucker lunged at the Indian and drove his blade into the man's belly, ripping upwards. He seemed to dance at the end of Tucker's blade, seemed to swing the war club a final time when he dropped it on the forest floor a moment before Tucker drew his knife back. The Lakota sank to his knees next to his war club. He reached for it, then looked with disbelief at his innards popping out of his gut before toppling over, dead.

Tucker ran as another shot from somewhere impacted a tree, and Tucker heard Blue Boy bark commands to his warriors. Sounds of Indians running into the forest grew fainter, and Tucker wiped his Bowie on a clump of switchgrass before sheathing it and drawing his pistol.

He walked cautiously into the trees, where he spotted another warrior shot through the pelvis and bleeding out on the ground. Sounds of the rest of them fleeing through the forest reached Tucker, and he frantically looked for the shooter.

Another shot. Cries of anguish in the distance from Blue Boy or his men, and Tucker saw a faint *puff* of smoke drifting in the wind from a high butte west of the trees.

Tucker would have to run toward the base of the butte, to find out how the man climbed up to such a height. The only man Tucker knew who could hit another man as far away as the high hill was surely reloading now — Simon Cady.

CHAPTER 23

"They *must* be gone by now," Erin said.

Jack put his finger to his lips, though it was too dark inside the cave for Erin to see him. "They moved on, but they're known to leave a warrior or two behind in case their quarry bolts."

"But you didn't see any Indians on your way here."

Jack had not. When he sneaked to the Indians' camp, he thought they might have returned to ride out the storm, waiting for it to break before resuming their search. That the camp was empty except for the wounded Swan — in the middle of a thunderstorm — told Jack that Iron Hide must really have wanted to find them very badly. Especially Erin.

"How long we gotta' stay in this here cave?" Erin swatted something on her arm. "It gives me the creeps being confined to this tiny place."

"At least it's better than the last over-hang." Erin had followed Jack's directions and found the cave in which he'd once rode out his own storm in the hills when scouting for the army. This cave had saved him that time. And it saved him again this night.

Jack reached inside the sack he had stolen from the Indian camp. He grabbed a candle and propped it against a rock before feeling around for a lucifer. He struck it against a fire starter he had also taken, and the match flamed up, illuminating the cave, and Jack touched it to the candle. He took in a short breath when he saw Erin's condition. Mud was pasted on the side of her patchy head, tendrils of hair Iron Hide missed hanging down. Dirty and muddy. Bags sagged under her eyes, and her dress was torn up the side, with more cuts from branches and brambles than he could count. "I'm thinking you better have something to eat." He upturned the sack, and a can dropped out along with several strips of dried buffalo. "All I could steal on the moment's notice was this can of hardtack and dried meat."

"And that bow and quiver you dropped down there," she chin-pointed to the mouth of the cave.

"Only 'cause there wasn't a gun to be had in their camp. I stole the bow because I had to have *some* weapon if the Indians found me besides this little skinning knife of Swan's. Though I don't much know how to use the bow."

He held the can of hardtack close to the light and opened it. He smacked the can against the side of the cave wall and four biscuits dropped into his hand. He handed Erin two and had broken off a corner for himself when she said, "Ew! There's worms in this . . . stuff."

Jack swallowed and thought he felt something wiggling down his throat. "What do you expect — they took the hardtack off some soldier. Don't worry about the worms — you'll probably chip your teeth on the biscuit before the worms get you." Jack wasn't exaggerating much. Without something to soak the flour and water wafers in, a body could chip a tooth. He leaned over and held out his hand. "Now if you're not hungry enough to eat it —"

Erin jerked it back. "I'll force it down," she said and soon had one of the biscuits devoured.

"As for how long we have to stay here," Jack said, "I figure we can't stay long. They'll eventually work out our sign. They always do."

Erin ripped off a piece of dried meat and

looked at the cave entrance ten feet away. "I got no desire to go through what Pa did when they found us that day," she said, her voice breaking. Without her father by her side, the thought of losing him finally caught up with her. She began to sob, and Jack scooted closer to her. He hesitated putting his arm around her, until he recalled his own parents' deaths at the hands of a Pawnee raiding party, and he gently draped his arm around her shaking shoulders.

They sat in the dank cave lit by that single candle, two people perched on the edge of their own eternity, with only a hollowed-out piece of Black Hills granite between them and the killers who hunted them.

After what seemed like an hour — if Jack judged the diminishing candle wax — Erin sat up and moved away from him while she swiped her hand across her wet cheeks. "We need to make a break for it," she said. "You're right . . . they *will* find us, just like they found me and Pa. It's only a matter of time. Besides, we have a weapon now."

Jack chuckled and held up the quiver of arrows. "What are we going to do, get close enough to stab them with one of these? I'm not the handiest with a bow. Now if you give me a rifle —"

"I can use a bow."

Jack chuckled again. "Sure you can."

Jack saw her face and neck flush red even in the dim light. "I grew up using a bow. Made it myself. Made my own arrows, too."

"I'm listening."

"Ma was a catalog girl Pa brought out from Chicago. After she had me, she hung around the ranch for a few years before she found some travelling drummer to whisk her away. And take all of Pa's seed money with her, little though it was. So, somebody had to hunt supper while Pa was working cows. That was me." She reached in back of Jack and hefted the quiver of arrows, taking one out and holding it to the candle. "Metal trade points." She put it back. "As deadly as that pistol of yours. In the right hands."

Jack poked his head out of the cave and looked about. Nothing moved in the forest, but Jack knew they were not free of the Indians. He and Erin had managed to escape from their hasty overhang long enough to move to this cave. Jack dragging Mick's body off into the trees would fool them only for a brief time. And when he'd sneaked away from the Indian camp last night, he carefully erased what little tracks he had left. Jack had spent two weeks here riding out that blizzard three years ago, and he felt safer then than he did now; the Lakota *would* find them if they remained here.

Jack thought back to his approach to the Indian camp, with Swan huddled shivering over a dying fire he was too weak to keep hot. The man had been easy prey, still suffering from the wound he received at Slim Buttes and traipsing through the hills as a decoy for the raiders. Jack had sneaked up behind him as the rain was pelting the blanket draped around his shoulders and hit him from behind, snatching his knife from his belt as Swan toppled over onto his back. Jack straddled him, the heavy blade poised overhead, ready to smash the warrior's head. Swan had looked into Jack's eyes, showing neither fear nor a pleading look. All Jack saw was a young Indian, his sin fighting to preserve his own way of life.

Jack had turned Swan over onto his stomach and tied his hands. Had he been careful not to put any more pressure on the wounded shoulder? Jack dismissed it. Swan was, after all, an enemy, and one that did not deserve life, let alone to be treated with kid gloves. The only time Swan had shouted a protest was when Jack took his bow and quiver full of arrows.

"You ready to leave?" Erin asked, quiver slung over her shoulder, clinging to the bow as if it were a lifeline to their survival. *Which it might be if Erin was telling the truth about her abilities with it.*

She caressed the feather fletching expertly slid into tiny grooves around the top of the arrow, and she smiled. "I almost hope they *do* find us."

CHAPTER 24

Simon clung tightly to Soreback's saddle as he rode slumped over, letting the mule pick his way down the steep shale hillside, thinking back to an hour ago when he had shot Blue Boy's second warrior. After the man had dropped, he had glassed the area, certain they would have seen the puff of smoke high atop the butte. But they hadn't, and Blue Boy and his warriors had run off into the woods, not knowing whom the next heavy slug would tear into. Simon knew they would scour the area, looking for the source that had killed two of their men.

But not now.

Now they would be far away licking their wounds, discussing how to find the shooter.

But not now.

"Hold up there, pard'ner," Simon said, his arm draped around the mule's neck. He used the horn to sit erect, blood seeping from his opened shoulder wound. The last shot from the heavy-kicking Sharps had torn stitches apart, and he needed time to recoup and lick his *own* wounds. Time to throw more thread to close the wound. Time to . . . he shook his head to clear his vision while he stuffed his bandana deeper under his shirt, the sticky blood caking under his shirt. He nudged Soreback, and the mule resumed his downward journey, even as Simon's eyes were closing.

Strong arms grabbed onto him, and he jerked away, nearly falling backwards off the mule as he forced open his eyes.

"Whoa!" Tucker said as he stopped Simon from toppling from the saddle. "Take it easy, big man. I gotta' get you off this mule, and you're not helping any."

Simon shook his head, long, gray hair falling over his forehead, his eyes looking at *two* Tucker Ashleys before his vision converged into *one.* "Thought the Indians might have lifted your scalp down in those woods," Simon managed to get out.

"Not yet they haven't." Tucker worked Simon's moccasin out of the stirrup as Soreback nudged Tucker. "I'm glad to see you, too, though I have no treat this time," he said to the mule.

Tucker wrapped his arms around Simon

as he slid off the saddle. He landed on the ground, teeth-rattling, agonizing pain shooting through his wound, and he moaned. "We'd better get you lied down so's I can take a look at that shoulder of yours."

Simon felt himself collapse before Tucker *grunted* and helped him over to a stand of pine trees where Tucker laid him gently down onto the ground. "I'll be back," he told Simon.

He rubbed his eyes. How long he'd been unconscious collapsed over the mule he didn't know. All he did know was that he was lucky to be alive judging by the amount of blood that had soaked through his shirt. And lucky that Tucker had found him and not the Indians.

He spotted his rifle propped against a fallen log, and he had started for it when he fell back down. He might need the Sharps, for the Indians couldn't be far off, or could they? How long had he been unconscious?

Tucker grabbed Soreback's reins and led him to a tree in the middle of lush mountain grass and tied him off. The mule nudged Tucker, and he nearly toppled over before turning to Soreback. Tucker wrapped his arm around the critter's thick neck and spoke things Simon couldn't hear before he stripped off the saddle and blanket and laid them on the ground.

He snatched his water bladder before reaching into his saddlebags. He came away with a bottle and walked to Simon, but he waved it away. "You know I never drink."

"After what I'm about to do," Tucker said, "you'll *wish* you'd have taken a long pull. Now let me take a look-see at that wound."

He sliced through the bloody fabric of Simon's shirt and spread it apart so that he could look at the damage. Tucker whistled and squatted next to Simon. "Bullet went in your upper back and travelled down and out your shoulder. Hacksaw be my guess?"

Simon nodded. "The bastard shot my sorrel out from under me, too. I loved that horse."

"Losing your horse is the least of your worries right now." Tucker uncorked the bladder and trickled water over Simon's back and shoulder, carefully scrubbing the dried and caked blood off with a bandana. "I'd say you did a passable job of stopping the blood before you busted stitches out and opened it back up."

Simon forced a smile. "The stitches would still be there if I hadn't run off Indians about to ambush *someone.*"

"Don't think for a moment I don't appreciate it." Tucker took the bottle he'd grabbed from his saddlebags and uncorked it. A lavender-like fragrance wafted past Simon's nose. "What you got there?"

"Lydia E. Pinkham's medicinal compound," Tucker answered.

"Let's see what you're fixin' to pour over me." Simon squinted and held the bottle to the sun. "This says it's for menstrual difficulties and such. That why it's in your saddlebags — to treat your female problems?"

"No," Tucker answered. "I keep it around because there's a whole lot of alcohol in it."

"So, you like to drink it now and again?"

Tucker shook his head. "Not me — Jack. If I kept regular whisky around, he'd drink the bottle dry. No, I keep a bottle handy for this," he said and trickled the liquid into the open wound.

Simon winced. "You could have given me some warning."

"You might have hurt me," Tucker said, "in your moment of pain." He carefully massaged the muscle around the bullet hole before pouring more disinfectant in while Simon grunted in pain. "You should have sewed this hole up better."

"With what?" Simon said, pain contorting his face. "When my horse was shot from under me, I was lucky to come away with just this," he motioned to his shoulder. "I dared not go back to get my saddlebags . . . didn't know if Hacksaw was still up on top of that canyon or not. Didn't have anything *to* sew the hole up with until Soreback came along. I used your heavy canvas patching thread in your saddlebags." He nodded to Soreback grazing beside the tree. "Hadn't been for him coming onto me, I would have been dead for sure."

"I saw how he was allowing you to ride," Tucker said. "I figured the mule had better taste than that."

Tucker walked back to his saddlebags and rooted around. He came out with a saddle needle and some fishing line.

"Where'd the line come from?" Simon asked.

Tucker knelt beside him and threaded the line through the needle. "In the bottom of my saddlebag."

"If I'd have known that —"

"You still wouldn't have been able to reach your wound to stitch it up proper. Lucky you found what you did. Now you want a swallow of Lydia's compound or not?"

"I'll suffer." Simon stuck the shaft of an arrow into his mouth while Tucker started sewing the bullet hole shut. "Hold up a moment," Simon said after that first stitch as he reached for the tonic. "I might just sample a little of Lydia." He tipped the bottle up and took a long pull. Then, for good measure, took another and set it beside Tucker. "Now you can get it over with," he said, sticking the arrow shaft between his teeth again.

When Tucker had finished, he trickled more water over the wound before pulling Simon's shirt back over his shoulder. "The shirt's gonna' stink like hell until we get to a stream to wash the blood out." He stood and started for his saddlebags. "Some beans might help you —"

"I ate them," Simon said. "Had no choice — there was nothing else at the time. Ate your oysters, too."

"Guess you had to," Tucker said. "But at least you left the peaches." He looked at Simon. "You *did* leave the peaches?"

Simon shrugged and winced in pain. "I had to have dessert one of those nights."

Tucker slipped the loop off the thong over the hammer of his pistol. "Then I better hunt us some supper."

"I wouldn't advise it. Blue Boy and his men still be close. Here." He handed Tucker a small camp ax stuck into his belt. "Sharp enough for firewood, so it ought to be sharp enough to down a rabbit. You *do* know how to use one?"

Tucker wrapped his fingers around the ax and hefted it. "It's been a while, but I think I can get close enough to a rabbit or ground squirrel to bring home supper."

CHAPTER 25

Tucker sliced off a leg of roasting rabbit and handed it to Simon as he lay propped up by Soreback's saddle. Simon took small bites, savoring the meat, before he asked, "Why you sticking around? You could be long gone from those Lakota."

Tucker took one of the wild onions dangling over the fire by a forked stick and bit into it, wiping juice off his fingers before answering. "I owe you."

"For what?"

"For running off those Indians. If you hadn't opened up on them, I wouldn't be here."

"But we were never . . . friendly afore."

"Well, we sure weren't out and out enemies," Tucker said. "We just always had differences when it came to killin'."

"Meaning?"

"Meaning I killed just when I *had* to. You seemed like you . . . *enjoyed* it."

Simon choked on a bone and spit it out. "And you wouldn't enjoy killing the Indians who took Jack?"

"You know about the Indians what took him?" Tucker asked.

Simon motioned for Tucker to slice off another piece of meat. "We — the posse and me that is — come onto your ranch there by Custer City. Burned out. Your cattle left to rot in the sun. The raiders made no effort to hide their trail." Simon tossed a bone into the underbrush. "And neither did you. Made it easy for Hacksaw Reed to track you. He didn't need that Crow Kills the Deer. He could have followed you his ownself."

"Didn't figure on him bustin' outta' prison and coming after me."

Simon held up his cup, and Tucker warmed up his coffee. *I could get used to this treatment.* "Don't feel bad leaving sign a blind man could follow. Hacksaw did, too." He blew on his coffee. "Until they realized me and the posse was after them. Then they set an ambush." He gently massaged his shoulder. "I was lucky to get out alive, though I don't feel so lucky right about now."

Tucker took out his bible and rolled a smoke. He handed it to Simon, but he

245

waved it away. "Never smoked anything but a pipe since I was a little pot licker," he said as he fished his tobacco pouch out of his possible bag slung around his thick waist. He tamped the tobacco down with a stick and took the burning branch Tucker handed him.

Tucker lit his cigarette and watched smoke rings filter through the branches over their campfire. "I'd say you're *damned* lucky. Most folks don't live through Hacksaw's ambushes from what I hear tell."

"I wouldn't have either if I hadn't spotted one of his men in the trees with his bright yellow bandana flapping in the breeze."

"Jimmy Milk," Tucker said. He lifted his shirt and pulled Jimmy's bloody bandana out.

"That's the one," Simon said. "I saw his body beside two Lakota? They some who took Jack?"

"They were."

"Then you're wasting time tending to me. The longer you sit here being my nursemaid" — he chuckled as he nudged the bottle of elixir — "or my midwife, the less chance you have of catching up with Jack."

"Believe me, I thought of that," Tucker said, "and of how you managed to get ahead of Hacksaw. He's gotta' be right behind us."

"Ol' Simon has a few tricks up his sleeve, torn though it might be. I knew Hacksaw was following you as you went after those Indians that took Jack. And with Kills the Deer with him, I knew you wouldn't be able to shake them. So all I had to do was anticipate where *you* were headed and watch for Hacksaw and his men coming after you." He reached for the pile of branches Tucker had gathered and tossed another one onto the fire. He watched it catch fire as he said, "If I would have remained atop that butte, Hacksaw would have eventually come along. And I'd have had him in my sights."

"Until Blue Boy set his men on me. Still can't figure out why you didn't let them ambush me."

"You know that difference in killing we have?" Simon said. "We probably have some difference in living, too. I couldn't let them kill you when I could have done something," he said, leaving out his conversation with the mule.

"We might not be so far off in that livin' thing." Tucker dribbled the last of the coffee into his cup and tossed the grounds aside. "Just like I couldn't hardly leave you, hurt like you are."

"You could *still* take your mule back and

be on Jack's trail."

When Tucker didn't answer, Simon said, "That's what you're going to do — leave me afoot like Hacksaw left that coyote Lowell Tornquist, to fend for himself?"

"You saw him?"

"What was left of him, all shot full of arrows. Scalped. And his heels cut like he was going to run off on them or something."

Tucker explained to Simon how he crippled Lowell enough that it would *have* to slow Hacksaw down.

"That was cold of you," Simon said and grinned. "But smart. *If* Hacksaw would have helped his man. But he is a lot colder than you'll ever be. But getting back to leaving me —"

"I'm not going to leave you." Tucker sighed deeply and shook his head. "But as soon as you can sit the back of my mule, we're back on Jack's trail —"

"I can sit a saddle now," Simon insisted. "The sooner we find Jack, the sooner I can get back to finding Hacksaw."

"You can't ride now," Tucker said. "But we'll see how those stitches are holding up in the morning."

Simon's head began to droop, and he woke up when Tucker eased him back against the saddle propped against a rock.

"I hope you're able to sit Soreback tomorrow," he told Simon. " 'Cause the Indians might already be too far ahead to find."

"We might not be able to find them so easily," Simon said. "It appeared they began hiding their tracks a couple miles back like they figured someone was on to them. My guess they'll leave a bunch of false trails. Just like that fork in your false trail led you."

"What you babbling about?" Tucker asked. "Must be the elixir having its effect after what, you finished the whole bottle."

"Not the elixir," Simon said, fighting to stay awake long enough to tell Tucker, "I think your mistake was thinking you could settle down and become a respectable rancher."

"I was doing just that —"

"Until you come onto the Indians who captured Jack. Then I suspect the excitement of being on the chase once again took over."

"Why you say that?"

"Because," Simon muttered as he felt himself lose consciousness, "you like the thrill of hunting men. Just like me. And the thrill that comes after you find them. Just. Like. Me."

CHAPTER 26

Killdeer squatted next to a faint impression in the dirt and circled it with a twig. "Tucker Ashley sat here. Waited for . . . two, maybe three hours, I think."

"Waiting for who?" Hack asked.

The Crow stood and held out his hand for Hack's plug of tobacco. "I do not know *who*. But I do know *what* he waited for." He walked another twenty yards along the trail before he squatted once again and circled a hoofprint with a branch. "*That* is what he waited for."

"He was waiting for someone on a horse?"

"Not a horse," Killdeer said. "A mule."

"A mule . . . not that jughead of Tucker's. Thought that critter had run off."

The Indian shrugged and spit a stream of tobacco that *splat* against a dragonfly passing over a log. "I cannot tell by these tracks if it is Tucker Ashley's or not. But the gait is a mule. Goes barefooted." He pointed to

Hack's horse depressions. "Your horse is shod. Mule is not. But the . . . strange thing is this." He pointed to a hoofprint, then another. "Man riding him is heavier than Tucker Ashley." He looked up at Hack. "Maybe as big as you."

Hack held out his hand, and Killdeer reached into his shirt pocket and handed the plug of tobacco back. Not that he didn't trust the Indian. "Not too many men as big as me . . ." He stopped abruptly, his heart suddenly racing as if he were running from an angry griz. *"Simon Cady,"* he sputtered. "Damn. But how the hell could he have lived after I shot hell out of him, let alone get ahead of us? And on a mule!"

Killdeer stood and tossed the stick aside. "If Tucker Ashley is clever, this Simon Cady is cunning." He looked around the woods as if expecting Simon to come busting out of the trees, scalping knife in hand, death scream erupting from his throat. "I have heard many stories about him."

"What have you heard?" Hack asked.

"That Simon Cady never gives up when he is on the hunt for a man." Killdeer met Hack's gaze. "Especially when a man has wronged him."

"And you wouldn't have killed his woman if she attacked you with that fleshing knife

251

of hers?"

Killdeer scanned the terrain. "I would not have been in the camp of the Oglala stealing pelts. Alone." He looked up at the clouds building for another thunderstorm. "As much as I hate the Sioux, I would not have killed Simon's woman. *Because* she was Simon's woman. I wish to keep this." He tugged at the braid lying on his thin chest, beside his medicine bundle.

"So you *are* afraid of Simon Cady?"

Killdeer looked up as if his answer was concealed on the clouds. "Not afraid. Just cautious. And wise."

Hack rode his horse just behind Killdeer, the Indian sometimes walking, sometimes running, stopping now and again to examine a mark in the dirt. A broken branch. A rock overturned with a different coloration from those next to it. The old man continued on the trail, never faltering. Never stopping long enough for a breather. In his younger days, Hack thought, the Indian could have run down a deer. *Hell, he could run down a deer now!* "We gaining on him?"

At the base of the tall butte, Killdeer had picked up the tracks of a man walking beside the mule and had followed it another half mile to where they had camped for the night. The Crow scooped up dark colored dirt and brought it to his nose. "A man bled here. A lot."

"Simon?"

Killdeer shrugged. "I do not know."

He had started back along the trail when Hack stopped him. "We need to take a breather."

Killdeer took the reins of his horse from Hack and tied it to a fallen log before taking his deerskin water bladder looped over the horn. He took a short pull before capping the bladder without handing it to Hack. "To answer your question: the man walking drags a foot sometimes. He tires. And he is cautious that he is being followed."

Hack sat on a log holding the reins of his horse with one hand as he took off his boot with the other. "Damn that breeze feels good," he said and held up his bare feet to the wind before asking Killdeer, "How can you know the man is afraid."

"I did not say he is afraid," Killdeer said. "I said he is cautious. Look here." He walked a few paces until he found what he was looking for. "This man stops and turns, his tracks showing where he looks back. Cautious. And cunning, I think." He threw a leg over his pony. "If we keep on his trail, we will find them tonight. I think."

Hack put his boots back on and used the stirrup to stand from the log. These last few miles, he had felt every muscle with every jarring step he took. *I'm just getting old,* he thought, then dismissed the notion. He had just been on Tucker's trail too many days and been through too many things that would exhaust any man was all. "When we catch that SOB he'll regret that beating he gave me in prison," he said, but Killdeer was already ten yards ahead working the tracks, looking back into the sun, studying faint marks left by their prey.

They followed the mule's tracks — and the man walking — all that morning and afternoon, Killdeer insisting they were gaining on them. By the time the sun began to set over the Black Hills, Tucker and the man on muleback had stopped to rest only once. But then, Hack reasoned, if *his* best friend were taken captive by the Lakota, he would do what it took to save him. "We need to kill us supper," Hack said. "We've seen some fat doe in these here hills —"

"Do not use your gun," Killdeer said, stopping abruptly and looked at their back trail. "Kill food, but do not use your guns. Too much noise."

"Then how the hell am I going to kill

254

anything?"

Killdeer laid his hand on the hilt of his knife shoved into his trousers. "Think like an Indian."

"Then you rustle us up some meat." Hack laughed. "You're the only one who *can* think like an Indian."

"No time to hunt," Killdeer said and started back the way they had come.

"Where are you going?"

"Back," the Crow said. "We are followed."

Hack was just turning the ground squirrel over as it dangled from a branch suspended over the fire when Killdeer materialized beside him as if dropped from the sky. Hack jumped, as he often did when the Indian crept back into camp so silently, and Hack often thought the Crow did so to frighten him. "So that is our deer meat?" Killdeer said as he squatted in front of the fire and warmed his hands. "It must have been a very small doe. A fawn perhaps?" he asked, grinning.

"This is all I could rustle up with my knife," Hack said and motioned to the black blood dripping scalp dangling from the Crow's trousers. "Looks like you found who's been following us."

Killdeer leaned over and sliced off a piece

of meat before sitting on his haunches. "Sioux." He fingered the bloody scalp. "But just two *now*. A half mile down that trail, I think."

"At least you stung them good, by the looks of that scalp lock. They'll think twice about coming for us."

Killdeer shook his head and looked at Hack like he was looking at a ghost. "The others will come after us," he said, shuddering, "even though I ran their ponies off."

Hack tore the back legs off the squirrel and started gnawing at the tough meat. "How can you be so sure? Were it me, I'd break off the track. I'd give up following us before any more men were killed."

"Do you break off your pursuit of Tucker Ashley after *your* men were killed?"

"That's different," Hack said. "I *have* to kill Tucker."

"And these two Sioux will *have* to kill us because I killed one of theirs."

"Why'd you kill a Sioux then?"

"I did not wish to. This time. After I spotted their camp I backed away. I thought there was no others in the woods and started to dig turnips for our meal. A warrior out hunting on his own saw me." Killdeer's hand brushed the bloody scalp. "I had no choice."

Hack licked grease dripping down his fingers. "I just don't see how you can be so certain they'll hunt us down."

Killdeer looked into the fire, flames reflecting off his weathered face, and Hack thought he saw the Crow tremble for a moment. "After I killed the young Sioux, I sneaked back into their camp to find out how many, and they woke up." His voice faltered. "One was Blue Boy."

"The Santee?"

Killdeer nodded. "The killer of white men. And killer of Crows. He *will* come after us, even though he has no pony." He grinned. "I cut their lines. Their ponies ran off and scattered into the woods like they were fleeing a fire."

Hack laid another log on to the fire and grabbed his bedroll. "Then we'd better make this a short night," he said.

CHAPTER 27

"Hold up here," Simon said, "and help me off'a your mule."

"Maybe you ought to take it easy —"

"I've been taking it easy since you found me yesterday. I feel good enough to stand for a bit. It'll help me to get back on my own feet, so grab on." Tucker helped Simon down from Soreback, and he stood for a moment holding onto the saddle horn while he caught his breath.

"See, you should've stayed in the saddle —"

"Never mind me," Simon said with a wave of the air. "You need help."

Tucker looked around. On three sides, the rock formation rose high with the trail passing through the stone, compliments of rushing water at one time cutting through the rock eons ago. "Does it look like I need help? There's no one around but you and me. Sometimes I think you enjoy taunting me."

"What I enjoy is working out a track. Call it a challenge. Something that you're having a hard time with right now. You need help. Another set of eyes."

Tucker hated to admit it, but he *was* unable to read the sign this morning when he and Simon had come upon a hastily broken camp of Lakotas. Tucker had no problem following the Indians, until he had walked right past an overhang not three feet off the ground that Simon spotted from the back of the mule. "That's no moccasin print," Simon said and had pointed to a partial boot print in the mud-caked ground, a track showing a man walking with the inside of his heel wore down. *Jack Worman.*

"Help me down there so's I can have a look-see," Simon barked, and he seemed to enjoy ordering Tucker around. He had entered the low overhang and immediately saw a footprint. Barefoot. And another, either a boy or a woman by the size of the foot. He laughed to himself: leave it to Jack Worman to find a woman out in the woods. Tucker had closed his eyes, putting himself in Jack's place. He and his companion had stayed under here until the Indians moved on, Tucker was certain. "But the tracks leading away show no barefoot person. It is two sets of boot prints, each leading in opposite directions."

They picked up the trail of the Indians following an obvious track Jack had laid for them. "Why you figure Jack's all of a sudden laying easy sign?"

"He's leading the Indians," Simon said.

"Where?"

"We'll see if you give me a chance to catch my breath again."

After a few moments, Simon nodded, and they walked the ground another fifty yards before Simon pointed to the decaying body of Mick Flynn. Tucker looked down at the corpse and said, "Ol' Mick never looked better," and Simon had thrown his head back and laughed heartily.

"Where's Mick's boots?" Tucker asked. "Indians have no use for them."

Simon shrugged.

But Tucker had lost *Jack*'s trail at the body, and — even when he backtracked — he failed to find where he and his companion had gone, Jack had confounded the Indians so good. The men had returned to the cave to work out the tracks from there once again. They had missed something. At least Tucker had.

Simon walked gingerly, a wide circle

around the outside of the cave, his arm in a makeshift sling Tucker had fashioned from Mick's galluses. As good a tracker as Tucker was, Simon was legendary. There was not a man Simon had hunted for the bounty that he hadn't found. "There's Mick's boots," he pointed to a toe dig in the ground. "Jack's friend was barefooted going into the cave. Wore boots coming out. Ugh! It would be a strong person to wear that smelly Irishman's boots."

Simon stopped and leaned against a tree to help him kneel on the ground. He scooped up damp dirt, letting it sift through his fingers before moving his position slightly to keep what sun escaped the trees between him and the ground he studied. "Give me a hand," he grunted.

Tucker draped Simon's arm over his shoulder and helped him stand. "The one that flees with Jack is small. Woman I'm sure now, just like we figured, probably snatched about the time they took Jack. You didn't spot it this far from the cave because she sets her toe down first before putting her weight down. Smart, that one is."

"What else can you tell by those Indian tracks?" Tucker asked, pointing to faint and indistinct moccasin prints beside the woman's.

261

Simon paused and got a faraway look to him before he sighed deeply and said, "The Indians who follow are led by a headman who will show them no mercy when he catches them."

Jack squatted and ran his hand over the moccasin tracks before looking up at Simon and said, "Even you couldn't tell who is leading these raiders by this track."

"No, I can't tell by that *one* track," Simon said. "But I can by tracks left at that Indian camp we found. A particularly nasty Lakota."

"And you didn't tell me back there?"

"I wasn't sure until now. The Indian who made that track is a heavy man. And he walked with his right foot a little pigeon toed." He leaned against a tree and caught his breath as he rubbed his shoulder. "It is Iron Hide."

Tucker stood and approached Simon. "I've heard of him. Bad reputation. How do you know him?"

Simon hobbled toward the mule. "Help me in the saddle."

Tucker lifted Simon's foot and put it in the stirrup. The big man grunted once as he grabbed onto the horn and swung his other leg over the saddle. He sat for a moment catching his breath before he said, "Iron

Hide is — was — Rain Water's brother."

"This is your brother-in-law?"

Simon nodded.

"At least when we catch up with them, you'll be able to reason with him —"

"There is no reasoning with Iron Hide. He and I had . . . words after Hacksaw Reed killed my woman. Iron Hide blamed me for her death. He thought I should have been in camp when Hacksaw slipped in to steal the pelts." Simon took the reins and nudged Soreback's flanks. "And he will not stop until he kills Jack and his friend. And us, if he knows I follow him."

CHAPTER 28

Jack lay on his stomach propped up on his elbow. "It didn't take them long to find us," he whispered, pointing to Grass and Iron Hide working the tracks no more than a hundred yards up a slight ridge. Pale Moon flanked them, one arm around Swan as he struggled to keep up, the white strip of Erin's dress still encircling his shoulder contrasting to the green of the woods.

"You sure they found our tracks?" Erin asked. "I was mighty careful sneaking here —"

"They found them," Jack said. "The rain threw them off some, but they picked up our trail all right."

Erin pushed Jack's bandana back from her eyes. She had given Jack his Stetson back and used his bandana to cover her baldness. Still — with only nubs of hair growing back and thin strands dirtier than a buffalo in a fresh wallow — he thought she was beautiful. Even prettier than the upstairs girls at the Bucket of Blood in Ft. Pierre. "If we're going to leave this place," Jack said, "we'd better do it now. Another hour and they'll find us. When we go, we go fast. You up for it?"

Erin nodded as she readjusted the bootstrings. Even though she was having a hard time getting past the smell of Mick's boots, she was having a more difficult time keeping them on her feet until she tore strips off her dress and stuffed them down the toes of the boots. She slung the rawhide quiver over her shoulder before grabbing the bow, running her hand along it almost lovingly. "I'm ready."

Jack led the way out of their cave, keeping an eye on the Indians as he walked hunkered over until he reached the crest of a hill, wet with yesterday's rain. The knoll sat on a meadow with ponderosa pine and a scattering of aspen, their leaves turning a vivid golden brown. He looked a final time behind him. He could see the Indians and motioned to Erin to follow him as he slid down the hill. Trees at the edge of the meadow below stopped them, and they brushed wet leaves off their backsides as they stood. At the edge of the shallow meadow, another hill would let them slide farther down, away from the

Indians.

"This will buy us some time," Jack said, out of breath. Any other time in his life, Jack was able to run up and down these hills and never break a sweat, never struggle for air. But these last weeks — with little rest and little food — had taken a toll on him. He sat on a rock as he looked at her. Though dirt and mud caked to her torn dress, and with his bandana covering little of her baldness, she stood looking around, breathing easy, ready to run if she needed it. *Damn if she wouldn't be a corker working my ranch. That I no longer have.* "How you holding up?"

She forced a smile. "Better than you, apparently." She scanned the hillside they had just slid down. "Where's that other Indian? That stocky one."

"Damn!" Jack said, louder than he wanted when he realized Stumpy hadn't been with the others tracking them. "They held him back. Watching. Using the others to flush us out."

Erin began trembling. "Watching where —"

A *blur,* rushing at Jack's back. He half turned to meet Stumpy's attack, the weight of the man crashing down atop him. They rolled on the ground and over the side of

266

the hill. A pine tree near the edge of the hillside twenty feet down stopped their descent, and a heavy *woooosh* escaped Jack's lungs as the Indian straddled him.

Stumpy grunted like a bull elk in rut. He thrust his knife at Jack's head. Jack jerked aside just as the knife went by him and imbedded into the ground.

Jack kneed Stumpy in the groin.

The Indian groaned, his face contorted in pain, straddling Jack, but he didn't budge.

Stumpy hit Jack in the face. Blood spurted from a broken nose, and he threw up his hands to block another blow. The bigger man easily shoved Jack's hands aside as he freed his blade from the ground. A broad grin crossed the Indian's face. He raised his knife overhead and . . .

The *thump* of the arrow seemed louder than the Indian's low groan. He paused, his knife poised for another thrust as he looked down in disbelief at the tip of an arrow protruding from his chest. Blood weeped from the wound, his innards dangling from the tip of the arrow like a worm on a fishing hook. Jack quickly rolled Stumpy off him, clamping his hand over the Indian's mouth to stifle his screams. He slumped to the ground looking about in disbelief. Looking for the other Lakota. Looking for Erin.

She stood on the hill above nocking another arrow. But no more was needed, and Jack waved frantically to her. She put the arrow back into the quiver and slid down the hillside, Stumpy's lifeless body stopping her descent. She regained her footing and stood looking down at the dead warrior, not a whiff of emotion showing on her face.

"You killed him!"

She shrugged. "That a problem?"

Jack shook his head. "Didn't figure you could *actually* use one of those things."

"Obviously, I can. Think the others heard us?"

"We're not sticking around to find out." Jack picked up Stumpy's knife and snatched his sheath from his trousers before he rooted through the bag tied around the Indian's waist. He came away with a flint and steel fire starter.

"Give me the steel," she said, and Jack handed it to her.

"There's a creek not a half mile through those trees," he said, motioning to the south, "and a cabin. If we can make it there without getting our hair lifted . . ." he stopped and felt his face flush as his eyes were drawn to her head. "No offense. But if we can make it there, we just might be able to throw them off."

Jack figured the Indians wouldn't see smoke if he kept the fire small in the hearth. The flames licked the side of the stone fireplace of the abandoned shack, with the half-collapsed roof on one side of that cabin that had blown over years before. Still, it was the first real shelter they'd had since they had been captured, and they could dry their bones from the rain that had begun an hour ago.

"The rain's a good thing," Erin said. "Rubs out our tracks."

It *was* a Godsend for them. When they reached the creek, Jack knew crossing it would kick up sediment the Lakota would have spotted. But they had made it to the shack he had stumbled across three years ago and were safe. For now.

"Where do we go now?" Erin said, sucking the marrow out of the bones of the quail. When she had bragged to Jack that she could hit a bird in flight, he laughed. He didn't laugh when Erin returned with two hen grouse.

He finished his own bird and tossed the bones into the fire where his socks dried over the heat.

"You said they'll find us," she said as she brushed a piece of meat off her dirty dress. Since Jack had first laid eyes on her, Erin's dress had gotten shorter and shorter each time she'd torn strips off to fashion some kind of bandage and to stuff in Mick's boots. This time, she had torn the dress itself off so she could clean up Jack's face. She had dipped her dress into the creek and washed the blood away. "I know this'll hurt a mite," she said and snapped his nose back into place.

"Sweet mother of God!" he cried out, fearful the Indian might have heard him. "You need to change your verbiage — that hurt like *hell*."

And it still hurt as he avoided looking at her knees and lower legs, now exposed for want of a dress to cover them properly. "We walked in that creek far enough and doubled back, so it would take them time to work out our direction. They might be on us now if it hadn't started raining."

Erin took the arrows out of the quiver and laid them in front of her in a neat row before reaching for Stumpy's steel fire starter. She picked up an arrow and held it to the light of the fire while she ran the steel along the metal trade point. After blowing metal filings from the point, Erin laid it beside the others before taking up another arrow, and Jack imagined she would love nothing more than to send every arrow into their pursuers. "There's gotta' be white folks in these hills. Miners. Bear or wolf hunters. Folks who could help us."

"Custer getting wiped out a couple months ago drove people into the towns. Deadwood. Custer City. Some folks have fled as far away as Ft. Pierre and Yankton they were so spooked, waiting until the army finds the Sioux and drives them back onto the reservations. You can bet there's no one hereabouts to help us." He shuddered, wanting to put more wood onto the fire but knowing better. As much as he still hadn't thawed from the cold rain, he did not want to send a signal to the Indians where they were holed up. He tested the dryness of his socks and slipped them on. "All I know is we better get some sleep. A couple hours would be better than nothing."

He laid close as he could to the fire, and Erin laid beside him. He resisted the urge to hold her when she slid nearer and draped her arm around him. "Let's just stay warm for a while. With these Indians hard after us," she said, "a couple hours sleep might be *all* we get before they find us."

CHAPTER 29

Hack reined his gelding at the edge of what had been a recent Lakota camp. The Indians left few things behind: a campfire that had been rain drenched yesterday, two ropes that had been tied and cut from around a tree. Nothing to indicate they intended returning. But Hack hadn't lived as long as he had by being careless, and he drew his rifle, even as Killdeer worked his way around to the far side of the camp. He had peeled off before they broke through the clearing, and Hack sat his horse, testing the air. The camp had been used recently enough that the odor of cooked meat lingered.

The Crow broke through the trees. He led his pony to the deserted campfire and motioned to it. "A half day," he said simply and walked to the tree. He picked up the cut ropes for a moment before tossing them aside. "They hunt for him that escaped."

"So you're saying Jack Worman managed

to get away from the Lakota?"

Killdeer walked a circle around the clearing and said over his shoulder, "There were three white people the Sioux took. I think they all escaped." He grinned. "The Sioux lost them. But" — he picked up a piece of blood-soaked rawhide — "another — a Sioux — had been left here. Tied up —"

"The Sioux tied up one of their own?" Hack asked.

Killdeer bent to study faint tracks and looked into the forest. "I do not know. The rain . . . it washed much of the tracks away. But the rain also soaked this rawhide. Stretched it so that this man they left in camp was able to free himself." The Crow chin-pointed to the trees. "I think that he catches up with the other *Snakes.*"

"What's that got to do with Tucker?"

The Crow held out his hand, and Hack handed him what was left of his plug of tobacco. "He was here" — Killdeer nudged the soggy ashes of the campfire with his moccasin — "looking for his friend."

Hack dismounted and gripped tight the rifle while he looked about the deserted campsite. "I don't see that Tucker was here."

Killdeer shook his head. "Have you lived this long to miss so much?" He motioned to the north. "He led the mule. Tied it off back in the trees. Approached the camp on foot sometime after this Sioux freed himself." He pointed to a boot print in mud, quickly drying in the hot sun. "Tucker's."

"How long?"

Killdeer studied the ashes and the boot mark closer before saying, "Five hours. Six. Maybe. He may not reach his friend in time. The Sioux might find him first."

"I don't much care about Jack Worman," Hack said as he walked to his horse. "What about Tucker?"

"Tomorrow we catch him," Killdeer said. "He cannot go so fast walking beside the mule —"

"Then we could catch up with Tucker tonight?" Hack untied the reins from around the pine. "If we head out now —"

"We wait until morning to hunt him again."

"Morning!" Hack said. "We're this close —"

"Do you not remember Blade? And the crippled ponies? This Tucker laid a false trail three miles back in the trees, and I thought any moment he would set another trap."

Hack waved the air as if waving away the notion that they wait until daylight. "I know. You told me that's why we were going too damned slow — figuring Tucker would spring one of his little surprises. But we're out of the thick trees now. Let's follow his trail . . ."

Killdeer sat impassively on a rock in the center of the clearing, and Hack recognized that look — there was nothing Hack could do to change the old man's mind. After many moments, the Crow stood and walked to his pony, stripping the saddle and hobbling the horse beside lush grama grass. "Get firewood," he said and bent to his bow and quiver of arrows. "I am going to find meat." He smiled. "And it won't be ground squirrel."

After they ate their fill of coyote that Killdeer killed and roasted, they tossed their blankets in front of the same fire that the Sioux had used the day before. Hack laid two large branches on the faintly flickering flames, the fire flaring up when the Crow kicked the branches away. "What the hell you doing? I'm cold."

Killdeer ignored him for the moment as he broke one of the branches in half and laid the other atop the wood pile. "We do not need a fire that every Sioux in these Black Hills can spot for miles."

"If we can see Tucker's tracks, that means

that he hasn't caught up with the Sioux yet. And we haven't run into *any* since we've been in this part of the hills."

"Do you forget about those Sioux I found at the base of the butte? The ones that I told you would follow because I killed one of theirs? They are not *these* Sioux."

"You also said you ran their ponies off." Hack tossed his cigarette into the fire. "I think we're safe."

Killdeer moved his blanket away from the fire and into the shadows that the fire couldn't reach. "With the Snakes, one never quite sleeps soundly. If one values his scalp."

Hack slept fitfully, due in part to Killdeer's warning about the Sioux, partly because he kept waking up to swat mosquitoes as big as fingernails off his face. And partly because this last week hunting Tucker had not gone as Hack envisioned. When he had broken out of prison, it looked like such a simple matter to find Tucker and kill him. No one tracked a man like the Crow, and Hack had three solid men riding with him, any of which could have been a match for Tucker. Except none had. He had confounded them at every turn, picking off each man one by one. And now it seemed he travelled with Simon Cady.

And that bothered Hack nearly as much as not finding Tucker.

He pulled his blanket over his head, the buzzing of the mosquitos loud as they hit the blanket, trying to get fresh blood underneath.

Until . . . the hitting of the blanket by the bloodsuckers abruptly stopped.

Hack lay under his blanket, grateful they had moved on to other victims. Perhaps they went to attack Killdeer, Hack thought as he dozed off once again only to awaken to wonder: why *had* the mosquitoes left him?

He pulled the blanket from his face, flames from the fire reflecting off a man even taller and heavier than he. A white man dressed like a *Sioux*. Standing by the fire looking calmly down at Hack as he held a pistol beside his leg.

Hack was clawing for his gun in his holster on the ground beside him when the Indian aimed his own pistol at Hack's head and said in perfect English, "Do you wish to travel the *Wanagi Tacanku* before it is your time?"

Hack withdrew his hand from the holster. "The what?"

"The Spirit Road," the Indian answered. "For as surely as you reach for your gun you will be dead. Stand and move away from your pistol."

Hack did as he was ordered, sizing the Indian up, looking for some weakness he could use when it came time to make his move against the Indian. He stood half a head taller than Hack and — where Hack had enough weight to push most men around — this man had that same weight. Except he carried the weight like a prize fighter.

"Where is the Crow?" the Sioux asked.

"He's . . ." Hack looked around camp. Killdeer's blanket — close enough to the fire he could get *some* heat when he turned in — lay where he had thrown it down. But the old man was nowhere in camp.

Two other Sioux emerged from the shadows shaking their heads. "My warriors have not found the Crow. But I know he rides with you. Where is he?"

Hack shrugged, feeling the handle of his knife rubbing his side, and his hand inched closer to it. "I don't know who you're talking about —"

The Indian's hand flashed quicker than Hack's eyes could follow and slapped him hard across the face. Hack staggered back. He was fighting to remain on his feet when the Indian stepped in and slapped him again, knocking him to the ground. Hack looked up at him while he wiped blood from his split lip as he recalled Killdeer's words. "You Blue Boy?"

"I am." He squatted in front of Hack, their face inches apart. "The Crow, killer of my people — where is he?"

Hack tried scooting away, but the other Sioux stood behind him.

Blue Boy drew his knife that — like Killdeer's — had flecks of dried blood crusted on the blade. He drew a shallow line down Hack's cheek, and sticky blood dripped onto his hand. "Okay," Hack said, holding his hands up as if to ward off the Indian. "He *was* here. But he lit out on me, the cowardly bastard. Left me to go after Tucker Ashley alone."

Blue Boy's eyes widened. "*You* seek Tucker Ashley, too."

"Oh," Hack said, "so you look for him as well?"

"He killed one of my warriors. And he walks beside the man who killed two others with a buffalo gun. I do want him" — he looked about the camp — "but I want the Crow even more."

Hack waved the air. "Leave the old man alone. He's harmless. Besides, you and me could team up. We both want Tucker, and we both want his agony to last as long as possible."

"Enough!" Blue Boy said. "We hunt Tucker alone *after* we find the Crow." He held the blade an inch from Hack's good eye. "Tell me where Kills the Deer is or surely you *will* travel the *Wanagi Tacanku* — "

The *twang* of a bowstring sounded like music to Hack's ears, followed by a sickening *thud* as the arrow drove into the thigh of one of the Sioux standing behind Hack. The Indian screamed in pain. Collapsing on the ground.

The other warrior yelled to Blue Boy in Sioux, pointing to the trees at the edge of the clearing twenty yards away. Blue Boy's head snapped around, straining to spot Kills the Deer, his focus off Hack.

For a moment.

Just a brief moment.

Long enough for Hack to snap a kick to Blue Boy's kneecap.

Blue Boy fell to one knee, holding the other as hate filled his face with a painful grimace while he dropped his gun in the mud. He drew his knife and cocked it overhead. Too late he realized that Hack had picked up a log from the pile of firewood and swung it at Blue Boy's head. Shards of bark flew from the log as the Sioux collapsed onto the ground, swaying as he sat up, struggling to gain his footing. He stood for a moment before his knee gave out, and he fell back again, his hand clawing for the gun on the ground.

The other Sioux — a seasoned warrior by the scar running down his cheek and neck, another across his shoulder blades — stood with an arrow nocked into his own bow, standing guard over the Indian with the arrow in his thigh, searching for Killdeer, paying Hack no mind.

Hack looked about for the Crow. The old man wasn't to be seen, and Hack gathered his legs under him and leapt onto the Indian. He drove a fist into the warrior's gut, rolling off, snatching his gun and holster as he went by, and was running for his horse when an arrow *whizzed* by his head. He spun around and snapped a shot, the .45 slug hitting the Indian on the forearm, and he dropped his bow.

Blue Boy regained his footing and stood, swaying, leaning off his injured knee. Reaching for his gun as Hack scrambled toward the horse tied to the trees. Killdeer stepped from behind a pine and handed Hack the reins of his sorrel. "Where the hell you been?" Hack asked and swung into the saddle.

Killdeer looked at Blue Boy hefting his pistol. Dropping the hammer. The gun misfired, and Hack thanked God for the rain. It would only be a moment before Blue Boy cleared his pistol. Only a moment to blow the dampness off the percussion caps and wing rounds their way.

The man Hack shot grabbed his bow and nocked an arrow as Killdeer drew his scalping knife and started for him. "Never mind him," Hack said and grabbed Killdeer's arm. "You can lift his hair another day. Let's just get the hell outta' here, or we'll be walking that Spirit Road Blue Boy was yacking about," he said as Blue Boy fired off a shot that clipped the tree beside Hacksaw, driving wood splinters into his cheek. "We better light the hell outta' here before that big bastard shoots again."

CHAPTER 30

Tucker sat upright at the sound of the gunshot.

"Came from the north," Simon said. "Pistol by the sound of it."

Tucker stood and started rolling his blanket. "That shot can only mean bad things." He held out his hand to help Simon stand, but he slapped it away.

"I can stand by myself."

Tucker stood beside Simon, who favored his injured shoulder as he stumbled to rise. The last thing they needed now was for his stitches to break loose. "Think that was Hacksaw?" Tucker asked.

"It had the crack of a cartridge gun," Simon said. "Has to be a white man — Indians usually carry cap and ball."

Simon's logic made sense. As he slid the britching under Soreback's tail so the saddle wouldn't slide off, Tucker thought of Indians he'd had run-ins with of late. Though many carried trade rifles or Springfields stolen from the army, their pistols tended to be cap and ball. Easier to mold round lead balls from most things lead they came across, and powder was easy to come by. Not like they could just come waltzing into a mercantile in a white man's town and buy a box of cartridges. Had to be cap and ball. Just like the Navy Colt Simon favors.

"My guess, ol' Hacksaw ran into trouble," Simon said. "He wouldn't risk firing a shot if he didn't have to. He'd not want to alert us that he's close. We could stay here. Nice place for an ambush —"

"We find Jack, *then* we hunt down Hacksaw. I want him nearly as bad as you, but I want Jack safe and alive more."

Simon bent to his Sharps tucked lovingly inside the deerskin sheath and walked to Soreback. Tucker finished saddling the mule, and he tied Simon's rifle to the side of the saddle before holding the stirrup for him. Simon looked at it for a long moment before stepping back. "I've ridden for long enough. It's your turn to ride."

"Not today," Tucker said. "You're still not mended up. You can barely walk. Now get your big behind up into that saddle."

Simon's head drooped in resignation before slipping his boot into the stirrup and carefully swinging his leg over. "The only reason I didn't stand there and argue with you is Kills the Deer. If he's still tracking for Hacksaw, there's nowhere we can hide. And we sure can't fool him, not with Soreback being as slow as he is with me atop him. But tomorrow . . . tomorrow you ride."

Tucker cocked his ear to the north but heard no other sound of battle. If it was Hacksaw, either he got himself killed or he prevailed and was hot on their trail. "We might not even *be* on this side of the grass tomorrow to worry about those shots."

They had to move slower than Tucker liked, doing what he could to confound Kills the Deer, though he knew it was futile. The Crow would be able to track them even if they were both afoot. But they could slow him down some.

They came to a fast moving creek, twenty yards wide and deep for a mountain stream even with a heavy snow runoff this spring. Jack's trail led straight into the water, but recent rains had washed out his tracks.

Simon climbed down from the mule and arched his back, stretching. He stood beside Tucker and looked at the creek bed. "That Jack's a cagey one, heading into the creek like he did." He looked upstream and down.

"Could be miles before they came out of the water on the far side. If whichever way we pick is wrong, we could lose hours coming back to this spot and going the other direction."

"That's why Jack walked into the creek." Tucker walked along the bank, Jack's boot marks all but washed out by the rain last night, thinking what his friend would have done. If he walked downstream, his tracks would have been washed away quicker. If he walked upstream, sediment kicked up and disturbed by him would be carried downstream, the discoloration alerting the Lakota what direction he and his woman friend fled. Tucker stood and motioned. "They went upstream."

"That wouldn't make any sense. Those Lakota would spot the discoloration in sediment right off."

"But it would make sense if you knew Jack Worman. Just his nature. If Jack read the weather right, he might suspect rain a-comin' and figured he and the woman would be safe walking thataway."

Simon held the mule's reins and started along the bank. "Then I guess we head upstream."

A flash, just for a fleeting moment and then

was gone. "Down," Tucker whispered, and Simon laid over on the saddle.

"What'cha see?"

"A reflection," Tucker said and helped Simon out of the saddle. He led Soreback to a stand of pine and dropped the reins. "There," he said, pointing.

"Can't see anything," Simon said, "but then my eyes are like me — getting a mite long in the tooth."

Tucker fished his ship's glass from his saddlebags and snapped it open. He scanned the hills beside a rock formation. "It was thataway . . ." He stopped, rubbing his eyes for a moment before putting the glass to his eyes once again. "Indian down there," he said and handed Simon the glass.

"Iron Hide," he breathed softly, as if the Indian could hear him a quarter mile away among the rocks. "And some others." Simon untied his Sharps from the saddle. " 'Cause if they saw us, I need to thin the herd a mite."

Tucker took the telescope from Simon. "Their attention is on something down in that valley."

"Let me have a look." Simon rested the glass on a twig protruding from the tree to steady it. "It's Iron Hide all right. Got him three warriors and they're pointing . . .

there!" He handed Tucker the telescope back. "To the right of that huge boulder at the edge of the clearing. Something moved. White. My old eyes can't quite make out what."

Tucker steadied the telescope against the tree and studied the boulder but saw no movement. He brought the glass down for a moment before looking again, the powerful glass straining his eyes. A white cloth fluttered beside a pine tree for a brief moment and was gone.

Tucker turned his attention back to the Lakota. They pointed down the valley to the boulder, seeing something from their vantage point that Tucker could not, and he looked once again to where the Indians pointed when . . .

. . . a flash of white. A . . . dress, worn by a white woman who walked behind Jack Worman, visible for only a moment before disappearing down a steep bank. "Jack. And a woman, but you ain't gonna' believe this — she carries a bow."

"Sure she was white?" Simon asked. "If she was an Indian, it wouldn't be odd for her to carry one."

"I don't know," Tucker said. He brought the glass to his eyes once again, but the Indians and Jack had disappeared behind a cluster of rocks. "I saw them for only a second."

"*If* the Indians head right toward that boulder like it appeared they was fixin' to, we can drop down below that ridgeline." Simon pointed to a ridge down in the valley. "It's high enough to hide a critter even as big as Soreback. We could get to Jack and his woman before the Indians do." He took his pipe from his possible bag around his waist and filled it with tobacco as he studied the terrain. "There's an abandoned wolfer's cabin about two miles in the direction they're heading. Jack just *might* know about it."

"How do you know about this shack?"

Simon blew smoke rings upwards where they dissipated among the branches. "The wolfer had a hundred-dollar bounty on his head for robbing a mercantile in Omaha. I tracked him to his cabin."

"By any chance did he make it to trial?"

Simon shrugged. "He tried to escape, and I had no choice . . ." He tapped ashes out of his pipe on the heel of his boot.

"What I figured." Tucker stowed his ship's glass in his saddlebags and motioned for Simon to saddle up.

"I'm not going to get any better riding that mule of yours like I have been. I need to stretch my legs. Besides" — he patted Soreback's neck — "he could use a rest. And we might find Jack sooner without the mule burdened by all my weight."

Tucker began to argue but decided it was futile. "Suit yourself if you think you're up to it. I haven't been to this part of the Black Hills before, so you'll have to lead the way."

Simon looked over the ground to the east. "We make it to that ridgeline, there's a game trail that'll take us right to the cabin. A mile closer than the way the Indians are headed." He looked at the blackening sky. "Especially if we get a rain that wiped out their tracks."

"And if Jack's not headed to that cabin?"

"Then we'll have lost too much time, and the Indians will have lifted his scalp by the time we find him."

"So it's no more than a guess?"

"About it," Simon answered.

Tucker took Soreback's reins and followed Simon down a steep hillside when . . .

A shot.

Simon stopped and cocked his head. "Close."

"Gotta' be Hacksaw and that nasty old Crow tracker of his," Tucker said.

Another shot echoed off the canyon walls to the north. "Cap and ball," Simon said. "And at least one cartridge gun." He chuckled as he rubbed his itching shoulder. "My guess is Blue Boy caught up with Hacksaw." The smile faded. "Hope that Santee didn't kill him."

"Thought you hated Hacksaw?"

"I do," Simon answered, grabbing bushes, picking his way down the hill. "But I want him for myself. Kill him so's he knows it's me at the other end of the gun." He looked down the steep trail leading to the rocks below. "If it weren't for Jack needing help, I'd go back and find the son of a bitch now and kill him."

"If there's anything left after Blue Boy gets done with him," Tucker said, "he's yours."

CHAPTER 31

Killdeer stopped abruptly and turned towards their back trail.

"You hear something?" Hack asked.

The Crow said nothing, and Hack thought he hadn't heard anything over the light rain that had begun an hour ago. He looked back the way they had come along one of a thousand game trails intersecting in the Black Hills. This morning when Killdeer voiced a notion as to where Tucker and Simon were headed, Hack told the Indian to take the lead. Now, he stood looking back along the trail, a worried look on his weathered face. "Perhaps," Killdeer said at last as he turned back in the saddle, "it was nothing. A deer. Bear maybe. There are more things unseen in these Black Hills than a man knows."

"Then we wasted time with your little lesson about deer and bears —"

An arrow *whizzed* through the air and

thumped into the side of Hack's sorrel. The horse's legs buckled, and it stumbled, frothy blood spewing from its mouth, fighting to stand as another arrow missed Hack's head by inches. He hurled himself out of the saddle just as the horse collapsed. Hack had scurried to a clump of juniper when Killdeer grabbed Hack's leg and hurriedly dragged him deeper under the bush.

Silence.

Hack peeked under the juniper but saw nothing. "I don't see —"

"Quiet!" Killdeer said.

Hack strained to hear movement. Nothing. But he knew the Indian who'd shot Hack's horse still lingered within killing range.

Hack looked over at his horse, the sorrel's head flat on the ground, blood sputtering from its mouth every time it took a breath. *Lung shot.*

He drew his Colt and aimed over the backstrap, sighing with deep sorrow at killing his sorrel, and he touched off the round. The horse shuddered a final time before its lifeless eyes started glazing over.

Hack quickly shucked the spent cartridge and thumbed another one in before closing the loading gate. He looked around the bush, leading with his pistol, expecting a

Sioux charge any moment. But none came. "Where the hell *are* they?" he whispered to Killdeer.

The Crow put his finger to his lips and scooted deeper under the bush, looking around. He moved back and tapped Hack's shoulder while he pointed to thick choke-cherry bushes. A single eagle feather — five, perhaps six feet off the ground — seemed to float through the forest just above the foliage until . . . a Sioux passed between two bushes, an eagle feather tied to his braids, and was gone.

"Bastard's flanking us," Hack said to Killdeer, who nodded and worked his way out from under the bush, preparing to attack the Sioux when the warrior made his move.

Hack pulled his hat farther down on his head to shield his face from the rain, watching for the Indian to spring from the trees or launch another arrow. He held his pistol in front of him, waiting. They were lucky Killdeer spotted the Sioux working his way around to attack their flank, and Hack thought it more than luck — more like the Sioux got careless.

Or *wanted* to be seen!

"Shit!" Hack said, "he's a decoy . . ." He heard footsteps behind them, and he and

Killdeer turned as one to the sound, pistols ready, looking up at Blue Boy towering over them. He held his Navy Colt to Hack's head, and a sinister smile crossed his face. "You I can kill right this moment." He turned his gun on Killdeer. "Him . . . I will take my time with. Perhaps" — he kicked Killdeer in the thigh, and the old man groaned in pain — "I will skin off a piece of flesh for every Lakota he has killed."

He whistled, and the Indian shielded by the chokecherry bushes emerged, a bow slung over his shoulder as he walked toward them. "Drop those guns," he ordered Hack and, to Killdeer, "drop that scalping knife of yours, too."

The Crow tossed his pistol aside and was beginning to draw his knife when Blue Boy cocked his pistol and aimed it at his head. "Do not even think about it. Toss the knife."

Killdeer seemed to be weighing his odds before throwing the knife away. It landed at the foot of the other Lakota, and he picked it up. "Cloud," Blue Boy said to his warrior with the bandage around his arm — the one Hack had shot at the campsite — "grab their pistols."

"Now what?" Hack asked.

"Now I kill you and take the horse."

Hack sat back, looking up and into the

barrel of the pistol. If he lunged at it, maybe he could surprise Blue Boy . . . "You're going to waste your time on us when Tucker Ashley is down that mountain? I can find him for you."

Blue Boy waved the air with his gun. "Tucker I can kill anytime."

"But there's more white men for you —"

"*Wasicu* I can find in these hills. But *Kangi Wicasa*" — he kicked Killdeer again — "I have been looking many years for Crow Man. I will waste my time on, as you put it."

"And after that? You *will* want Tucker Ashley's scalp, I'd wager."

"I'll get it —"

"You have no idea where he is!" Hack shouted. "You could traipse these hills until the next snowfall and never find him. Especially now with the rain washing out his tracks. But I can find him." Hack inched his way closer to the guns lying in the mud twenty feet away guarded by another Indian, favoring the leg that Killdeer had shot back at the campsite. His bow was slung over his shoulder, seeming to pay Hack and Killdeer little attention as he looked around, Hack's pistol in his hand, cocked.

"If I thought you were a religious man," Blue Boy said, "I would tell you to pray."

He cocked his gun and aimed it at Hack's chest. *Too far away to rush him,* Hack thought, wondering if it *was* too late to become a religious man. He recalled somewhere about an eleventh-hour teaching that a man's never too late to speak to the Lord, and he started to pray as . . .

Blue Boy's finger whitened as he applied pressure to the trigger, smiling as he aimed through the narrow notch cut in the hammer that served as a sight . . .

The hammer dropped!

Hack flinched, steeling himself for the round ball to his chest when he realized . . . Blue Boy's gun misfired. As it had back at the campsite.

The Indian quickly cocked the hammer to fire again and pulled the trigger.

Nothing but the *snap* of the trigger falling on a wet percussion cap.

Damn fool, Hack thought, swiping water off his eyes, *should have traded that for a cartridge gun,* and threw himself against Blue Boy's legs. The Indian went down into the mud. Hack lunged for his pistol.

Killdeer screamed as he ran to Cloud and knocked him to the ground. He clawed at the Sioux's skinning knife stuck into the top of his moccasin. Meanwhile the Indian with the arrow-shot leg was stumbling in a circle, trying to get a clear shot without hitting Blue Boy, when Hack swung his leg hard. It hit the warrior on the ankles, and he fell to the ground. Hack dropped Blue Boy's pistol and grabbed his own right before he hit the Indian on the bad leg. He screamed in pain while Hack rolled over onto his back, expecting Blue Boy to be writhing in pain, but instead he was running for the cover of the chokecherry bushes.

Hack snapped off a shot at the fleeing Indian but missed, and Blue Boy disappeared into the cluster of bushes.

Hack turned to Killdeer fighting with Cloud. He thrashed around, trying to grab the skinning knife that the Crow had raised overhead. He missed it, and Killdeer plunged the blade into the Sioux's chest. Cloud coughed violently, throwing Killdeer off him, clutching his chest for the briefest moment until he bled out, and his head dropped lifeless into the mud.

Almost before the Sioux had died, Killdeer ran the skinning knife around Cloud's hair and lifted his scalp. The Crow shook off blood before standing and hanging the scalp off his trousers. He was starting off in the direction Blue Boy had run when Hack stopped him. "Where you going . . . where's that other Sioux?" Hack asked, expecting the man to be writhing in pain. Not disappeared.

Movement out of the corner of Hack's eye, and he spotted Killdeer running towards the trees. "Where are you going?"

"After Blue Boy."

"Blue Boy hell! We need to find Simon and Tucker. We've already lost time with these Sioux, and the rain washed away much of the tracks. Get on back here."

Killdeer turned back to Hack and said, "I know where he is going." He seemed to be weighing bucking Hack and going after Blue Boy when he started for the horse. "He heads for a white man's cabin left empty some time ago."

"We can find and kill Blue Boy later. It'll be easy killing the bastard now that his powder is wet. Now that he has no more warriors with him, except that one hobbling after him."

"As you say," Killdeer said.

Hacksaw looked at Killdeer's buckskin. "Think that mustang's gonna' carry us both?"

Killdeer shook his head and grabbed the reins tied to a tree. "No. She could barely carry you. You ride. I walk. In that way we reach the cabin faster. Then we find Simon

Cady and Tucker Ashley when you are done
with them. At the cabin."

Chapter 32

Jack ran back to the shack and burst through the dilapidated door. "Get your boots on. I spotted Grass not two hundred yards along that ridge we skirted."

"How could they have gotten onto us?" Erin hurriedly slipped on Mick's oversized boots and tied the laces tight. "It's raining. Our tracks ought to have been washed away—"

"Remember me telling you how they always seem to work out sign eventually?" He tossed water from a bowl they'd set out to catch rain water into the fire, plunging the cabin into darkness. *No sense letting the Indians age the fire any easier.* "Just because they can't find our footprints, don't mean there's not other things we disturbed walking through the woods — a broken branch. Rock displaced. Piece of cloth on a bush that we didn't notice."

Erin slung the quiver of arrows over her

shoulder, a wry smile crossing her face. "Grass was the one who killed Pa. If he's close . . ." She trailed off.

Jack shoved the scalping knife he'd lifted from Stumpy's dead body down the top of his boot. "If he's close," Jack said, "the others will be close as well. You might get off that one arrow. But you wouldn't get off another one before our scalps would be hanging from their lodges."

Jack motioned for Erin to follow him, bent over, not making the same mistake he made before when Stumpy had laid back and caught them unawares. She held an arrow in her hand, ready to defend them, as she stumbled in the darkness and . . . tripped on a tree root bulging from the ground. Falling, the razor-sharp arrow gouging a furrow in her leg.

Jack turned and dropped beside her, ignoring her protests when he took hold of her leg to examine the wound. "Settle down," he whispered. "That's a nasty cut you got. We need to find some water to clean it —"

Erin slapped his hand aside. "Leave me be. It ain't much more than a deep scrape. I'll be fine."

She stood and tested her balance. "Like I said, it's fine." She walked behind Jack for twenty yards when she stopped and patted the blood off her leg with her dress.

"Your leg is giving you fits."

Erin waved it off. "Just tell me if Grass is the only one you seen," she whispered.

"He is," Jack answered, looking slowly all around for any movement, any reflection in the half moon however small to tell him where the hunters were. *But where were the other Lakota?* Close, he was certain, waiting for Jack or Erin to snap a branch underfoot or frighten off sleeping deer or quail or rabbit. Anything that would alert them to where their quarry was. And just because Erin killed Stumpy, that didn't mean she'd be able to sling her arrows fast enough if Iron Hide and his Indians attacked.

Jack motioned for Erin to head out just as the first faint rays of the sun peeked through the trees. In another hour it would be sunup. In another hour the Lakota would have prime hunting light. In another hour, they would be in even more danger.

Erin and Jack huddled together under layers of overhanging pine branches. The rain had stopped about the time the sun rose, flooding the forest with bright light that — any other time — would look beautiful bouncing off the green pine and the aspen that had started turning golden.

"I tell you," Erin insisted, "I can take out that Swan and Pale Moon before they even know where the arrows came from."

"And at least one of them would scream loud enough to alert Iron Hide and Grass."

"Then what *do* we do? If we do nothing, they'll be on us, and what chance will we have?"

Jack had wondered that, too, since it became obvious they were being herded like cattle to the slaughterhouse. The Indians knew Erin and Jack were *somewhere* in this valley, he was sure. The Indians had split — Iron Hide and Grass one direction, Swan and Pale Moon another. They walked a loose perimeter where Jack and Erin hid, working closer, herding them for . . . "Erin, do you trust me?"

She looked up from behind the buffalo-berry bush they squatted behind, a painful grimace crossing her face as she dabbed at the blood crusted on her leg. "Why wouldn't I?"

"I mean do you trust me to do the right thing when the time comes?"

Erin faced Jack and said, "Whatever are you talking about?"

He pointed toward a granite wall a hundred yards away with a twenty-foot rock face they could never scale. "*That's* where they're herding us."

"How we ever gonna' climb . . ." The blood drained from her face, and she began to tremble. "We can't slip out through the hills without them spotting us, and we won't be able to climb up that rock. We're not gonna' be able to get away from them, are we?"

" 'Fraid not," Jack answered. He draped his arm around her trembling shoulders and drew her near. "Looks like we're going to be trapped right at the face of that big ol' rock. But" — he pulled her away — "with that bow of yours and this scalping knife we can make it more difficult for them. And I promise" — he tapped the handle of the knife — "the last thing I do in this life is make sure they don't get a chance to . . . take you."

"Thought you said the Lakota ain't about violating women?"

"Not in that way," Jack said, catching a glimpse of a braid walking between two trees fifty yards up the hill. "But Iron Hide wants you. That might be worse than death. And when the time comes" — he tapped the knife again — "I'll make sure he *doesn't* take you."

■ ■ ■ ■

Jack ran his hand over the cold, damp moss-splotched stone wall behind them. They had tried a last futile time to skirt around the Indians, only to have Iron Hide and Grass come within killing range of where they had hidden. If they'd known Jack and Erin were that close, lying in a shallow ravine listening to them walking by, they would have found them. The Indians were herding them to that granite wall twenty feet tall that might as well have been twenty miles high. And there was nothing he nor Erin could do about it.

"I'm scared, Jack." Erin trembled as much from the fever that was setting in from her leg wound as from fear. She remained defiant as she held the bow tight in her hand, the nocked arrow ready to send into the heart of whichever Lakota showed his face. She knelt in front of the remainder of the arrows that she'd stuck into the mud in front of her for a faster reload. Frightened though she may be, she'd do her best to kill as many Indians as she could before they overran them.

"Tell you the truth, I'm almighty scared my ownself," he said.

She scooted close to him and took his arm, draping it around her shoulders. She looked up at Jack and drew his face close. She kissed him lightly, then kissed him again, deeper this time. "If I'm fixin' to die," she said, "I figured I'd better at least get kissed once before I go."

"You never been kissed?"

Erin shrugged. "Not like I had any time for sparkin', working the ranch with Pa . . ." A branch broke somewhere in the trees surrounding them. She jerked back and clutched her bow. "Came from the east."

Jack fingered the hilt of the knife, not that it would be any good for saving their lives when the Indians attacked. He held it for the other job — killing Erin before the Indians overtook them — that he didn't want to think about. "I heard another sound . . . from the west. Won't be long before they break through that clearing —"

"And then we're dead."

"Not before you take out a couple. At the first sign of an Indian, you wait a moment. Another will come through the trees soon after, and you'll have two targets. Narrows it down to where we might have a chance —"

"Jack . . ." She drew his face close a last time. "I know what you're doing, but at this point I'm resigned." She kissed him again. "But at least I can take out one of them bastards."

Jack had worked out a scenario this past hour as he waited for the Indians to find them. At the first sign of one, he'd rush them. Catch them off guard. Who the hell ever rushed an armed man with only a knife? The Indians would be stunned for a moment, just long enough for Jack to wrest a gun from one of them and hope it didn't misfire from the rain . . . who the hell was he fooling? When Iron Hide and his warriors busted through the trees not twenty yards away, they'd see him and Erin butted against the rock wall. Clear targets for their pistols *and* their arrows. There would be no time to rush them with Stumpy's scalping knife. He looked over at Erin trembling but determined to shoot as many arrows into as many Lakota as she could before . . . he shuddered himself thinking about what he'd have to do — plunge the knife into her heart *quick.* Sudden. And hope her final seconds of life went quick. Sudden.

A rabbit bolted into the clearing in front of them and veered off into the brush as if not wishing to see the impending carnage.

"They're close." Erin nocked into the sinew bowstring. "I'm awfully scared, Jack."

He stood behind her and laid his hand on her shoulder. "Me, too."

"Will you . . . do it fast?" she asked. "Kill me quickly when it looks like they'll get us, 'cause I sure don't want to live the rest of my life as Iron Hide's woman?"

Jack drew in a deep breath and had begun speaking when a *slapping* noise against the side of the rock caused him to look over his shoulder. The end of a lasso dangled from up above, the wind causing it to smack against the wall.

Jack shielded his eyes and craned his neck up. Tucker lay on his belly looking over the lip of the rock. He motioned to the rope and said, "Unless you want your scalp adorning their lodges tonight, you best tie that rope around you. And grab onto your lady friend."

Erin turned halfway to look up while her eyes darted to the trees where the Indians would most likely come. "Who's talking to you?"

"A crazy man." Jack sheathed the knife and grabbed the rope. "Stay close," he told Erin while he tied it around his waist, looking over his shoulder for the Sioux.

"We're both barely able to stand," he told Tucker, "weak so bad you'll have to help us on up there."

"Soreback'll haul you two up. Soon's you get a grab onto your woman; Simon Cady will lead the mule away."

"Simon! What's that killer doing here?"

"Right now," Tucker said, "I'd say he's helping me save your scrawny butt. Now hurry before those Lakota come onto you."

CHAPTER 33

Hack reined his horse beside Killdeer, still not used to the randy mare. After Hack and Killdeer had come onto Jimmy Milk's horse, the reins stuck in the low branch of a tree, Hack figured the critter would welcome being freed. But the horse, the whites of his eyes wide, glaring at Hack as he mounted him, had proven almost too frightened to ride the trail.

Killdeer sat looking over the forest. Since they had lost Tucker's and Simon's tracks at the cabin, Killdeer figured the quickest way to find Tucker and Simon was to find Jack Worman. "What you see?"

Killdeer remained silent, studying the ground. He slid off his pony and handed Hack the reins before he bent and ran his hand gently over tracks leading up to the sheer rock wall. "I am not sure."

Hack threw up his hands. "Like you

weren't sure why we missed them at the cabin."

Killdeer ignored him and walked slowly around the clearing, stopping at the granite wall and running his hand over scuffed rock. He picked up a piece of moss that had been abraded off the face and brought it to his nose. After a long moment, he tossed the moss aside and smiled wide. He reached high and plucked a single thread of white fabric from a crevice.

"What the hell you grinning at?" Hack asked

Killdeer showed Hack the thread. "Jack and his woman escaped up *there.* To get away from the *Snakes.*"

"Up that wall? I don't think so. Why climb up there rather than run into the trees and hide from the Sioux?"

Again, Killdeer grinned and shook his head. "I think the *Snakes* think the same. Here." He pointed to faint moccasin tracks. "Sioux broke through the clearing. Expecting those two to be easy prey, I think. They were not."

Hack rode across the clearing and looked at the sheer wall, searching for natural handholds, places to anchor your feet as you ascended, but there were none. He took off his hat and stood in the stirrups looking up.

"How could they get up there?"

The old man walked along the rock until he found what he looked for: a single frayed piece of hemp rope wedged into a crack in the stone five feet off the ground. "Someone up there threw them a rope." He waved his hand around the empty clearing. "It saved their lives."

Hack stepped from the saddle and bent over, looking at the ground where Killdeer indicated. Moccasin prints — as many as three or four by the difference in the size of the tracks — had come into the clearing. "Tucker," Hack breathed. "Tucker Ashley's the one who saved Jack and his woman."

Killdeer arched his back and stretched before holding out his hand for tobacco. "You make coffee. I am going to find out where the Sioux went."

"I ran out of tobacco."

Killer smiled. "I know that you did not. You want to find them?"

Hack grunted a protest and handed Killdeer his plug of tobacco. "Vulture," Hack muttered under his breath.

Hack picked his teeth with the tip of his knife after he finished the dried deer meat that he'd washed down with weak, tepid coffee. He had reached over to refill his cup when Killdeer appeared at the edge of the clearing. Hack jumped — as he often did when the Indian sneaked back into camp. Killdeer said nothing as he walked to the fire and bent to the coffee pot. "We soon catch the Sioux," he said as he poured a cup.

"How do you figure that?"

Killdeer spat tobacco juice that landed in the fire with a *sizzle.* "The *Snakes* rode around the rock wall. Losing ground to Tucker and Jack Worman." He spit out the coffee before tossing the grounds into the fire. He stood and kicked dirt over the coals.

"What the hell you doing? That fire felt mighty good —"

"Do you wish to catch your Tucker Ashley or do you wish to be comfortable for the night?"

"I got a feeling we'll be riding out." Hack stood and walked to the dun, shaking the dirt out of the blanket before draping it over the horse's back. "Let's hear it."

"We are close to the Sioux," the Crow said, untying the reins of his horse. "And they follow Tucker. We will catch the *Snakes* . . . soon. But . . . they left a man behind."

"Like a rear guard? Damn!"

"Not a rear guard. I think this man was left to slow us down."

"So, they know we're right behind them?"

"This is what I believe."

Hack laid his hat over the mare's eyes. He didn't need the horse to whinny or snort and alert the Sioux. "Easy, girl," Hack softly soothed as Killdeer returned with news of the Sioux.

"One *Snake*," he said softly, "sits by a fire. Bow in hand. Arrows stuck into the ground in front of him."

"How far?"

Killdeer looked toward the trees as if he could see the Sioux. "Fifty yards. Maybe."

Hack lowered his voice. "Was this man left to ambush us, or lure us into the open?"

"I do not think so," Killdeer said. "I think he waits to slow us down."

"Just one man?"

The Crow nodded.

"Surely the Indians — and this one Sioux — must know we'll kill him if he is alone."

Killdeer looked to the stars, studying them as if his answer was among them. "He is injured. Blood spots the ground in front of this man. This man may be close to meeting his *Wakan Tanka*. His Creator. This man is brave."

"Don't go soft on me now," Hack said.

The Crow shrugged. "I said he was brave.

One to be . . . respected even in death. I did not say he does not deserve to die. I will make that happen soon." He fingered the shaft of his knife. "I can approach this man from his blind side. Through the trees —"

"I don't want him dead."

Killdeer tapped the bone handle of his knife. "No Sioux deserves to live."

Hack tugged tight on the saddle's front cinch that had loosened up this past mile riding through the hills. "I didn't say you couldn't kill him. I just need to talk to him before you do."

Killdeer smiled. "I will signal you when I have taken this man's bow and knife from him."

Hack watched the Crow disappear into the trees. No movement. No sound. Nothing to indicate that he was ever there, and Hack thanked God that the old man was not *his* enemy.

Hack sat on a stump and massaged his legs. He wasn't as young as he used to be, certainly not as young as when he robbed and killed his first man — a mercantile owner down Denver way foolish enough to try stopping him and two other toughs with Hack. They had ridden for days, then, the posse after them. And, like other posses that chased after Hack over the years, they had given up in exhaustion. *Smart lawmen. I'll kill any man that comes after me and my gang.*

His gang. What a joke now with just him and the Crow left.

After Tucker was worm food, Hack would find others wishing a better life on the backs of those with money to be taken. He chuckled — it will be little problem finding men to follow him. With his reputation, Hack will soon gather another *gang.*

He stood from the stump and walked a tight circle, working out the kinks in his legs when he kicked a rock and silently cursed his bad luck. And cursed Simon. Any other posse would have turned back. Any other posse would have realized who they chased after and given up. But those weren't led by Simon Cady. Not to worry. When they caught up with Tucker — and after Hack killed him — Simon would be an added bonus for this week of busting up his *gang.*

A *whistle* followed by another that sounding eerily like the call of a lake loon filtered through the trees. *Killdeer.*

Hack left his horse tied to the tree and walked cautiously towards the sound of the whistle. He ducked under an overhanging pine bough and skirted a large granite rock before walking into the clearing. Killdeer stood holding a bow, a quiver slung over his shoulder as he lowered his voice. "I do not know if this *Snake* speaks your language. He will not speak to me except his name."

Hack walked around to face the man, a pained look in his bloodshot eyes. He sat cross-legged on the ground. Blood stained what looked like a strip of a woman's dress. Hack squatted in front of the young warrior and said, *"Kola,"* addressing the man as a friend and asking him in Lakota, "where are your other warriors?"

"Khanyela," the man answered.

Hack smiled. "You claim the others are close by but" — he nodded to Killdeer — "he says they are gone. That they have left you here."

The Sioux glared at Killdeer but said nothing.

Killdeer stepped close to the Sioux and hit him on the head. He fell over but pushed himself erect, defiant as he swore at Killdeer in Lakota. "This man is Swan. I am certain Iron Hide left him here to . . . how you say it, buy the others time."

Hack bent closer to Swan and said in Lakota, "Iron Hide left you here to die. Abandoned you." Hack shook his head. "Something *I* would never do. If you tell me how many are left with Iron Hide and how close they are to finding Tucker Ashley and Jack Worman, I will let you live," he lied.

Swan spat at Hack, spit *splattering* against his cheek before turning as best he could to look off into the trees. He began his death chant, the *trilling* rising and falling, seeming to unnervingly bounce off the granite rock and tall pine trees of the sacred *Paha Sapa.*

Hack wiped the spit from his cheek before standing and drawing his Colt. Swan looked up at Hack — pistol pointed at the young man's head — and there was no fear in his fierce eyes. Nothing to show that he knew his life would end in mere moments . . .

Hack's shot sounded loud in the confines of the woods. Swan fell backwards onto the ground, adding his blood to that already soaking the dirt.

Even before Hack replaced the spent cartridge with a fresh one, Killdeer had lifted the Sioux's scalp. He stood and shook blood off the hair before looping it over his trousers. "The Sioux . . . they are worried, I think, that they are followed."

"So you'll be able to pick up their sign?"

Killdeer smiled. "Have I ever failed?"

CHAPTER 34

"You both best rest for a minute," Tucker said.

"Don't fret about me," Jack said. "It's Erin I'm worried about. She caught a fever from that wound in her leg."

Tucker took off his coat and rolled it up before placing it under Erin's head. Jack had helped her stay on Soreback the last half mile while he stumbled and staggered, his own strength waning before he had to set her down atop clumps of soft buffalo grass. Her head lolled from side to side, incoherent words escaping her chapped and split lips as she tried focusing on Jack.

"Here," Simon said. He handed Jack a water-soaked bandana. "Wash some of that blood off her leg before you drape this over her forehead. It'll help bring the fever down."

Jack sat beside Erin and followed Simon's instructions.

Simon motioned Tucker aside and lowered his voice. "As much as I'd like to hold up here until the girl pulls through, we need to move. Those Indians are out there in the hills close. Hunting us."

"Don't you think I've agonized over that?" Tucker looked around the trees as if expecting Indians to burst through. "Besides Blue Boy's band, Hacksaw and Kills the Deer's gotta' be close, too. And Iron Hide's there somewhere. But I'm afraid if we move Erin, she'll slip even further into her fever."

"Give me a mile," Simon said, filling his pipe with tobacco and raking a lucifer across a rock to light it. "A mile as the hawk flies. I know a place that's shielded on three sides by rock, and the fourth offers a good view of those Indians *when* they find us." He glanced over at Jack pouring more water onto the bandana before draping it over Erin's forehead again.

"A mile as the hawk flies," Tucker said, "can be miles on foot in the Black Hills."

"Not if you know a cut-through leading between rocks. It's an Indian trail some Cheyenne showed me many years ago. We can put the girl back on your mule and be there before the Indians catch us."

Tucker nodded. Once again, Simon was right.

Tucker walked to where Jack tended to Erin. "We have to move from here."

"Can we go slow? Erin's in a bad way."

"She'll be in a worse way if those Lakota find us." He motioned to Simon untying Soreback's reins. "He knows a place that's defensible —"

"Now you're trusting the word of *him*? Last I knew, he killed most people he ever met."

"Can't argue with you on that. But right now, he's the *only* one who knows where we can fight off these Indians."

That morning, a light, cool drizzle fell on them as they made their way steadily higher. Jack had insisted on walking beside the mule, holding Erin in the saddle as she slumped over, her face wet from the rain and the fever, spittle drooling from her mouth as she talked to someone only she saw. Now and again, Erin's bow slapped the side of the saddle with more noise than Tucker liked. But Jack had insisted on taking it, along with the two arrows still in her quiver, all she had left when Tucker and Simon hauled them up the rock wall moments before Iron Hide burst through the trees into the clearing.

Simon walked in front, his great bulk

under his tattered shirt moving like the prairie grass in a light breeze, pushing aside tree branches so they wouldn't hit Erin in the face as she rode slumped over Soreback. Tucker brought up the rear and was checking their back trail when Simon said, "We can rest under that overhang." He led the mule towards a divot in the side of a rock wall barely big enough to shield them from the rain, the mule's ears scraping the stone wall.

As Tucker helped Jack lift Erin from the saddle and under the protection of the shallow cave, turkey vultures circling overhead caught his eye. He stood watching them as Simon came up beside him. "I saw them, too. Something's been killed not long ago."

"Could be a man."

Simon shrugged. "Could be a deer or other game those Lakota killed and butchered. Could be what's left after a cougar or bear found whatever's dead. Vultures could be circling the gut pile."

"Can't take a chance with the Indians. I'll know soon enough," Tucker said and went to his saddlebags. He had grabbed his ship's glass when Simon asked, "Where you going?"

"To find out just how close they are."

"As good a woodsman as you are, I'd better have a look-see."

"With your shoulder and back still mending, you'd best stay here."

"Your own arm ain't doing so good where that Indian cut you."

"Better than yours. Besides" — Tucker jerked his thumb in Jack's direction — "he'll need help with the girl."

Before Simon could argue, Tucker walked into the trees. He picked his way between thick juniper and chokecherry bushes, sharp spines gouging his arms. He continued looking above him, guessing where the dead deer — or man — might be. He had walked a couple hundred yards into the trees and squatted beside a large bur oak, looking over the terrain below when . . .

. . . movement on the ridge line that had shielded them from any pursuers not an hour ago, and he brought the telescope to his eyes. Iron Hide walked behind an Indian nearly as big as he — the one Jack said carried a grudge because Jack had killed his friend the day of the ranch ambush — Grass. Behind them stumbled another warrior little older than a boy, looking nervously around the woods. Tucker watched as they stopped under a low hanging tree at the edge of a clearing of lush grass.

Tucker snapped the glass closed and

walked as quickly as his worn-out legs would carry him. When he arrived back at the overhanging rock, Jack still tended to Erin. Simon kept watch with his rifle straddling his knees, the big gun so adept at long range but near useless at close distances with his Sharps. "We'll never make it to your spot," Tucker said. "The Indians could be here within the hour. We got to get moving now." He took a twig lying on the floor of the overhang and drew a hasty map in the dirt of what he'd seen through the ship's glass. He drew the logical place for the Indians to camp for the night and emphasized how close they were. "With Erin slowing us down, they'll come on to us come morning *if* I don't slow them down."

"What do you mean *if* you slow them down?" Jack asked, keeping Erin's face out of the dirt as he cradled her head.

"Disrupt them if I can. If I put the sneak on them tonight . . . puncture their water bladders, that'll slow them. Even with the rain, they'll need fresh water. And, they're bound to have a cache of dried meat in their camp."

"Do you know what you're even saying?" Jack asked. "You're going to *injun* up on those Indians. Figuring they won't hear you."

325

Tucker hitched up his holster from falling down his trousers. These last weeks, he'd lost weight, as his baggy pants showed. "Seems like we got no choice. We won't stop them, but if they figure we can sneak into their camp, they'll be even more cautious. Make them wary of every step they take."

Jack gently laid Erin's head on the rolled-up coat before duckwalking under the rock to where Tucker squatted. "Oh, we got us a choice, all right — you stay here and get Erin ready to ride while *I* sneak into their camp."

"You?"

"Yes. Me. I don't know if you realize it, but you're a little big to be putting the sneak on *anybody.* I've heard you trying to be quiet before, and you ain't. But I can be. I'll go."

"He makes sense," Simon said. "Even if Jack is exhausted from these last weeks, he can be a whole lot quieter than you *ever* thought of being."

Tucker didn't want to admit it, but Jack's logic was flawless. He had known his little, wiry friend for years — scouting for the army, chasing renegade Indians and owl-hoots together. And it had always been Jack sneaking up on the enemies when the time came. "All right," Tucker said. He took off his holster and handed it to Jack. "I only have those six rounds left, so let's hope you won't run into any more Indians than that."

"I hope I don't run into *any* that spots me." Jack hefted the Remington. "But if I do, I might just be able to take out all of them." He looked down at Erin fighting the fever. "Lord knows they deserve it."

"Jack," Simon said, "you might be able to get one. You might even be able to kill two if you're lucky. But it's that third one that you *didn't* see who will be your downfall."

Jack tucked the pistol into his trouser front and looked around Tucker. "Take care of Erin."

"You just worry about the Lakota," Tucker said. "And don't use my gun unless you have to. I suspect Hacksaw and that Crow are close enough that they'd hear any gunfire."

"You think he's still after you?" Jack asked.

"He's still after me," Tucker said, scanning the woods. "How close he is I can't even guess."

CHAPTER 35

Jack squatted beside thick skunkbrush bushes, their orange leaves turning with the change in the weather coming, their sticky red berries a sour taste, their leaves crushed underfoot an unpleasant odor. Jack had lived in the lodge of a Shoshone for a year of his youth, and women of the tribe would send him out to pick the sour tasting berries to be boiled as medicine and given for colds during the winter months. But it wasn't any illness that made Jack tremble, but the sight of Iron Hide and Grass and Pale Moon wrapped in their trade blankets sleeping around the dying fire across the clearing.

Jack rested his hand on Tucker's gun. He could get one or two, like Simon said — the Indians were that close. But which one? He answered his own question: he would kill Iron Hide for his humiliation of Erin cutting off her hair, and Grass because he had savagely killed her father right in front of her. Pale Moon, Jack was certain, would hesitate enough that Jack could kill him, too, if he chose. Jack brought his hand away from the gun butt, for Simon was right, too, when he said gunfire could alert Hacksaw Reed and that murdering Crow tracking for him. They would be drawn to the gunfire like flies to a gut wagon.

Jack squatted closer to the ground and cocked an ear as he studied the Indians five yards away. Their heads were tucked inside their blankets, and Jack fought the temptation to kill them. It would be that easy, with Iron Hide nearly within touching distance. Probably Grass on the other side of the fire by Pale Moon.

Jack took quiet breaths as he listened intently. Sleeping men breathe differently, most often with some labor, and he had learned to recognize when an enemy feigned sleep. After many moments, he was satisfied the Indians' snores were genuine, and he sat on the ground. He slipped off his boots and laid his hat on top of them before resting the pistol and holster beside them. When he crept into the camp, he wanted nothing jangling or making noise that could alert the Indians.

He took hold of Stumpy's skinning knife

and cautiously stepped from the safety of the bushes. *This is for Erin.* He approached the camp. With each measured step, he tested the ground, sidestepping leaves and branches and pine needles that would snap in the night air as loud as any gunshot right this moment. He avoided loose rocks that — when overturned — would tell the Indians when they awoke in the morning when Jack had raided their camp.

He avoided looking at the fire that would destroy his night vision and instead eyed the camp. Four water bladders hung from a makeshift stand of branches, and he silently poked a hole in three of them as he passed, the water leaking gently and noiselessly out onto the already-damp ground. The fourth one he slung over his shoulder. Erin would need fresh water.

He paused once again, closing his eyes, listening, verifying that the three Indians yet slept before moving back and looking into the trees. The warriors had hung their meat bundle high off the ground against marauding animals, and Jack spotted a small, canvas pouch suspended from a branch by a thin rope. He stood and moved toward it, each step as careful as the previous one until he was close enough to cut the line. He clutched the pouch, grateful for more meat, and kept an eye on the Indians as he backed out of the camp.

When he reached the skunkbrush bushes, he sat on his haunches, studying the three Lakota. None of them moved. None were aware that their water supply had been drained and camp meat had been stolen. But they would when they awoke in the morning. Chaos would ensue as each man blamed the others for allowing their meat cache and water to be taken. They would awaken to no water and no food at hand, and the thought caused Jack to smile.

He slipped his boots back on, grabbed the pistol and hat, and carefully made his way back to his own camp with the meat and water bladder slung over his shoulder.

Jack had gone a half mile into the forest, stopping now and again to see that he wasn't followed, feeling proud that he had slipped in and out of a Sioux camp until . . . too late he heard the *snap* of a twig. By the time he'd turned and started to draw Tucker's pistol, Grass stood mere yards away, sighting down a nocked arrow, the bowstring trembling at full draw. "Throw down your gun," Grass said. "And kick it over here."

Jack hesitated, wondering if he could draw

331

and fire before Grass could send his arrow into Jack's heart. He wisely picked the gun out of the holster by a thumb and finger and dropped it onto the ground. He kicked it toward where Grass stood, and he picked it up.

"I would think that Jack Worman — killer of Lakota and scout for the horse soldiers — would know a blanket stuffed with grass from a sleeping man."

Jack said nothing. His eyes darted around the woods. Looking for anything he might use for a weapon when the time came, when the hilt of the scalping knife rubbing his back reminded him that he *did* have a weapon. Even if it was no match for the arrow still aimed at his chest. If he could agitate Grass. Anger him. Distract him . . .

"Little Squirrel," Grass's voice broke, "was my . . . brother. We lived our life together hunting. Fishing. Free Lakota. No reservation." His jaw clenched, the neck muscles straining with the rage inside him. "And you killed him."

Jack's hand inched closer to his back, to the knife as he judged how far it was to Grass. He'd have to dive out of the way of the arrow, drawing his knife . . . *if* he could rile Grass enough that his fury would override his skills with the bow. If Grass was a few inches off with his aim . . . "You forgot that you and Little Squirrel lived your life killing *wasicu*. He was a warrior, and he died as a warrior. I had no choice. He would have killed me." Jack stepped closer, now ten feet from Grass. "And if it were in my power, I would have killed *all* your band that day for what they did to my ranch and cattle. So go ahead, you cowardly bastard — put that arrow right here," he said, pounding his chest.

Grass's lips trembled, his anger seething, his teeth grinding loud enough Jack heard it across this distance between them. Grass relaxed tension on the bowstring until it was slack, and he laid it on the ground before setting the quiver of arrows beside it. He pointed Jack's gun at him for a moment before laying it beside his bow and quiver.

He drew his knife — long and crusted with dried, blackened blood — and began circling Jack, keeping between him and the bow, cutting off any attempt Jack might make to lunge for the arrows with their razor-sharp trade tips. "I have thought long about this moment, Jack Worman," Grass said, the rage replaced by a broad smile of anticipation. "Thought how I will slice pieces of flesh off you and toss it to the buzzards."

"You're going to kill me without a chance. What warrior would do that?"

"Our water bladders were cut with a knife. I think you have one hidden in your back."

Jack drew his knife and matched Grass's movements, working around the clearing. Each time he got close to Tucker's pistol, Grass would move to block him.

Jack sized the man up. His torn shirt revealed a muscled arm as he held his knife low. He stood several inches taller than Jack and forty pounds heavier. The deep scar running down his neck and one on his cheek told Jack this wasn't the first knife fight the man had been in.

And the smile never left the Indian's face.

Jack's strength had waned these last weeks, his legs moving like two stunted sticks, feeling the weight of the scalping knife in his hand. Jack had been in his own knife fights, and he'd be a match for anyone. Even Grass. *If* Jack still had his strength and power.

He would have to make this quick. If possible. He couldn't afford a protracted fight weak as he was; he would be good for a minute of intense battle. Maybe less.

He feinted to his right. When Grass moved to confront him, Jack stepped into the Indian, thrusting with the knife. But Grass deftly sidestepped the blade, his own knife flicking out in a wicked arc. Stepping into Jack. Slicing across his shirt. Cutting Jack's forearm.

Sticky blood dripped down onto Jack's hand. He wiped it off as Grass hopped out of range.

Grass bent low and — when he tossed his knife to his other hand — Jack instinctively focused on the blade. Grass lunged. He raked his blade across Jack's stomach. Cut through his shirt. Jack felt the cut oozing blood as Grass leapt back out of Jack's reach.

Jack chanced a quick look down and saw he had been a fraction of an inch from having his guts spill onto the ground.

"Jack Worman bleeds like me," Grass said, laughing. "And he does not fight well."

"You get beaten and dragged by a bunch of savages for more'n a week with barely any food and —"

Grass rushed in, flicking his blade out once again, slicing a piece of flesh off Jack's cheek a moment before he hit Jack hard on the nose where it had already been broken. Jack fell backwards, the knife sailing through the air and hitting a tree five feet away.

Grass walked calmly to Jack and straddled him, his knife poised overhead. "Now,"

Grass said, "I will avenge the death of Little Squirrel."

"I don't think so." Tucker walked from the trees into the clearing so quietly neither Jack nor Grass had heard him during the intensity of their fight.

"Damn, Tucker, where'd you come from?"

"Figured you were overdue in camp —"

"So, this is the great Tucker Ashley," Grass said, shifting his knife from one hand to the other while he stepped away from Jack to face Tucker.

Tucker's eyes darted to the pistol lying where Jack had dropped it. Grass saw the movement, too, and stepped to block him as Tucker drew his Bowie. "I'm not as worn out as Jack . . ." He lunged at Grass, slicing the blade across his stomach.

Grass stumbled back, regaining his footing but not before Tucker's knife carved a deep, red line across the Indian's stomach.

Tucker rushed in and was cocking his knife overhead when Grass kicked him viciously in the belly. Tucker staggered.

Grass flicked out his blade once. Twice. Each time cutting Tucker's arm holding the knife. He dropped the Bowie. Caught it as . . .

Grass darted in, lashing out, cutting a corner off Tucker's ear before stepping back and forcing a smile. "This is the mighty Tucker Ashley my people fear?" He laughed. "He is nothing more than —"

Tucker lunged.

Grass backhanded his knife, cutting only air.

Too late. Tucker had closed the distance and plunged his blade into the Indian's chest. Tucker set his legs and ripped the blade upwards before jerking it out and stepping back.

Grass dropped his knife as he sagged to his knees. Blood seeped through his hands covering the wound, trying to keep his guts inside as he looked up at Tucker with disbelief in his dying eyes.

Tucker eased Grass onto the ground a heartbeat before the life left his eyes.

"He should have done more fighting than talking," Jack said.

Tucker wiped his blade off on Grass's shirt before turning to Jack and helping him stand. He looked closely at Jack's knife wounds.

"I'd worry about mine more if'n I was you," Jack said. "He cut you in a bunch of places."

For the first time, Tucker assessed his own injuries. The cuts on his forearm hurt like hell, as did the piece of flesh dangling from his face. "My ear'll heal, but I won't be as pretty as I was before."

"Tuck," Jack said, "you weren't pretty to start with. Besides, that gut wound is worse than all the other ones."

Tucker pulled his shirt up. Grass had cut him deeply enough that the blood flowed freely, and he thanked God the warrior's blade hadn't gone a hair's breadth deeper. "Fetch that water bladder. We need to wash our wounds." He bent to his pistol and stuffed it into his waistband. "And grab Grass's bow and quiver. Neither of us are too champion using one, but we'll need all the weapons we can get if those Indians catch us."

CHAPTER 36

Simon sat on a rock beside Erin. Her fever had broken during the night, and she struggled to sit up. He put his hand on her back and helped her up before propping the saddlebags behind her. "This is the last of our good water until we find a creek," he said as he handed her the bladder.

She tipped it up and took long, deep drinks. Water ran down her cheek, her chin as she sucked in great gulps of air before handing it back to Simon. Looking around the campsite, she asked, "Where's Jack?"

"Went to slow down the Indians."

"Then where's Tucker?"

Simon stood and looked down the hillside, seeing nothing. In minutes the sun would rise, and perhaps the ship's glass would help . . . "Jack was overdue, and Tucker went to the Indian camp to find him."

Erin gathered her legs beneath her to stand, and Simon put his arm around her waist and helped her up. She looked to where Simon said Jack and Tucker had gone. "Have you looked with that telescope?"

Simon shook his head. "No use. Sun's not quite up yet, and my eyes ain't what they once were . . ."

"Can you at least try it?"

Simon paused. He wasn't used to women bossing him around. But Erin standing on shaky legs, so fragile, with the only thing in her life mattering right now being Jack Worman, Simon felt a twinge of humanity for the briefest moment. He bent to the saddlebags and grabbed the ship's glass. Snapping the telescope out, he brought it to his eye. Nothing. Perhaps with more light . . . "There's no movement."

"Can I look through it?"

Simon handed her the glass, and she panned it down the valley. He had turned to the pot of coffee he'd nursed through the night when she cried out, "There!"

Simon turned around. "What do you see?"

She brought the telescope from her eyes and handed it to Simon. "Jack and Tucker. Running through the trees. But I don't think they'll outrun those Indians."

Simon looked through the glass once more, his eyes straining, concentrating on the direction that Erin pointed. *Hell to get old,* he thought when he spotted movement in the woods down in the valley. Jack broke through the trees first, Tucker only steps behind him, into a clearing before disappearing into other pines on the other side of the small meadow. A long minute later, two Sioux broke through the trees into the same clearing, studying the ground. *A reunion, then,* Simon thought. His brother-in-law. *Iron Hide.* And another Lakota looking young enough to be his son.

Erin snatched the telescope back and looked down into the woods. "Those Indians will be in arrow range of Jack and Tucker in moments," she said as two shots echoed off the trees, the rocks. He looked once again. Tucker had fired two shots at the Indians gaining on him and Jack. Erin was right — the Sioux would be in arrow range of their prey in moments.

He walked to where he'd stashed his rifle under a tree out of the drizzle last night. He slipped the Sharps out of the scabbard and fished cartridges out of his waist pouch.

"Hurry!" Erin pleaded.

Simon took the sight out of his bag and screwed it to the tang before grabbing two long, thin branches from the firewood pile to use as shooting sticks, crossing them into a *V* to rest his rifle on.

"They're almost on them!"

Simon loaded one of the big cases into the breech and set it on half cock. He held the branches and laid the rifle's forearm in the crook they formed and sighted through the tiny aperture. He picked up the front sight. The woods were too thick to actually hit either Indian; the trees would deflect the bullets. But the sound of the big lead slugs hitting the trees or whizzing by would cause any sane man to pause.

The shot — when it came — surprised him, as it should, and he opened the breech and shucked the spent case.

"You were over their heads by a foot," Erin called out, and Simon loaded another cartridge. Then, "They're not twenty yards in front of those Indians. Four hundred yards away from here if it's an inch."

Simon was watching for movement when . . .

Tucker — holding Jack by the waist — stumbled into a clearing, staggering towards the rocky hill that would take them back to camp.

Except Iron Hide had other ideas as he stepped into that clearing and took aim with his pistol.

Simon touched off a round. The slug hit

342

the tree beside where the Indian stood. Bark flew into his face, his own bullet going awry and hitting the ground beside Tucker just as they dropped back into the trees. "Can you saddle the mule?" Simon asked over his shoulder as he fished another shell from his pouch.

Erin laid the ship's glass down and stooped to grab the saddle blanket. "It might take me a mite longer but, by Gawd, I'll do it."

"Good. If I can keep those Indians' heads down long enough for Jack and Tucker to make it here, we just might have a chance to reach that summit I told you all about," he said as he fired again. The bullet tore into another tree, knocking a large branch down, and Simon picked up the telescope. Iron Hide and the boy had dropped back: Jack and Tucker were no longer in immediate danger from the boy's arrows or Iron Hide's pistol.

Simon spotted Jack and Tucker breaking through the trees thirty yards from where they had been, stumbling along like drunks in a three-legged race, Tucker holding Jack up. Headed toward the steep trail that would lead them back to where Erin saddled the mule.

As Simon stuffed his rifle back into the

scabbard, he knew this was no time to relax. For if Iron Hide Lakota didn't attack, others roaming the Black Hills might. Perhaps Blue Boy's Sioux.

Chapter 37

Hack stopped abruptly and turned his head to the sound of the gunfire. "Pistol shots. Close."

Killdeer held up his hand when the next shot — louder, more distinctive than the first — followed within moments. "A white man's gun, I think. Maybe your old friend."

Hack spat tobacco juice, nearly too exhausted to wipe the spittle running down his chin stubble. "It was a Sharps. And I'm thinking you're right — it's gotta' be Simon. Difference is that now I'm the one that's hunting *him.* And he don't even know for sure if I'm still alive."

Killdeer shook his head. "That one . . . he *knows* you still live. That one is cunning."

They waited for more shots, but none came, and they stood for minutes, listening.

Silence.

"The *Snakes* hunt him also. Your Simon Cady shoots at the Indians, I think. They shot once. But they do not shoot back now."

"How do you know that?" Hack asked.

"Did you hear gunfire from one of these?" He held up his Navy Colt, fed by a powder horn, not a cartridge gun. "A gun that makes a distinct sound when fired."

By mid-morning, Killdeer had picked up the Lakotas' trail. "Two *Snakes*," he said. "Hampered by the small one." He stood and brushed the dirt from his fingers. "He has not yet learned the ways of battle. This small one — a boy maybe — not learned to pace himself. He does not keep some . . . strength in reserve. He tires." The Crow pointed to moccasin tracks, faint, yet showing where the walker had started dragging his feet. "He holds Iron Hide back."

Hack stepped from the saddle and unbuttoned his trousers as he stepped to clumps of rabbitbrush bushes. "That's all right by me," he said over his shoulder. "Last thing I want is for them Sioux to catch up with Tucker and kill him before I get a chance. As long as they just lead us to him that's dandy." He turned around and buttoned. "I will kill that bastard myself."

Hack watched as Killdeer fingered the handle of his scalping knife. He'd love nothing better than to jump ahead of the Sioux and ambush them, lift their hair. That'd lose them valuable time though, time Tucker and Simon and now Jack and his woman would use to get as far away as possible. And Hacksaw would let nothing get between the end of his blade and Tucker.

He thought about that this last week chasing after Tucker. He'd proven to be an apt enemy, confounding Killdeer now and again, picking off Hacksaw's men one at a time. More than once, Hack had wondered if Tucker was *too much* of an adversary. But chasing the man — afoot until he'd met up with Simon Cady — he would be exhausted, beat after trekking up and down these Black Hills. Hacksaw grinned. That was all right, too. It would just make killing him easier. Even if the man was a half step from the grave, killing him would still feed the need for sweet revenge coursing through Hack's veins.

They'd decided to give their horses a rest, and Killdeer led his horse up a fifty-foot-high hill leading to a rock ridge, following the tracks of the young Indian, easy to spot as he shuffled along behind Iron Hide. Just as Hack shuffled along behind Killdeer. "Hold on up there a minute."

The Crow walked back to where Hack bent over sucking in air. "For a young man, you have never kept up."

"Young! I *am* not young anymore."

"Much younger than me," Killdeer chided.

Hack waved the air. "Let's just take a few minutes breather. This altitude is kicking my behind."

Killdeer shrugged. "If you feel you really *need* the rest —"

"I do," Hack said and grabbed the water bladder hanging from the saddle horn. He took a long pull and handed it to the Indian, who waved it off.

"We cannot rest for long," Killdeer said. He grabbed a twig and walked to where the tracks faded, and he circled one. "We have crossed this track before." He held his explanation like a trained actor. "Blue Boy."

Hack looked down at the track like he knew what the hell he was looking at. "Can't be Blue Boy. We left him afoot ten miles back in the tree line."

"It is him," Killdeer said. "He follows Iron Hide."

"Crap!" Hack said and stood up, feeling older than his fifty years. "How close?"

"Half a day behind the other *Snakes*. Maybe more."

"Blue Boy must be after Tucker. He sure as hell wouldn't go to all this trouble to meet up with other Sioux. If he finds Tucker, he'll kill him. Cheat me outta' the pleasure." He swung into the saddle. "And that I can't abide."

CHAPTER 38

Soreback's ears perked up, and Tucker instantly stood from his bedroll beside the fire.

"I heard something, too," Simon said, using a rock to help him stand. "To the northeast."

"What is it?" Jack asked. Since coming back from his fight with Grass and nursing his knife wounds, Jack's ordeal of the last few weeks had caught up with him. He was grappling to stand when Erin came back from the bushes wrapped in a horse blanket and helped him off the ground. "I heard something but don't know what it was," she said.

"Don't know myself." Tucker looked around the camp. "Darker'n all get out. All's I know is something spooked the mule, and I'm gonna' have a look-see."

"That wise?" Simon asked. "You didn't exactly come away unscathed from your last encounter." He motioned to the strip of Erin's dress encircling Tucker's torso holding a makeshift dressing on his knife wound. "You don't want *that* to open up again."

Tucker tightened the belt hiding his holster and winced in pain. "Jack can't go, and you're not mended up yet. Erin's barely recovered —"

"I ain't gonna' be labeled a burden," she blurted out.

Tucker walked to where she stood beside Jack. She had draped her blanket over his shoulders while she helped him remain standing. "You are *not* a burden," Tucker said. "It's just that you had a fever, and your leg is not healed. It's just reality — I'm the only one fit enough to go out and scout the situation."

"But I'm the only one who can use that," she said, nodding to the bow and quiver of arrows beside it. "You *might* hit an Indian with it, but I *will* when the time comes."

"That's *if* there's Lakota what spooked Soreback," Tucker said. "It could be Hacksaw Reed, at what point you wouldn't get close enough to use it."

Tucker turned to Simon and said, "Keep it a cold camp. I don't want whoever's out there knowing *exactly* where we are."

Without another word, Tucker slipped

down the hillside and blended in with the trees lining the game trail. He'd do his best to put the sneak on whoever trailed them, recalling what Jack had said. Tucker might not be as stealthy as Jack, but — once he found the enemy — he was far more lethal.

When Tucker had gone down the trail as far as the tree line, he stopped, listening, looking with his peripheral vision, knowing he would pick up more movement looking to the side than he would head on. He walked a few paces and stopped again.

Silence.

He entered the trees, the moonlight filtering through the pine casting long shadows, and Tucker imagined each one to be a Lakota with their arrow nocked and waiting. Or Hacksaw Reed waiting in ambush with Kills the Deer. He closed his eyes, swiveling his head slowly, straining to pick up whatever had alerted Soreback. Leaves blown by the gentle breeze? A prairie lawyer calling other coyotes far off? Tucker didn't know, but something had worried the mule.

Once again he closed his eyes. Once again willed his heart to slow when . . .

A branch snapped. Somewhere in the trees.

Tucker opened his eyes and squatted

behind a pine, looking around when . . .

. . . another *snap.*

The brush of cloth against a pine bough.

The faint form of a figure stumbling over a dead tree, stubbing his foot on a rock, barely stifling a cry. A Lakota wearing the feather of a hawk in his braids that bounced on his thin chest as he faltered, illuminated for a moment by the moon before the shadows engulfed him once again.

Tucker remained immobile while he drew his gun. *If I can waylay him, talk to him special-like, I can find out where the other Indians are.*

The warrior picked his way along the dark game trail.

Tucker flattened and moved to the far side of the tree as . . .

The Lakota walked past him, never knowing Tucker knelt there until . . . his hand firmly grasping the barrel of his heavy Remington he hit the Indian on the back of the head as he passed. The Indian collapsed, and Tucker caught him and dragged him to one side of the trail. He took a moment to study the woods. Even though this man had been alone, others were around. Iron Hide had to be close. Had this warrior and his headman split up, searching for Jack and Erin?

Tucker waited for long moments, listening. Satisfied no others trailed with this Indian, Tucker tied his bandana around the man's mouth before cutting his bowstring and tying the man to a birch tree.

When he was done, Tucker sat on his haunches and waited for the man to regain consciousness, and once again he closed his eyes. Even though he heard nothing, he knew this man did not walk at dark in the Black Hills alone. Indians rarely did. It made them lethal against their enemies.

Tucker dug a lucifer from his pocket and cupped it in his hand as he bent to the Indian. He struck the match and held it to the man's face for a moment before blowing it out. In that brief instant when the flame illuminated the Indian's face, Tucker saw he was little more than a boy. Of Jack's height, the Lakota was thinner than Jack in his exhausted and depleted condition, and Tucker hoped he hadn't hit him *too* hard.

After long moments when the Indian hadn't come around, Tucker squatted in front of him and shook him. When he got no response, he slapped the Indian lightly, but his head remained on his chest until Tucker slapped him harder. The warrior's head finally raised, and he looked wild eyed up at Tucker. The Indian struggled against the bowstring to free himself from the tree. "The more you pull against your hands," Tucker whispered, "the tighter it'll become. Best to just settle down."

The Indian's head slumped against his chest for a moment, and Tucker saw a large lump already forming on the back of his head. Tucker parted the Indian's hair and brushed fresh blood away. "You'll live through this," Tucker said, "*if* you tell me what I want to know."

He untied the bandana from the boy's face and drew his Bowie, holding it to the Indian's face. "I'll finish taking this off so's we can jaw a little. But one little *peep* outta' you, and I'll just have to use this. *Oyakahniga huwo?*" he asked and brought the bandana away so the boy could answer.

"Hau," the Indian said. "I understand."

Tucker took the bandana off and set it within easy reach. "Now what do they call you?"

"Pale Moon. Son of Here's the Fire and Pretty —"

"I don't need your family history," Tucker said. "I just want to know where the others in your band are."

Pale Moon looked straight ahead and said, "I am Pale Moon, son of Here's —"

Tucker slapped the flat of the Bowie hard

355

against the boy's cheek. The Indian's eyes widened as Tucker waved the large blade in a circle in front of his face. "One last time now: where are the others?"

The boy defiantly met Tucker's gaze. "There are no others left except Iron Hide and Blue Boy."

"They together?"

Pale Moon nodded.

"Why's Blue Boy running with Iron Hide? I heard there's some bad blood between them."

"Blue Boy came into camp last night," Pale Moon said and smiled. "He will kill you."

"Do they know where my camp is?"

Again, the boy smiled. "We heard the mule . . . talking, when the wind carried his braying in the night. They . . . we, are going to your camp." He sat up and strained against the bowstring once again.

"What are you doing out here alone?"

"Alone?" Pale Moon said. "I am not alone on this night." He leaned his face close to Tucker's. "Kill me. I am warrior. But know that you cannot reach your camp in time to save your friends from Blue Boy and Iron Hide, for they are surely there by now."

CHAPTER 39

Simon shouted a warning to Jack. He threw his blanket away and sat, feeling for the scalping knife under the blanket, but he was too slow. Iron Hide stood in front of him, his pistol pointed at Jack's head while he motioned to Erin with the barrel of his gun. "Get ready to ride. I will take the mule."

"Then what?" Erin asked. She stood from the far side of the fire and walked to stand beside Jack lying close to the heat. "You will kill Simon and Jack before you leave?"

"I will not," Iron Hide said, "but my brother might."

Blue Boy emerged from the trees holding his Colt loosely beside his leg. Erin took a step back, and Simon looked up at the Santee. He didn't have to point the pistol — the man's size alone would bend most folks to his wishes. "All I want to know," Blue Boy said, stepping towards Jack, "is where is Tucker Ashley?"

Jack shrugged. "I don't keep track of him."

Blue Boy aimed his gun at Jack's head, a look of determination in his eyes that Jack recognized well. *The man will kill me if I don't tell him where Tucker is.* But right this moment, even Jack didn't know exactly where his friend was.

"Where . . ." Blue Boy turned the gun on Erin and cocked the hammer, "is Tucker Ashley?"

"Enough!" Simon said. "Stand down, and I'll tell you what you want to know."

"Don't tell him nothin'!" Erin shouted.

Jack slid his hand slowly under the blanket, his hand coming to rest on the hilt of the knife. If only he were ten feet closer . . .

"I'll tell you where Tucker is" — Simon nodded to Erin — "if you leave the girl here."

"I agree," Blue Boy said without any thought about it.

"But I do not." Iron Hide kept Simon and Jack in his side vision as he approached Blue Boy. As big a warrior as Iron Hide was, he had to look up into his brother's eyes. "You wished to come with me for *your* own reason. I have *my* own reason for hunting these *wasicu*. And it is the girl."

Blue Boy stepped around Iron Hide and asked Simon, "Why is it that you walk the road with these people?"

"Hacksaw Reed," Simon said. "He broke out of the territorial prison."

"Ah," Blue Boy said as he pointed his pistol toward Simon. "I know the story. He killed your woman. Left your boy to die in the cold. And now you want him?"

"In the worst way."

"We came upon tracks many miles back. A big man's tracks. Over Tucker Ashley's. But the tracks were not yours."

"What's your point?"

"There is no point!" Iron Hide said. "Leave them. Or kill them. Either way, I take the woman when we ride away."

Blue Boy turned his back on his brother as if shutting out the noise. "The point is, I have a chance to kill Tucker Ashley. After I find Kills the Deer. I have heard where Hacksaw goes, so goes the Crow. And him I want even more. I think that he follows Tucker Ashley." He turned to Simon. "You know where Tucker is, Simon Cady, killer of Lakota children —"

"He has killed no children." Iron Hide approached Blue Boy and stood looking up at him.

"You defend him . . . that is right — he *is* your sister's husband."

Iron Hide spat on Simon's moccasins.

"*Was* my sister's husband. I would plunge my blade into his heart myself if I thought he had killed Lakota children. Warriors. But no children."

"It is of no consequence," Blue Boy said. "Tucker Ashley will be bait to lure Kills the Deer close. And I can kill them both who have violated the scared grounds of our *He Sapa.*" He holstered and drew his knife, the foot-long blade glistening and slicing the air in front of Simon's face. "Tell me where he is, or I will take the girl and slice flesh off her. Slowly."

"No!" Iron Hide said. "The woman is mine. I will take her. You learn from this Simon Cady where Tucker is . . . any way you can. But leave us."

Jack slipped the knife out from under the blanket, taking advantage of the two Indians' arguing, and hid it under his leg.

Blue Boy flicked his knife out, and it gouged a furrow into Simon's cheek. "Where is he?"

Simon wiped blood off his cheek and onto his trousers. "I told you," he said, looking to Jack, who showed the very tip of the blade before hiding it again. "I stand by my offer — I will tell you *if* the girl goes free. As soon as she's away from this mountain, I will take you to Tucker."

360

Before Blue Boy could agree, Iron Hide brushed past his brother and grabbed Erin roughly by the arm. "We go —"

"No!" Blue Boy yelled to his brother, and . . .

Jack sprang from the ground. He jumped on Iron Hide's back, slashing his knife at the big man's chest.

The Indian deflected the blow.

He threw Jack off his back, Jack's knife cutting the Indian's shoulder as Jack raked the blade across as he fell.

Iron Hide yelled a deathly scream as he flung himself onto Jack. Jack rolled away. Iron Hide landed on the ground where Jack had been a moment ago, when a shot — loud and close — caused Jack to flinch. Blue Boy cocked his Colt for another shot. He aimed his pistol at Jack, as Simon ran at Blue Boy as best he could scramble. He threw his great weight against the Indian as he pulled the trigger. *Misfire,* and Jack once again thanked God for the drizzle this morning.

Iron Hide drew his own knife, the handle wrapped in deer hide, with dried blood on the blade. Before he picked himself off the ground, Jack ran at him, slicing the air, the scalping knife finding the Indian's leg. Jack ripped upwards, cutting deep into Iron

Hide's thigh muscle.

The Indian howled in rage, catching Jack with a fist that knocked him to the ground. Jack rolled over onto his back as the Indian staggered to his feet, blood spurting from Jack's broken nose.

Iron Hide raised his knife overhead and leapt on Jack as he . . .

. . . held the hilt of his own knife hard onto Iron Hide's chest, the blade pointing upward . . .

And Iron Hide impaled himself on Jack's knife.

Frothy blood *spurted* onto Jack's shirtfront as the Lakota struggled to raise his own blade, realizing he had dropped it, staring at his empty hand when he . . .

. . . collapsed atop Jack. Dead.

Jack wriggled beneath the enormous weight of the dead man. He shoved Iron Hide off him when he saw Simon fighting with Blue Boy. Simon circled him, holding a stout log from the firewood pile with his good arm, swinging it in front of him, driving the Indian back. Blue Boy feinted right. Simon stepped wrong, and Blue Boy rushed Simon's left side. Blue Boy kicked him hard on the knee, and he collapsed, his leg at an odd angle, losing his grip on the branch that fell to the ground a moment before he did.

Blue Boy snapped another round at Simon. Another misfire. He tossed the pistol aside, drawing his knife, was rushing Simon with knife poised overhead when . . .

. . . the *whump* of the arrow hitting Blue Boy's shoulder stopped the Santee. He staggered forward, nearly losing his footing as blood seeped from the wound. The metal arrowhead stuck from his muscle, the shaft protruding from his back as he looked at Erin. She stood at the edge of the campsite, grabbing for another arrow.

Simon grabbed the branch and used it as a crutch to stand, shuffling toward Blue Boy as he snapped the shaft of the arrow. Jack pulled the knife from Iron Hide's body and stumbled toward the Santee. Blue Boy looked from Jack to Simon to Erin as she nocked another arrow meant for him; then he disappeared into the night.

Simon collapsed on the ground, and Erin ran to him. "My leg's busted," he said between clenched teeth. "Get me a bottle of that elixir, and I'll be all right."

"Nonsense." Erin laid her bow on the ground close to her. "I'll fashion a splint for you. When Tucker gets back you can ride the mule outta' here."

"To where?" Simon said, holding a painful grimace.

"Deadwood, of course," Erin said. "Only place in this part of the hills that has a sawbones to set that leg."

"That's if Blue Boy doesn't come back," Jack said. He bent to the Indian's pistol. There were four primed cylinders left. He took off the percussion caps and blew dirt off each one before snapping them back on the cylinder nipples and stood as if expecting Blue Boy's return.

Jack sat with his back to Simon and Erin, watching for Blue Boy while Erin splinted Simon's leg. "Need some help here," she said, and Jack turned to her. "Take holt of his foot and pull. Gently."

Jack did as Erin ordered, holding Simon's leg steady while she wrapped strips of her dress around two thick branches on either side of his leg. When she finished, she rested his leg carefully on the ground. "Now I'll fetch that elixir."

"Thank God," Simon said, breathing hard. "It'll help ease the pain of seeing my dear brother-in-law killed."

Jack looked to the woods where Tucker had disappeared hours ago. He had been gone longer than he should have, and Jack wanted to go search for him. As Tucker had done for him. But as he looked over at Erin — the weeks and the fever taking a toll on her strength — and Simon in a bad way, he knew he had to leave now. For Deadwood. Now. Jack would leave signs that Tucker could see even in the dark. Tucker would catch up with them.

CHAPTER 40

"That shot we heard an hour ago came from their camp." Killdeer looked at the campfire. "There is no coffee."

"We ran out this morning," Hack said. "And salt. And plug tobacco." Hack never thought that finding Tucker would take this long, and he hadn't stocked up on supplies. If it weren't for Killdeer bagging a deer or grouse, they would have half starved chasing after the man.

Hack stood, his trousers nearly falling down, and he hitched them up. Once they got back to civilization, he'd put the pounds back on. "Important thing is if one of those shots took out Tucker."

Killdeer sat on his haunches and warmed his hands over the fire. "I do not think so. At their camp is Iron Hide. Dead."

"Tucker?"

"I could not tell. But his heart had been stabbed. And something else." He reached into the bag around his waist and withdrew a broken arrow shaft that he handed to Hack. He held it to the fire a moment before giving it back. "Lakota. Where'd you get it?"

"Their camp," Killdeer said. "A lot of blood on the ground. Not Iron Hide. Another Sioux I think."

"Thank God it's not Tucker's blood."

"I do not know that for sure. But the two — Jack Worman and his woman — walk beside the mule carrying a heavy load. Toward Deadwood."

"Deadwood! Thought Jack and his woman were running from the Sioux?"

"With Iron Hide gone . . . and the other one who hunted with him, Blue Boy not seen . . ." Killdeer slapped a fresh scalp on the ground beside Hack. "I found him trying to free himself from a tree. He was tied with a bowstring to a tree. A boy. *But* a Sioux."

"How far?"

"A mile perhaps," Killdeer answered. "Maybe more. They left camp hours ago. One rides the mule — Simon Cady I think."

"Then let's get after them." Hack stood and walked to his horse and was tightening the cinch and slipping on the spade bit when he realized Killdeer wasn't moving.

"Well, saddle up."

The Crow remained squatted beside the fire, and Hack walked to stand over him. "I said —"

"They are no longer any threat," Killdeer said. "If we go . . . to Wyoming, perhaps, we can find trains that need to be robbed. Banks with white people's money —"

"You suggesting we break off the track?"

"We can find money. Women. If we leave —"

"I don't believe this!" Hack said. "Never thought I'd see Kills the Deer turn yellow."

Killdeer's jaw muscles tightened, his teeth clenching. He fingered his knife as he stood and looked up at Hack. "Kills the Deer is no coward."

Hack stepped back, his hand resting on the butt of his gun. "You ought to think twice about pulling that blade."

Killdeer seemed to be mulling taking on Hack when he stepped back, and his hand came away from his knife. "We have beaten them. We can go —"

"You figure if there's no more Sioux to kill, we might as well go on? Forget what Tucker did to Blade and Lowell. And even that smart ass Jimmy Milk?"

Killdeer looked away.

"Well, you can go and hunt Sioux scalps

once we find Tucker. Now saddle up, and let's not hear about heading to greener pastures until I find that bastard."

Killdeer stopped at the bank of a free-flowing creek several feet deep and dis-mounted. He cupped his hand and drank of the cool water while he ran his hand over a deep track in the muddy bank. "They try to hide their trail. But they tire. Like us."

"Go on."

"Tucker Ashley joined them here." He pointed to a boot print. "At the creek. They move east." He stood and looked over the rocks and trees, a faint trail leading through the forest — once used by Sioux? Or the Cheyenne before them?

"How old?"

Killdeer crossed the creek and stood with the track between him and the sun. "Two hours. Maybe more. Maybe less if they stop and rest."

"Then let's move faster," Hack said and spurred the mare across the water. "We can catch them unawares, long before they get to Deadwood."

"No," Killdeer said matter of factly.

"What do you mean 'no'?"

The Crow motioned to the forest. "It is true they are moving slower than us, and we can catch them, I think. But you remember that broken arrow shaft . . . one of their group knows how to use a bow. Tucker?" He shrugged. "Simon Cady? And they took the pistol off Iron Hide, so they are armed better now."

"But we are so close —"

"Do not forget Simon Cady's buffalo gun. If we find them — and attack them in daylight — they have an advantage. That Simon Cady . . . he shoots from a long ways."

Hack nodded, thinking how, once again, the Crow's logic was sound. "What do you suggest — we wait until night to jump them?"

Killdeer swung a leg over his saddle. "We catch up. Follow them. When night falls and dark lulls them to sleep, we attack their camp. When they least expect us. And we kill them."

CHAPTER 41

Tucker sat on one side of Simon, Jack the other, holding the big man's leg positioned between two branches. Erin had looked at Simon's broken leg after several miles riding the mule in the hills, a jarring ride, through rocks that had fallen across the old game — or Indian — trail. Simon had not complained, yet Erin saw he was not doing well. "If we don't resplint the leg now, infection could set in." She had used Simon's axe to sheer off branches from two stout, straight limbs and torn another strip off her dress that she laid beside the branches. "This is gonna' hurt just a mite," she said.

Simon drank the last of his elixir. "Get it over with," he said and stuck a thick branch between his teeth.

Erin looked at Jack and Tucker. "When I cut the wrap off the old splint, you" — she nodded to Tucker — "pull gently on his foot so's the leg don't move. And Jack, when I take these old branches away, you hold the new ones on either side of his leg."

Erin breathed deeply. "Ready?" she asked and sliced the wrap with Jack's knife. Tucker pulled on Simon's foot as the old splint fell away, and Erin quickly wrapped the new branches Jack held on either side of Simon's leg. He ground the branch between his teeth so hard Tucker thought he'd break his choppers. "Ease his leg to the ground," she ordered. When she had tied the strips of dress off, Tucker gently laid Simon's leg on the ground.

Though the night was chilling cold with the setting of the sun, sweat beaded on Simon's face, and he let out a long sigh. "Once again, girl, it didn't hurt 'just a mite.' It hurt like *hell.*" He forced a smile. "But I thank you for doin' this for ol' Simon."

"And thank you for being so sloppy that I can waltz right into your camp." Hacksaw Reed stood at the edge of their campsite, his pistol leveled at Tucker. Killdeer stood off to one side, his own pistol drawn, bow and quiver slung over his back. "Now shuck that gun of yours, and that Bowie as well. And, Jack, that old Navy Colt's not going to be much use in this weather anyways, so lob it over in those juniper bushes yonder along with that scalping knife."

They each disarmed and stood facing Hacksaw.

"You all get right cozy with one another. Huddle together so's I can watch you. Go on."

Hacksaw sat on a fallen tree and waved a lazy figure eight at them with the barrel of his Colt. "Simon, Simon. I hear tell you're after my hide. Something about killing that pretty little woman of yourn."

Simon's face flushed, the veins on his forehead throbbing with rage as he struggled to stand.

Erin eased him back to the ground. "You're in no shape to do anything."

"Good advice, missy." Hacksaw winked. "You and me'll have a little visit later." He snapped his gun up when Tucker started to stand. "First me and him's got a little matter to resolve."

"Give me my gun, and I'll show you how to resolve our problem," Tucker said.

Hacksaw tilted his head back and laughed. "I wouldn't go agin' Tucker Ashley in a stand-up gunfight for all the gold on the Deadwood stage."

"Good," Simon said, jerking away from Erin as he used a branch to stand. " 'Cause Hacksaw Reed's going to die by *my* hand."

"Like missy there said, you're in no condition to fight anyone. Especially me."

Tucker looked around for a weapon. Any weapon. But with his gun and Bowie in the brush twenty feet away, he'd stand no chance of rushing them. "I'm thinking Simon could beat hell out of you even in his condition," he said, taunting Hacksaw. If he could rile him, get him off his track . . .

"How you figure that?"

"As easily as I beat you in prison, Simon could right now."

"Come here," Hacksaw ordered.

Tucker stepped toward Hacksaw, looking down the barrel of his .45. "So now you're going to kill me without a fight, you cowardly bastard."

"No," Hacksaw said. "But this brings us to just why the hell I've been tracking you for the last two weeks." He took off his belt and holster and laid them neatly on the ground along with his knife. "What I aim to do is beat you to death. You caught me with a lucky shot in prison that day. Then put the boots to me bad enough I lost an eye." He stripped off his eye patch and tossed it along with his coat. He motioned to Tucker with his finger to meet him in the middle of the clearing. "There won't be no lucky punches today."

Tucker motioned to Killdeer. "And as

soon as I beat you again, the Crow will step in."

"Killdeer," Hacksaw said, his eyes never leaving Tucker, "keep an eye on the other three, but *do not* interfere. Understood?"

The Crow nodded and relaxed the muzzle of his gun as he moved to better watch Erin and Jack and Simon.

Tucker stepped into the middle of the clearing, sizing Hacksaw up, something he'd had no chance to do that day in the prison mess hall before Hacksaw jumped him. He stood half a head taller than Tucker and — recalling the prison fight — had a considerable reach advantage. At thirty pounds heavier — forty now that Tucker had lost so much weight this past week — he also recalled that Hacksaw fought like a big man — slow and awkward. Clumsy. Relying on his bulk and strength to win the fight. Tucker *had* beaten him in prison that day. But then, Tucker *had* landed the first punch that day.

Tucker stripped off his coat and draped it over Simon.

"Don't fret over him," Hacksaw said. "He'll only be on this side of the grass as long as it takes to beat you to death." He began circling Tucker, smiling, taunting. "You look a mite played out. Maybe this

375

last week running from me did you no good."

Tucker matched Hacksaw's movements, circling around the clearing, each staying out of the other's reach. Tucker looked Hacksaw over, from his thickly muscled arms to his head that seemed attached onto his shoulders with no neck. The big man had the advantage of size. But Tucker had his own advantage — he'd beaten Hacksaw badly once before. And that can weigh on a man's mind once he's been whipped. "I think I'll break your ugly nose," he said.

Hacksaw motioned Tucker in. "Take your best shot."

They continued their deadly dance. Each time they circled by Killdeer, Tucker watched the Indian leaning against a tree, gun loosely pointed at Erin and Jack and Simon. That the Crow would avenge Hacksaw if Tucker beat him, he had no doubt. When the time came to stomp Hacksaw into the dirt, Tucker would have to rush the Crow.

But first, he needed to stay out of Hacksaw's powerful grip.

"Don't kill him all at once!" Simon shouted from where he leaned against a large rock in front of the fire. He winced in pain and repositioned his broken leg. "Beat hell out of him if you want, but I want to kill him my ownself."

"Keep quiet, old man," Hacksaw said. "I'll take care of you soon's I put Tucker away. I'll —"

Tucker rushed in. He set himself and threw an overhand right that landed flush on Hacksaw's chin. He staggered backwards, was struggling to keep afoot when Tucker hit him again.

Hacksaw fell to the ground. Tucker's blow should have finished him, but he merely shook his head to clear it while he rubbed his jaw.

Tucker jumped to Hacksaw's side and flicked out a jab. Hacksaw blocked it and kicked Tucker's leg. He leapt back, but Hacksaw's foot caught Tucker's ankle. He shook off the numbness of his foot and jabbed again, falling short of Hacksaw's face as he hit Tucker on the side of the head. He collapsed on the ground and was trying to stand when Hacksaw kicked him hard in the stomach. Air *whooshed* out of Tucker, and he rolled and rolled again to avoid another kick.

Hacksaw ran after Tucker, who stood and caught Hacksaw's foot, twisting it. The big man lost his balance for a moment, and Tucker slapped him across the face before moving out of Hacksaw's range.

"Hurts, don't it?" Tucker said, watching Hacksaw's face flush red, the veins in his neck standing out while he rubbed the imprint of a hand on his stubbly face. "But then, it hurt that day in the mess hall when I beat you like an ornery stepchild."

Hacksaw howled and rushed in.

Tucker sidestepped him. His stomach still reeling from Hacksaw's kick, he sucked in deep gulps of air as he circled, keeping Kills the Deer in his peripheral vision.

Tucker saw Jack watching Kills the Deer intently while he moved closer to the guns, and Tucker was sure the Indian caught Jack's movement as well. "You don't move so good for being some kind of killer," Tucker said.

Hacksaw rushed in, his fists flailing the air. He threw a straight right that Tucker sidestepped, and an uppercut thrown too far away when . . .

Tucker stepped in quickly, closing the distance. Setting himself. Drove his fist deep into Hacksaw's side. His face contorted in agony from the liver shot Tucker delivered, and he fell writhing in the dirt, holding his side.

Tucker was inching his way closer to Hacksaw's gun on the ground when Hacksaw yelled, "Kill the son of a bitch!"

Kills the Deer smiled and walked toward Tucker as if prolonging the dread.

"So much for staying out of the fight," Tucker said, moving backwards carefully. He could not get to Hacksaw's gun before the Indian shot him, but he might be able to get to the only other weapon at hand — a burning log from the campfire. If he could distract Kills the Deer long enough to make a play for the gun . . .

Kills the Deer said nothing, grinning as he approached Tucker walking backwards, close to the fire when . . . he dropped on his knees as Kills the Deer shot, the bullet passing where Tucker had stood a moment before. He seized a long, burning limb and pivoted, facing Kills the Deer, who had cocked his pistol again and aimed it at Tucker's head. Tucker let the log fall, and the Indian said, "You were a worthy enemy these past weeks." His finger tightened on the trigger . . .

A scream erupted from his throat. He dropped his gun, kicking at Jack, who had grabbed Tucker's Bowie and stabbed the Crow in the leg. Jack stabbed his leg again, and the Crow went down.

Tucker was scrambling for his gun when . . . "Don't *even* pick it up," Hacksaw said wheezing, catching his breath, his face still contorted in pain. He had stood and massaged his side with one hand, the other leveling his Colt at Tucker and Jack. He motioned to the Crow, and he dragged himself away from Jack. "You look in a bad way," Hacksaw said. "Best sit still. We'll doctor those cuts soon's I finish with these fools."

He stepped away, creating distance. "I would have preferred beating you to death. But, in the end, this will have to do," and he was sighting down the top strap when . . .

. . . Simon's axe *whizzed* though the air, surprising Tucker almost as much as it did Hacksaw. A sickening *thump* broke the night air. Hacksaw looked down at the axe embedded in his chest, his fingers failing to stop the blood spurting from the wound. Blood dripped from his mouth in a bizarre drool, his eyes quickly glazing over, and he dropped face down into the dirt as light left his eyes. Dead.

Jack threw himself at Hacksaw's pistol.

Tucker lunged for Kills the Deer's gun before he could grab it. Tucker snatched it and turned. Cocked the gun . . .

The Crow was gone. Melted into the forest without a sound despite his leg wounds.

As if he'd never been there.

"Lucky you threw that coat of yours over me when you did," Simon said, "or Hacksaw might have seen my camp axe." He laughed and winced once again as he repositioned his leg. "I told you *I* would be the one who killed him."

"Well, you could have killed him just a little bit sooner."

"I was waiting for Jack to make his move on the Crow."

Jack stuffed the pistol down his trousers as he headed for the trees.

"Where you going?"

"After Kills the Deer," Jack said. "He'll be easy to follow gimped up like he is. And won't be so fast I won't be able to catch him."

"We can go after him once we mend up a bit —"

"I would say you will not be going anywhere." Blue Boy walked into the clearing, covering them with his pistol held in his good hand, the other arm tied to his side. Blood crusted his shirt from Erin's arrow, but he showed neither pain nor emotion as he said, "I have long waited for Tucker Ashley's scalp to adorn my lodge pole."

Tucker stood sideways from Blue Boy, wondering if he could spin and fire before the Santee could. "Drop your gun. And you, too," he said, motioning to Jack. He sighted down the barrel at Erin and nodded to the bow. "Do not pick it up. I have seen your skills."

"So now you're just going to kill me?" Tucker asked.

Blue Boy nodded.

"And then what . . . Simon kills you?"

Blue Boy laughed. "Simon Cady is in no position to kill anyone."

"No?" Tucker said. "Look at him. Under my coat draped over his lap is a gun pointed at your chest. Simon can't miss from this close."

Blue Boy's smile faded. "You lie."

"Want to make a side bet on that?" Simon asked, pushing against the jacket covering him with *something.*

"Then why not kill me right now?" Blue Boy asked.

"Because your gun is cocked and aimed at Tucker," Simon said, picking up on the bluff. "I shoot you, and your gun might go off."

Tucker forced a smile. "See, we have a standoff."

"A standoff. I have heard of that," Blue Boy said.

"And have you also heard of another . . . offer?"

"I am listening."

"Kills the Deer. It is said he has killed many Lakota through the years."

Blue Boy's neck muscles tightened. "The Crow has murdered many of my people. Warriors. Women and children. Makes no difference to him whose Lakota scalp he lifts."

"I'll tell you where he is," Tucker baited him.

"I do not believe you know. The Crow drifts with the wind —"

"Recently, his wind drifts a mite slower."

"He has never been caught," Blue Boy said, his voice becoming excited.

"What if you *could* catch him?" Tucker said. "Would you avenge the deaths of all your people?"

"Many times over. *If* I could catch him."

"You leave us . . . walk out of here, and none of us will get hurt," Tucker said. "And you will have your Crow at the end of your blade. I have seen him."

Blue Boy paused. "I think that you . . . bluff. I can kill you three and still go after the Crow —"

"If you knew where he might be," Tucker said. "And *if* Simon did not have you covered with his gun."

Blue Boy took a long moment to think about that before lowering the barrel of his pistol slightly. "Where did you see him?"

"Here," Tucker said. "Standing right where you are now."

Blue Boy looked down as if he could see his enemy in the dirt. "I do not believe you."

"No?" Jack said, pointing to the ground. "That's his bow and quiver over there. Kills the Deer's bow and quiver. He left them when he ran from us."

"And that blood is his leg wound," Simon said. "He is hurt bad. You follow that blood trail" — he motioned to the trees in the direction Kills the Deer fled — "you'll have that scalp of his dangling off your lance. Just like you want."

Blue Boy stood silent.

"And you will have the rest of your life to hunt us *wasicu*," Tucker said. "So what is it — the Crow or the possibility your people will never be avenged of that murderer because he got away?"

"And because I shot you through the heart," Simon added, moving the coat once again as if he *had* a gun barrel under it.

Blue Boy kept his pistol pointed their direction as he backed away. "Next time, Tucker Ashley, we will fight once again, you and me." He turned and disappeared into the forest, his eyes on the ground following Kills the Deer's blood trail.

EPILOGUE

Olaf opened the gate to Tucker's stall and kicked his boot. "Dat Simon Cady is driving me to drink."

Tucker sat up and spat a piece of straw out of his mouth before slipping on his boots. He stood, using the wooden stall slats to stand, and massaged the kinks out of his back. But he needn't complain. After he and Erin and Jack had brought Simon to Deadwood to see the sawbones here, no one else would rent a room to the bounty hunter until his leg mended. Olaf had, though it sounded as if he had regrets. "He told me to go down to Lou's Meal Tent and fetch him breakfast."

"What's wrong with that? It's only a block away."

The big Norwegian held out his hand. "Dis is vat he says he vil pay me vith — nothing. He said the next man he bring in for da bounty he vil pay me back."

Tucker slapped his hat against the side of his leg, and more straw fell away. "Simon Cady's a lot of things, but he's no piker. If he says he'll pay you, he will. Just as soon as he's on both feet again."

"I know dat," Olaf said as he started walking through the livery. "Problem is, every man Simon hunts dies before he can get to da law. That vil be blood money."

"But it will be *your* blood money," Tucker said, grinning.

"Ah, to hell vit you," Olaf said and handed him a note. "Deadwood stage dropped it off dis morning. From Jack Worman. He has been rebuilding your ranch, him and dat new woman of his."

"You read the letter already?"

Olaf shrugged. "Just as a courtesy. I am, after all, a *professional* man. I get breakfast now for *him.*"

Tucker watched the big man waddle out the door on his way to the meal tent, and Tucker walked into the stall Jack and Erin had set up for Simon. He sat on a stool atop a cushioned seat, a cup of coffee on an overturned peach crate beside him, his broken leg propped on another crate. Smoking his pipe. "Anybody tell you not to smoke in a livery stable?"

Simon looked up and sent smoke rings

overhead. "Sure. Olaf. But he thinks I'm crazy, so he won't push it."

"Who's to say you're *not* crazy?"

Simon paused, thinking. "Got a point. What you got there?"

"Letter from Jack."

"Well, let's hear it."

Tucker grabbed a milk stool and sat while he opened the letter. "Jack and Erin got the dead cattle cleaned up, and they cut logs for a house."

"Won't do much good without cows to graze on the place," Simon said. "By the way, go in Olaf's office and refill my coffee cup, will ya? I'd do it myself, but" — he tapped his splint leg with his cane — "it's a mite difficult getting around."

"I heard just how hard it is for you to get around."

"How's that?"

"Nuthall and Mann's," Tucker said. "I heard you cleared out the saloon last night. Did someone carry your big butt there and back, or did you hobble over there on your own?"

Simon looked away.

"That's what I thought." Tucker saw why Olaf had been pulling his hair out, not that he had much to lose. Tucker went into Olaf's tiny office and returned with a cup of what Olaf affectionately called coffee for himself and Simon.

"As I was saying," Simon said, "it'd be hard for the new couple to make a living raising turnips or corn in that part of the hills."

"They won't have to," Tucker said. He explained that Ramona Hazelton — who had originally deeded Jack and Tucker the land *and* given them the bull and starter heifers — had arranged for another bull and six bred heifers to be driven to the ranch. "She told us, 'be more careful with the cattle this time' Jack's note said. Guess she heard about the Sioux killing the others."

"You said she gave them to 'us.' Regret what you did, walking away from a ranch?" Simon asked.

"Giving my share of the ranch to Erin so she and Jack can make a go of it?" Tucker laughed. "I'm sure one day I'll regret it. But not today." As Simon was mending in the days after arriving in Deadwood, he and Tucker had talked more about that fork in the road that Tucker had taken some months earlier. He and Jack had talked of little else these past years than getting their own spread. Raising cattle. Maybe running some horses. So when Ramona Hazelton set them up in the ranching business, it seemed like a Godsend. Until they had begun building the ranch. Jack had been a natural, but Tucker had to force himself to rise in the morning and tend to their cows.

"I think we're a lot alike," Simon said.

"Not hardly," Tucker said. "We're not any alike."

"Can you scratch those toes," Simon said. "I've got a powerful itch."

Tucker shook his head and scratched Simon's toes beneath the splint as he explained. "My pappy once wanted me to go into the legal profession, and I was going to, too. That was my false trail, just like ranching was yours."

"Your point?"

"My point is that — when I took that fork in the road — it was as if a big ol' bull buffalo sat on my chest. I felt constricted. Like it was a chore to get up and just live every day. But that *wasn't* living. That was doing something someone else wanted me to do. What I thought someone else wanted from me."

Tucker tossed the dark, smelly liquid onto the floor and hoped Olaf would return with *actual* coffee. "So how did you manage to get onto the *right* fork?"

"I was blessed," Simon said. "Dirk Roberts murdered the banker."

"I'll bet the banker didn't feel like it was a blessing."

Simon tapped the ashes from his pipe and stuffed it into his shirt pocket. "The blessing was, the town put up a reward for capturing Dirk. Now I had a passel of law books I needed to buy, and I knew about where Dirk was headed. From the moment I lit out after him and picked up his track, there was a tremendous feeling that that ol' buffalo on my chest just rolled off."

"Let me guess — poor ol' Dirk never made it back to stand trial?"

Simon waved the air. "A small matter. Point is, after chasing Dirk and dodging his bullets until I put the *habeous grabbus* on him, I never looked back. I'm thinking that's what you're going to have to do."

For all Simon's bravado and ruthlessness, Tucker knew he had a point. As Tucker was returning to the ranch that day the Indians raided it, all Tucker could think about was how much he'd hate rising the next morning to work it. Only when he saw what the Indians had done — and knew he would have to hunt them down — did he feel that old exhilaration overcome him, the feeling that only that fork in the road could give him.

"But you gotta' come with us," Jack had

said, practically begging Tucker. "It's *our* ranch."

"It's yours and Erin's now," Tucker said. "When I come for a visit, just you give me a roof over my head and a soft mattress, and we'll call it square."

"Where you figure on going?" Simon asked as he filled his pipe bowl again.

"Heard Montana had need of folks with tracking skills. Maybe Wyoming. There's a bunch of owlhoots that the law wants caught there."

"Might go there my ownself," Simon said. "Maybe we can work those wanted posters together."

"I don't think so," Tucker said. "Most of my wanted men would make it back alive."

Simon shrugged. "A small matter."

Olaf returned to the livery carrying a tray covered with a flour sack and handed it to Simon. He took the cloth and tucked it under his chin before grabbing the fork and knife. "Olaf," he said, "they didn't send any salt. Do you mind . . . ?"

"See vat I mean?" Olaf said.

"I have salt in my saddlebags," Tucker said and walked beside Olaf toward where Tucker's tack lay in his sleeping stall. "Won't be long now — Simon will be mended up."

"And not a moment too soon," Olaf said and handed Tucker a turnip. "For Soreback. Compliments of Lou."

Tucker had started down to the far end of the livery when a chill wind blew through the stable. He reached for his coat, but it wasn't where he'd hung it. It hung by a nail on the stall *next* to Tucker's. He bent to the chaff and dust floor and spotted moccasin tracks stopping beside Tucker's stall before walking out of the livery. He stood and asked Olaf, "Any strangers been in here?"

"Strangers all over Deadwood but . . . dere vas one. A big guy. Bigger than me," Olaf answered. "When I asked him vat he vanted, he said 'just checking out the livery.' Said he might board his stallion."

"White guy?"

"*Ja.* As white but bigger than me. Why?"

"These are moccasin tracks. Did you know this big feller?"

"Never saw him before. He just walked through and left. I paid him no mind."

"Probably nothing," Tucker said and grabbed his coat. Beneath it hung a fresh scalp. Black hair with a hint of gray.

And woven into one braid was a small, beaded leather lizard. A medicine bundle. Just like many Crow Indians wear.

ABOUT THE AUTHOR

C. M. Wendelboe entered the law enforcement profession when he was discharged from the Marines as the Vietnam War was winding down.

In the 1970s, his career included assisting federal and tribal law enforcement agencies embroiled in conflicts with American Indian Movement activists in South Dakota.

He later moved to Gillette, Wyoming, where he found his niche and remained a deputy sheriff for the final twenty-seven years of his law enforcement career.

During his thirty-eight years in law enforcement, he served successful stints as a police chief, policy adviser, and other supervisory roles for several agencies. Yet he always felt most proud "working the street." He was a patrol supervisor when he retired to pursue his writing career.

He writes the Spirit Road Mystery Series, Bitter Wind Mystery Series, Nelson Lane

Frontier Mystery Series, and the Tucker Ashley Frontier Fiction Series.

He can be reached at spiritroadmysteries .com or cmwendelboe.com.

The employees of Thorndike Press hope you have enjoyed this Large Print book. All our Thorndike, Wheeler, and Kennebec Large Print titles are designed for easy reading, and all our books are made to last. Other Thorndike Press Large Print books are available at your library, through selected bookstores, or directly from us.

For information about titles, please call:
(800) 223-1244

or visit our Web site at:
http://gale.cengage.com/thorndike

To share your comments, please write:
Publisher
Thorndike Press
10 Water St., Suite 310
Waterville, ME 04901